Madame Delafloté,

Impeccable Spy

D0869464

OTHER BOOKS BY SUE CHAMBLIN FREDERICK

The Juan Castillo Spy Series
The Unwilling Spy

The Ivy Log Series
Grandma Takes A Lover
The Boardinghouse — Return to Ivy Log

Madame Delafloté,

IMPECCABLE SPY

Sue CHAMBLIN Frederick

ISBN: 978-0-9852104-5-8

Word Jewels Publishing

ACKNOWLEDGMENTS

To my five brothers and sisters who thought my wild imagination was dangerous – see, you guys, I've channeled that imagination into a terrific novel!

To Robert (Rob) L. Bacon of "The Perfect Write" who tirelessly contributes his wisdom of the writing world to both published and unpublished authors. His manuscript evaluation and editing are solid gold! You're the smartest guy I know, Rob!!

To the most handsome Frenchman I know: Olivier Plomion. Olivier ensured the technical aspects of the weaponry used in "Madame Delafloté, Impeccable Spy" were amazingly correct. My darling Frenchman also critiqued the French language in the manuscript so you cannot blame any "colorful French language" on the author.

To Steven W. Johnson, the best layout person in the world and author of *Not Much of a Crime*.

To Sherri Crawford, Brenda Cochrane and Gary Frederick for their expert proofing of the manuscript.

VISIT THE AUTHOR AT: www.suechamblinfrederick.com

Prologue

On the Place de la Concorde, the Hotel de Crillon was in deep shadow, its grand façade dimmed by the fading light of a January evening. In Room 308 where King Louis XV's architect had designed an opulent suite for the King's mistress, a young woman lay grieving the death of her husband. Outside her window, the sounds of Nazi soldiers marching throughout Paris rang loud and proclaimed it a German city, revered by Hitler himself.

Eléonore Delafloté yearned for death. The loss of her husband opened an abyss of deep despair and she entered without the slightest struggle. The British spy, Avery Gannon, became enthralled at the very mystery of her, exciting him as though she were a locked box that had no key. The frailty of the young Parisian woman caught his heart and whispered to him that she was no ordinary woman.

CHAPTER ONE

It was to be her last indulgence, seven thousand francs for a Russian sable. A rare jet black with white tips said the sly man at the *boutique de prêteur sur gages,* a pawnbroker on Rue Royale, not far from the Place de la Concorde. *You will be the most beautiful woman in Paris. Not only that, you will never be cold again. Yes, it is made for you. Just give me the francs.*

Late afternoon had settled on *The City of Light* and the young French woman left the little shop and crossed the alley, the collar of the soft fur pressed against her neck. She turned onto the Place de la Concorde as two women, squatting together like fat hens, watched her with suspicious eyes, perhaps thinking she was a *prostituée.* A *prostituée? Non,* she was nothing other than a young woman whose wealth allowed her to buy a luxurious fur.

Their laughter trailed her as she walked toward the Hotel de Crillon, the same lavish building where Marie Antoinette had taken music lessons so long ago. It was a vague memory from her days of studying French history at the University, long before the war had made France a prisoner of the Germans.

Only steps from the hotel, she stopped to look at her reflection in a store window, a dress shop where alabaster mannequins wore frozen smiles tinted claret, their eyes seductive with long black eyelashes that swept across their lids like feathers. Her attention was drawn to the fur, the exquisitely matched pelts of the sables glinting in the light. For a moment she thought of the sleek animals alive and loping atop a Siberian snow bank, their whiskers weighted with ice crystals. She shivered involuntarily and turned to see three Nazi soldiers briskly marching down the avenue in her direction.

Entering the hotel, Madame Eléonore Delafloté saw Monsieur Claude Bedeau bow his head slightly, his hat erect and formal, the words "Hotel de Crillon" embroidered into the wool. He exxtended his arm and led her through the lobby to the ancient elevator.

"Madame Delafloté, I have never seen you so beautiful," he said, his eyes alert as he leaned closer and lowered his voice. "I don't know why, but the Germans are everywhere today. Perhaps you should stay in your room."

He smiled and lightly touched her on the arm. "Shall I bring you hot tea? or wine perhaps?" The gaunt little man cocked his head and waited for her reply.

Eléonore shook her head in refusal and stepped into the elevator. The door closed with a soft clang, the rumbling and rocking of the cage sounding ominous as it rose to the 3rd floor and its operator released its lone passenger.

"*Merci*," she said to the attendant and glided down the dim hallway.

Room 308 was quite grand, a suite, with an authentic Louis XVI bed and a pair of blue and white silk balloon-back chairs on either side of a dainty Marquetry side table. The French neoclassical design so treasured by the King seemed out of place, too beautiful for a city hosting Nazis.

The view from the tall windows that lined the west side of the room extended across buildings spared by German bombs. The avenue below lay in deep shadow, perhaps in mourning for the tragic death of Paris when German troops had marched down the Champ-Élysées and celebrated the fall of France.

Eléonore pulled the drapes together and the room became dark and still, as if the sun had set on a quiet evening. She removed the black fur, but only long enough to take off her clothing. Naked, she wrapped the fur around her once more, like a butterfly in a cocoon, her face barely visible. The five pills lay on her dresser. In moments, she would swallow them. Nothing else mattered, not the war, not the death of Édouard. Her life would simply fade away and with it her grief and loneliness.

***

The playwright Balzac would have described Avery Gannon as "the vanishing man," an apparition whose body heat lingered only a moment before evaporating into a mist of mystery. MI6's master spy had played a vanishing act for His Majesty's Secret Service for eight long years.

He pushed his body against the cold stone wall of The Church of the Madeleine and swept his eyes down Rue Royale to the buildings around him, his breath leaving his lungs in quick spurts while he contemplated how he might elude the Germans.

Nothing was familiar. In his frenzied flight, his bearings had become distorted. He had been followed first when he left the footpath along the Champs-Élysées earlier that morning and again as he hurried toward the Place de la Concorde. None of his well-honed diversionary tactics had worked, but he reassured himself by patting the Webley Mark IV pistol he carried and hurried to the little gardener's cottage that hugged the rear grounds of the church. Perhaps the cottage would provide a semblance of cover before he made his way to the safe house.

His last instruction from MI6 had been three days earlier and quite specific. *Get out. They know.* Of course, they knew. At the moment, the only thing they didn't know was where he was hiding. The city crawled with Hitler's feared Gestapo, their agents frantically searching for "the vanishing man," the British assassin who throughout France had terrorized the Germans for eight months.

In the middle of the garden, he slipped behind the cover of a fountain and waited, studying the door of the small cottage fifty meters away and obscured by vines of ivy and overhanging tree limbs. There was no padlock, yet there was something else strange about the door. The color, perhaps. Or maybe, the shape.

His heart pounding, he eased past the thick ivy that ran atop a stone fence and hid behind a climbing rosebush, its thorns catching the sleeve of his coat. Closer to the cottage, his gaze once again fell on the door. *This is not a cottage.* He cursed silently as he examined the intricate artwork of some obscure

painter who, on a warm spring day, had decided the dreary wall
of the fence needed the whimsy of a door.

Trapped. Trapped in the garden of a church where an imita-
tion cottage refused his entry.

Gannon heard guttural shouts and the unmistakable hurried
footfalls of Gestapo soldiers. He turned toward the street.
Nothing he could do but shoot it out, go down firing. He pulled
his pistol and crouched his body. Perhaps a few bullets would
stop the soldiers and gain him precious time.

He pushed himself farther into the veil of ivy and waited.
Two soldiers, guns drawn, swept around the corner of the
church. Now only ten meters away, they hesitated. This brief
pause was all Gannon needed. The first bullet struck the forehead of the soldier on the right; a moment later, the second
bullet struck the neck of the other.

Quiet and stillness. Another chance to run. He turned to his
right and saw the obscure back entrance of the Hotel de Crillon,
its doorway marked *De Concierge et les Livraisons.*

More soldiers ever closer, he sprinted across the alley and
through the doorway and found himself in a dark alcove that
reeked of rotten potatoes and soured milk.

Breathing hard, he stepped behind a stack of wooden crates
and waited. Perhaps he should have obeyed MI6's order to leave
France and cross the English Channel immediately. Instead, he
had chosen to stay; there was one more thing he had to do.

***

She was a mound of black in the grand bed, the room dark,
waiting for her last breath. The opulent fur was still, perhaps
aware that the young woman who lay within was content to be
alone in its darkness. An opera by *Massenet,* appropriately
named *The Girl in the Black Sable,* would portray a beautiful
French woman who takes her life and is found wrapped in a soft,
silk-lined fur. Nothing else. Only her tears, dried on her cheeks,
would expose the most revealing clue as to why. *Elle est morte
d'un coeur cassé,* the tenor sang. She died of a broken heart.

***

It took Gannon only a moment to pick the lock of Room 308.
From below, he heard loud voices. German voices. Then, the fright-

ened voice of a Frenchman, a voice that at first seemed aloof, then submissive. The sound of footsteps echoed throughout the hotel, up the stairs, across landings where doors were opened and slammed.

The spy quickly removed his gun from its holster. How many shots could he fire? One? Two? He moved inside the dark room, his hands trailing along the wall. A slight glimmer of light slipped beneath a drapery and his eyes found the bed and the mound of black fur.

***

"Please, please. I beg you. Only the Madame occupies this room."

A German officer, his left eye strangely crooked, and four soldiers pushed Monsieur Bedeau aside and stepped into Room 308. The officer scanned the room with his good eye, then the bed and the mound of black.

"The bed?"

"The Madame. She has been ill and sleeps long hours. Please, do not disturb the poor woman."

The four soldiers searched the room, underneath the Louis XVI bed, the armoire, behind the draperies. In the semi-darkness, the officer studied the heap of black fur. With his pistol, he pushed aside the collar and saw the still face of a sleeping woman. He lingered a moment and looked around the room once more.

"Next room!" he shouted.

CHAPTER TWO

Hiding beneath the dark fur, Gannon thought of his grand-mother, recalling things she had told him in his youth. He even envisioned her standing over him, not exactly a happy face on the thin woman whose raspy voice, rising and falling like an ocean's tide, admonished him until he had withered into a sub-missive little boy of ten. "Pictures of naked ladies are not to be looked upon by young men," she had scolded, spittle flying into his face. A childhood of blame, accusation and, finally, humilia-tion had placed within him a desire never to disappoint those who expected him to rise above the sins of the flesh.

Fortunately, he had long ago dismissed the idea that pictures of naked ladies were sins of the flesh. Instead, he had evolved into what he considered a well-adjusted man who, despite the predictions of his sinister grandmother, succinctly enjoyed the sins of the flesh. Now as he pressed against the naked body of the lithe woman who lay beside him, he wondered what his grandmother would think.

Long minutes had passed since he crawled under the black fur and flattened his body into the mattress. Her body had been cold, then warming slightly from his body heat. Still, she had not moved. He knew she was breathing, but barely.

The Germans had stormed from room to room, shouting and threatening. "The Englishman! Where is the Englishman?" Monsieur Bedeau had said there were no Englishmen registered at the hotel. Only French and German. No Poles. No Spanish. No Jews. "If you are lying, you will be shot," the German officer had shouted. Then, like an autumn mist, a ghostly silence crept up the stairs, from room to room, until the only remaining sounds were the faint notes of a piano from the lobby below.

The spy eased his body upright and left the warmth of the bed and the woman, who remained still, her lips pale, slightly open, a lock of dark hair across her cheek. At the window, he pulled back the drapery and watched the street below. Two soldiers walked smartly toward the Arc de Triomphe, a shrine commissioned by Emperor Napoleon to honor his victories as well as flaunt his genius.

The Germans delighted in Paris – it gave them the culture they craved, despite the fact the French perceived them as *babouins sots,* empty-headed baboons. The Germans believed there was no culture in Warsaw and had bombed the city into oblivion. But, Paris? *Ah, Paris. Let us capture Paris and steal its culture.*

Gannon considered himself an above-average spy. How else could he have stayed alive while he lied and murdered his way from St. Petersburg to Berlin to Paris? Despite his loyalties to the monarchy, as well as his own integrity, he had decided to do things his way. Unorthodox, but productive, to say the least.

His last face-to-face conversation with MI6 had been in the summer, in London, where Whitehall produced spies by the thousands. His turn in spy school had been eight years before, a number of years after his graduation from City University. For four years, he had trekked to the Angel tube station in Islington to his parent's home in Finsbury, only to obtain a mundane degree in mechanical engineering, a degree that did nothing to satisfy his desire for adventure.

Auspiciously, becoming a member of Britain's elite espionage society had provided him with every imaginable means by which he could satisfy his longing for . . . intrigue. He was a young man and young men liked to explore.

At first glance, he resembled a college professor, forty-two, salt and pepper hair, intelligent hazel eyes and an expression of deep thought resting on his brow. His smile was quick, engaging. Trustworthy? One would trust him with their lives. His grandmother, however, would have been aghast at his ability to kill a man in mere seconds with only his hands. Even worse, the brittle woman would have protested loudly from her grave if she had observed him seducing a beautiful woman. A beautiful *naked* woman.

He scanned his eyes across the tops of buildings that silhouetted the darkened sky that covered a winter Paris. He saw movement, a flushing of air across the sky that seemed almost musical. Snow. Large wet flakes pummeled the window in front of him.

Gannon watched as a white Paris emerged, pristine, disguising the darkness of war and emanating a muffled quietness that somehow soothed the soul. The flakes piled one on top of the other on the sill of the window. His heart quickened and he felt himself smile as he made a decision. Once again, a decision totally without the input of His Majesty's Secret Service.

From the opposite end of the room, a voice drifted toward him like dandelion pistils floating through the air.

"Is there someone in the room?" The words came delicately through the darkness until they rested upon his ears.

Unmoving at the window, Gannon heard his own breathing as he contemplated a conversation with the woman. Whether she knew it or not, she had been a refuge for him, she and the black fur. He had lain pressed beside her and smelled her soft perfume and wondered why she was wrapped in the coat, naked, oddly still. She hadn't stirred when he lifted the coat and lay beside her. There was no response to his burrowing into her back, his knees behind hers.

His eyes strained through the dark and sought the woman whose voice he had heard.

"You have saved my life, Madame." His words drifted to the end of the suite where the large bed and its occupant lay. He heard the softness of his own voice, the indebtedness that wrapped itself around each syllable.

From the bed: "Your French has a slight accent. Are you English?"

From the window: "I am English."

From the bed: "Where in England?"

From the window: "Finsbury."

From the bed: "Why are you in France?"

From the window, a pause. "To find a woman who wears a black Russian sable."

From the bed, a pause. "And now that you've found her?"

He could hear the humor in her voice as well as the calmness of someone who was neither afraid nor concerned that a French-speaking Englishman happened to be in her hotel suite. He once again lifted the drapery and looked out the window.

"Did you know it is snowing?" Then, without waiting for a reply, "Now that I've found her?" He laughed quietly, a laugh that surprised him, and he began to find his way through the darkness to the bed.

He heard the strike of a match, saw the flicker of a candle, then the gun in the hand of the woman in the fur coat.

CHAPTER THREE

"**M**adame, are you aware there is no safety on your gun? If
you simply *breathe* on the trigger, it will fire." Gannon's
steady gaze never left the eyes that watched him. He said
nothing more as he calmed his breathing and waited.

"Well aware," she said. She sat queen-like in the middle of
the bed, fur clad, dangerous. Had there been a crown on her
head, he would not have been surprised. She was that lovely,
that regal.

His experience in negotiating with an enemy did not apply to
his present quandary. An incongruous situation, to say the least.
From the beginning of his entry into espionage, he had envisioned his death in the line of duty from a volley of gunfire from
a 9mm pistol held by a ruthless German or perhaps a fanatical
assassin from Russia. But never, in his wildest imagination,
would his demise be at the hands of a fragile Frenchwoman who
presently, without the least bit of compunction, aimed a gun at
his heart. Though he admitted his life could end in a hotel suite
in the middle of a Paris snowstorm, he refused to have it end
that way.

His voice slid into a cajoling temperance. "Is it possible for
you to lower your pistol for a moment while we decide what is to

happen here?"

"There is no *we* in this decision, monsieur." Her voice rose, "Perhaps you would be so kind as to remove your coat."

"Remove my coat?"

"Are you having difficulty understanding my French? Shall I use English?" Her words were not kind.

"I understood you, Madame." Gannon reluctantly removed his coat, exposing his shoulder holster and within it, his weapon. The uncertainty of the moment caused an anxiety in him that he did not like. His life undercover did not permit him to expose the very means by which he made his living – namely, brandishing a weapon whenever the need arose, whether it be in Paris or in the dark alleys of Moscow, but certainly not in a hotel room with a woman who wore only a fur coat and currently pointed a pistol at him.

She looked at him for a long moment. Her French was very clear. "You now see why I am holding my own gun." She motioned him to the blue and white silk chair. He grimaced as he watched her wave her pistol.

"Sit for a while," she said. "We must have a conversation."

Reluctantly, he settled in the chair and waited while her eyes followed his every move. He noticed she was pale, even in the soft yellow light of the candle. The black fur hid her thinness, hid the bones in her back that had earlier pushed against his face. Now, as he looked at her, he thought of what lay behind the large, sad eyes that watched him. Perhaps pain as well as a deep longing, a longing for tranquility, for a peace she had lost. Her stillness was so disconcerting, he hesitated.

When she spoke, he thought of snowflakes, her words weightless, floating, looking for somewhere to light as they drifted out into the cold room.

"My name is Eléonore Delafloté and you are in my hotel room. May I ask why?"

"Why?"

"Again, you are having difficulties understanding my French. Again, shall I use English?"

"No, French will do." His eyes expressed anger. "My name is Avery Gannon and I needed a safe house."

"A safe house? As in a place of refuge? To hide?"

"Yes. A place to hide."

"Why did you choose my room?"

His frustration caused him to flush and he fought to retain his patience.

"It was a random choice." How much should he tell her? He had no idea who she was, her loyalties nor her alliances.

"And from whom are you hiding?" she asked, her chin rising slightly, an obvious dominance in her voice.

He stalled. "It is the war, you know." Instinctively, he knew she was an intelligent woman, as well as analytical, probing. He did not want to be caught in a lie.

"How well I know of the war, Monsieur Gannon. That is something everyone in Paris knows." Her eyes fell to the holstered gun strapped around him. "Tell me why you are armed." She paused and spoke again. "And you have yet to tell me from whom you are hiding."

Gannon turned his gaze from the woman to the flame of the candle. There were no simple answers. He was certainly smart enough to concoct a believable lie, a lie with numerous details that could convince just about anyone of its feigned authenticity. Leaving the confines of MI6 and their policies and procedures had allowed him carte blanche. Perhaps he should have listened to his grandmother after all, a life as a Catholic bishop might have been much safer and certainly less complicated.

"I find your curiosity quite amusing." Was he stalling again?

"You shouldn't. Make no mistake, I am quite serious."

He nodded. "So you are." After a deep breath, "I'm hiding from the Germans. I carry a weapon because I fear for my life." He shrugged his shoulders as if to end the conversation.

Eléonore leaned forward, her eyebrows lifting in question. "The Germans?"

"Yes, the Germans. Do you not understand my French? Shall I speak English?" His words were harsh. He had not meant for his refuge in the woman's hotel room to end up in a lengthy conversation. His life was in danger, not only from the gun she pointed at him, but also from the Gestapo who knew very well he was alive and in Paris.

She didn't seem bothered by his gruffness. "What Germans? The SS?" Her eyes were alert, questioning. Color had returned to her cheeks.

"The Gestapo."

She leaned back and appeared thoughtful, the pistol lowering in a minuscule reprieve.

"What would the Gestapo want of an Englishman who obviously has French citizenship or he'd never be in France at this time. Unless. . ." Again, she studied him, her gaze falling to his gun, his clothes, his face.

A smile. It began slowly, an upturn of her mouth ever so slightly, the opening of her lips revealing a row of perfectly straight teeth.

"Monsieur Gannon, I do believe you are a spy."

CHAPTER FOUR

On the Right Bank, at precisely 12 Rue des Saussaies, the Hotel de L'Elysée no longer represented the carefree days of an unoccupied Paris. Instead, the building had been transformed into an establishment of various methodical, unabridged, polluted missions – missions whose purveyors would, in their estimation, bring about the intellectual reorientation of the French – of the world, for that matter. The hotel's only resident, the Gestapo, promoted the glorification of the ideals of a professional military. Even better, they rejoiced in the predominance of Germany's armed forces in the demonstration of their expansionist ideologies. Why not? The Romans had done the same thing.

The infamous Reichenau Order stated that the German soldier was the bearer of racial concept, as well as the avenger of all the cruelties that had been perpetrated on him and the German people.

Avenger? Enter Herr Horst Krenz. Head of Department E3 Counterintelligence in Paris. Born in an aristocratic Baltic German family, he was educated in geology at the University of Vienna. Herr Krenz' personal mission: destroy anything and anyone who compromised Germany's view of racial concept. He believed Germany should use their strong military capability to promote the exaltation of ideals . . . more specifically, a superior race. An ideology in perfect alignment with the view of Adolf Hitler.

When he arrived in Paris in a German Horch 852 in June of 1940, his poison green shoulder boards contrasting with his gray Gestapo uniform, he came no less than "god-like," with a tilt of his chin, the lifting of his nose into the air as if to avoid the odor of the French.

Today, however, he was alone in his office watching the depth of snow rise by the moment on the white streets of Paris. He hadn't bothered to drink the coffee his assistant had placed on his desk an hour earlier. His mind would not turn loose of Avery Gannon, the English spy who had eluded capture and was hiding somewhere in Paris.

He left his desk and stepped to the window. Down below, he saw a cat struggling in the snow, its body clamoring to stay above the drifts. *A fucking bad time for a blizzard.*

He called for his young corporal. "Herr Bauer, I would like some hot coffee."

Herr Bauer stood at attention, his eyes averting those of his superior. "Yes, Colonel Krenz."

The young soldier remained still. Krenz knew the man found it too difficult to look into his face, into eyes with vision that was oddly uncoordinated. His right eye rested with ease on another's gaze, but the other eye projected some distance to the left, as if contemplating something over one's shoulder. He was aware the soldier wrestled with a decision: which eye to look into or perhaps even wondered with curiosity if someone or something was lurking where the crooked eye gazed.

Krenz, a man who so intensely aligned himself with the Fatherland's mission to promote the glorification of a superior race, had a flaw. His awareness of it consumed him.

Alone again, Krenz returned to the window, brooding and wondering if the Englishman had escaped the city, was underground and in the safety of the French. His instincts told him the spy had not made it to a safe house, that he was hidden somewhere in Paris, perhaps even nearby – near enough . . . near enough to kill him. He knew Gannon would come for him. He would be ready. But, there was a better way. He would find

Gannon first. And, when he did, he would kill him. Just like he had killed the Frenchman.

He thought of Berlin. His last communiqué had arrived the day before. A brief, sixteen words: *Arrival 23 January. I expect success in capture or death of British agent. Hermann Göring, Reichsmarshall.*

Hermann Göring, Reich Marshal of the Greater German Reich and heir apparent to the Führer, commanded the arrest of the assassin who had in eight short months murdered twenty-seven high-ranking German officials in France.

If he was to survive, Paris' Chief of Counterintelligence Horst Krenz must hand the Reichsmarschall the head of the British agent Avery Gannon.

There was no doubt in Krenz' mind that, upon his arrival, the pompous Göring would orchestrate an end to the fiasco that presently haunted the SS in Paris, which, he surmised, would result in his removal as head of Paris' Counterintelligence.

Krenz shuddered. January 23. Three days away. Three days to find Gannon.

CHAPTER FIVE

Avery Gannon stared at the French woman. Uncanny as it was, she seemed to have a crystal ball, a supernatural ability to see things for what they really were. Yes, he was a spy. Yes, he was hiding. Yes, he was desperate. No, he wasn't going to lie to her.

"Madame, how do you know these things? These "spy" things?"

She smiled and, unbelievably, lowered the pistol.

"I don't know," she said softly. When she looked at him, her eyes clouded. "My husband . . . my husband was a member of some ... *group*. Sometimes he discussed . . . confidential things. Perhaps he would have made a great spy."

She leaned back into the bed and rested her head on a pillow. The candlelight touched her skin. He thought she had forgotten him when she lifted her head and turned to him.

"He's dead, you know. Killed in North Africa. I have been here for two months waiting for him . . . but, of course, the wait is over."

Gannon leaned forward. "I'm sorry. I'm sure he was a good man."

"But, of course. I loved him deeply. Still do." Her voice quavered. "I . . . I don't know that I can live without him, you see."

Her eyes found him. "Perhaps you did not know it, but you saved my life . . . instead of the other way around."

Gannon simply nodded.

She closed her eyes and pulled the fur closer to her chin. "When Édouard died, I felt my life was over."

Gannon leaned forward and saw the pistol had fallen from her hand and lay in the folds of the black fur. He made no attempt to retrieve it.

Her soft, wispy voice continued as if on the edge of sleep. "Monsieur Gannon, do you feel your life is over?"

He pondered her question while he studied her profile, the blackness of the fur contrasting with her pale skin, and was reminded of her fragility.

Her question had been remarkably insightful. There was no simple answer. He acknowledged his predicament was precarious, to say the least – trapped in a hotel room with the Gestapo ready to pounce upon him at some point was not where he wanted to be. Had he been able to reach a safe house, he would have had the means to escape – more ammunition, change of clothing, change of identity, escape route.

The safe house had been his only hope. The safe house – where he would have met his compatriot spy. Together, they would have gone underground, been led by the Résistance into the French countryside, hidden. But, his companion spy was dead. Working together at the command of MI6 had thrown them into the middle of French patriots who resisted the German occupation. And, now he had no fellow spy with whom to fight the Germans.

The Frenchman had been a brilliant spy. He had believed it was morally important to the survival of France to set an inspiring example of patriotic fulfillment. Before Paris fell to the Germans, he secretly made his way to England and presented himself to His Majesty's Secret Service, appearing as an arrogant Frenchman who humbled himself for the sake of his beloved country.

They adored him. The British had known he was a wealthy French aristocrat, the son of one of France's most revered diplomats, a man who had ignored his castles and wealth in order to serve his country. A rare man who obviously had set a good example for his son, who had followed in his footsteps, though it be in the capacity of an MI6 agent.

Gannon felt tightness in his chest. He had yet to mourn the death of his friend – he had been too engaged in his quest to stay alive. Ironically, that quest had nothing to do with the responsibilities of spycraft, his loyalties to Britain, the War. He knew himself well and profound introspection had proved once again the depth of his reverence for that which he believed. At the behest of his dead grandmother, there was no yawing in his confession of his weaknesses. And, now, it was that weakness, a weakness named retribution, that had ripened into a full-blown desire to avenge the death of his fellow spy.

"You have not answered my question." Her words were slurred, sleepy words that struggled out of her mouth and lay heavy in the room. She turned her face, cushioned by the fur, toward him but did not open her eyes.

"No, I do not feel my life is over." He saw her nod slightly as if satisfied with his answer.

"I'm glad to hear that." She turned away from him and pushed her body into a fetal position. "I'm very tired now. I shall sleep awhile."

He thought she would go to sleep quickly, but she did not.

"Monsieur," she said, almost inaudibly, "when I wake, we shall discuss a plan to save you from the Germans."

In moments, he heard the soft purring of her breath, cadenced, like angels humming.

He remained still until the flame of the candle spat loudly and consumed the last bit of wick and wax. The room fell into a cold darkness, the faint breathing of the Madame the only sound. From his chair Gannon walked to the window and pulled the draperies aside. The snow had blown against the glass and obscured the street below. Isolated, but only for a few more hours. When the snow stopped and the storm cleared, the war would continue. The Nazis would swarm from their holes and continue their joyous game of brutalizing and intimidating the citizens of Paris.

Gannon felt his body sag, his muscles heavy with fatigue. He left the window and touched his way along the wall. He had slept little in the past three days. Had eaten only a morsel of food. He found the bed and against his better judgment pushed himself deep into the warm black fur that hid the Frenchwoman. He fell asleep instantly.

CHAPTER SIX

The snows of January fell on the streets of Paris like a Siberian white breath. The winds gusted into a howling creature that raced around the corners of buildings, over rooftops and through the streets like a run-away locomotive, downing electrical lines throughout the city.

At 12 Rue des Saussaies, the Hotel de L'Elysée was shrouded in darkness. In his office, Horst Krenz sat at his desk reading, a candle on either side illuminating the file of Avery Gannon. *Intelligence Officer. Trained at Whitehall. Specialty: Counter Intelligence. Forty-two years old.*

Then, *"HI."* HI? Krenz leaned over and studied the entry. *HI.* Of course, 'highly intelligent." *So? Everything is relative. Highly intelligent compared to whom?*

Irritated, the German pushed back his chair and stretched his legs across the top of his desk and watched the flame of the candle with his right eye. If he was to capture this *highly intelligent* agent from Britain's MI6, should he compare his own intelligence to the Englishman's?

A feeling of unease crept over him. Exactly what was he up against? After all that had happened, he knew the agent was unusually dangerous. Even inside Gestapo headquarters in the heart of Paris, Krenz did not have a feeling of . . . of well-being. He leaned forward again to the file and turned to the next page. A photograph. Krenz opened his desk drawer and pulled out a small magnifying glass and placed it above the photograph. Gannon in a suit and overcoat, a muffler around his neck, a fedora, his face shadowed. Beneath the shadow, a man with an unusual mind was looking at him.

He leaned back in his chair and decided to call in four of his best officers, men just like himself, loyal to the Third Reich, to Germany's quest to avenge history's undeserved impieties against them. Together, they would find the spy and perhaps even hang his body from the same pole that once flew the French flag. How comforting, thought Krenz, as he extinguished the flames of the candles and closed his eyes.

CHAPTER SEVEN

At the first knock, Gannon pulled his revolver. By the second knock, he was flattened against the wall next to the door. On the third knock, he heard the voice of Monsieur Bedeau. It was three past midnight.

"Madame Delaflouté, it is I, Monsieur Bedeau. Forgive my intrusion, but I am concerned for you. May I come in?"

Breathing quietly, Gannon slowly released the safety of his weapon and waited. Another knock, louder. "Madame Delaflouté?"

Across the room in ink-black darkness, the black fur moved, a rustling of bed sheets, footsteps across the rug and finally the body heat of Madame Delaflouté only inches from where Gannon stood. Did she know he was there and did she know she was naked?

"Yes? Monsieur Bedeau?"

"*Oui!* Madame, it is I. May I come in, please? We must talk."

Silence. A shifting of feet, a deep sigh. "Is there something wrong, Monsieur Bedeau?"

A long silence from the opposite side of the door. Then, "Possibly, Madame."

Again, a shifting of feet, a palpable hesitancy. "*Un moment, monsieur.*

Madame Delafloté crossed the room to the bed. In a moment, Gannon heard the strike of a match, saw a small flame illuminate the naked body of the Madame. Once the candle was lit, she reached for the fur and placed it around her. She stood a moment as if forgetting something; then, a soft gasp. She turned slowly and saw Gannon by the door watching her. She said nothing as she looked at him and the gun in his hand. She placed a finger over her lips and pointed to the closet. Obediently, Gannon opened the door and stepped in.

"I am coming, monsieur. Please wait." She turned the lock and slowly pulled the door open.

Monsieur Bedeau held a lantern, a trail of black smoke lifting in the air and releasing the pungent odor of oil. The yellow light cast shadows on his weary face as he smiled at her.

"Please forgive me, Madame. I do not wish to disturb you. Yet, I feel as though you may be in need of assistance."

"But, of course." With one hand she clasped the front of her coat, with the other she opened the door wider.

Monsieur Bedeau seemed to shrink as he entered the dark room and placed the lantern on the small table between the two chairs. He turned and faced her, removing his wool hotel cap and uncovering a head of chaotic gray hair. He stammered somewhat as he searched for words. His eyes were wide, questioning. He moved closer and spoke in a whisper, which revealed the urgency that had compelled him to wake her in the disquieting hour of midnight.

"Madame, *Si je peux être au point . . .*"

"*Oui,* monsieur, please. Speak as you wish."

"The Englishman."

"The Englishman?"

"Yes, the Englishman who is hiding in your room?"

Eléonore stared at the old man. A charming smile, "Ah, monsieur, you are mistaken. There is no Englishman here."

"But, of course, there is . . . and we must discuss his leaving."

"His leaving?"

"Yes. His leaving. The Gestapo will most certainly return when the storm clears. We must have a plan." He was agitated; no more pretense. He looked around the room, his eyes searching while his hands nervously squeezed his cap. Then, a softened plea. "Madame, we are at war. There is no time to linger on the . . ."

The door of the closet opened and Gannon stepped out, the gun still in his hand, an intense alertness in his hazel eyes as he studied Bedeau. The lantern light cast an eerie shadow on the spy's lean figure as he moved across the room, his eyes never leaving Bedeau.

"Of course, monsieur. Let us talk." A calm voice, one used to command, solid and confident. He returned his weapon to its holster and motioned Bedeau to the chairs near the bed. "Please sit."

Gannon began the conversation with a question. "Monsieur, you are?"

Bedeau raised his eyebrows, the bushy hairs protruding upward into two half-moons that met his disheveled mane.

"Englishman, it is *you* who must tell me who *you* are. You are not a guest in my hotel, but someone who has commandeered himself into one of my finest suites." He looked at Madame Delafloté, "And, of course, interned the Madame."

His voice rose, its authority, whether real or not, quite discernable. "It would behoove you to tell me not only who you are, but also enlighten me as to your exact intentions."

Gannon smiled, his eyes vacillating between a humorous twinkle and a sage seriousness. "My apologies, monsieur. Of course, you are correct. In times of war, it is evident that protocol is not followed, as it should be. Perhaps, despite the Gestapo searching for me, I should have taken a moment to register at your fine hotel. Been escorted to a proper room, given the key and a wine list. Then, when the Germans arrived to search the hotel, they could have simply looked at your registry, found my room and shot me while I drank a glass of *Beaujolais*."

Gannon was not through. He stood and towered over the *petit* man. True, it was possible he had only hours to live. The probability of capture, torture, then death was very real. It was his *mode de fonctionnement* that had enabled him to survive under the auspices of His Majesty's Secret Service. His strength was in his ability to adhere to his instincts – instincts that were deeply embedded in every cell of his body. He turned from the old man and again sat in the chair.

A full minute of quiet followed while the two men considered the importance of their conversation. Bedeau, despite his small stature, seemed to lift himself up, raise his shoulders, stretch his neck and fill himself with resolve.

"Monsieur, your sarcasm does little to disguise the gravity of your situation. Perhaps, you should discuss your state of affairs with another member of the *Résistance*."

Gannon did not miss the inference of the *Résistance*.

Bedeau rose from his chair and bowed to Madame Delafloté. "My sincere apologies, Madame. Please return to your bed. I shall be back soon with some wonderful Port-du-Salut cheese – stolen from a German truck just last week. Perhaps also some wine."

He paused, a fatherly frown creasing his worn face. "You are too thin; you must eat."

Gannon lifted the lantern and held it out for the Frenchman. "I trust you will not mention my presence in the Madame's room to anyone."

Bedeau smiled from beneath his heavy mustache. "Englishman, your trust in me is well-founded." He turned and walked across the rug to the door.

"Monsieur," Gannon called, "there is no heat in this room."

The old man turned.

"Talk to the Germans if you want heat - they have all the coal in France." He closed the door behind him, taking with him the warm light of the lantern.

CHAPTER EIGHT

From her nest on the small couch, Madame Delafloté studied Avery Gannon. He seemed familiar to her. Not only his physical appearance, but a certain quality, a likening to someone or something. Maybe another Englishman she knew. Or, perhaps, from a dream. His movements had been cautious, deliberate, his words even more so. His demeanor was as proverbial as if she had known him a very long time. It puzzled her. She had met him under bizarre circumstances; yet, his presence was almost . . . almost ordinary. When her eyes swept his face, it was as though she saw an old friend. It startled her when she heard her own voice, clear and precise, surface in the room.

"This spy thing. Tell me how it is done."

"This spy thing?" Gannon's face was blank.

She laughed, her eyes becoming bright with amusement as she watched him.

"Ah, monsieur, you charm me so. It is as if you do not understand the French language. Why must I repeat my words? You speak our language well, but, perhaps, it is the translation that confounds you."

She leaned forward as she rearranged herself on the couch, her slim feet poking from beneath the fur. "The spy thing," she said in a tone that clipped her words. "It would delight me to know how it is done." She settled back against the couch and waited.

***

Avery Gannon faced the woman who no longer pointed a small, black gun at him. Rather, she seemed almost relaxed, as if settling down in her soft black sable awaiting a bedtime story. It angered him that she seemed almost flippant, droll in her question.

This spy thing? What did she think? That spycraft was a game to be played Sunday afternoons on the green lawns of a magnificent estate? That it was *pretend*? If he showed her the body of a man tortured by the Gestapo, would she still think it a game? His eyes held hers for a long moment before he spoke.

"What is it you would like to know?" He leaned forward and stared at the large brown eyes that seemed to be forever waiting. He noticed she had pinned up her hair, exposing her regal neck, long and white. When she spoke, he found her words somehow distant, as if they belonged to someone with whom he had never conversed.

"Perhaps I should be more specific," she said. "In your estimation, what is the most critical aspect of your work?" She spoke like a journalist, one who interviews a well-known person, a journalist who is sincere and offers one an opportunity to express themselves without fear of being misquoted.

Critical aspect? Even if he told her, she would never understand. Did he himself know? The conversation addled him — a polite conversation with a woman who had no idea of the workings of war, of the tradecraft of espionage. Hell, he had spent years honing the skills of spycraft. The *critical aspects* of spycraft were immense, too vast to critique them. *God, what is happening here? I must get to a safe house and away from the scrutiny of this woman.*

In an instant, the woman's eyes still watching him, he became the professor he knew his grandmother wanted him to be. His voice held an air of superior knowledge; he was an intellectual with a degree in a profession so dangerous that he was in hiding ninety-five percent of the time.

"Your question is vague, Madame. You have assumed many

things about me, one of which is my position as an Allied spy. That is all you need to know."

Eléonore lifted her chin and sent him a defiant look. "You seem to ignore the fact that I am, at this moment, your friend, someone who can help you. The more I know, the more I can be of assistance. I wonder why you are dismissing the benefits of my friendship."

Gannon became annoyed. "Friendship? Madame, I know nothing of you. You are simply a Frenchwoman who, like millions of other Parisians, awaits the end of the war, hoping to survive. There is no friendship here."

Eléonore pulled the black fur around her neck, the flame of the lone candle flickering in the soft sweep of moving air.

"No friendship?" Her words were low, almost guttural. "My dear spy, your perspective of your situation lacks reality. It may surprise you to know that most anyone who is not a German is your friend. It alarms me that you do not recognize this."

She paused, but she was not finished. Her voice rose, "Indeed, I question your ability to escape from the Germans." With a swirl of her coat, she stood, "Go! Leave my room and find a hole somewhere in the snow."

Gannon watched as she began to pace the room, her anger disappearing into the darkness with her. She returned from the shadows and passed in front of him, the candlelight framing her face and revealing something he had not seen before, not seen when he watched her pale face as she slept in quiet innocence. He saw a strength, a sense of purpose that had been hidden within her, beneath the black fur. When he leaned forward, she did not falter. She was poised, ready for him.

His breathing quieted and he found himself humbled. She and her black fur had saved his life. Of course, she was his friend. He heard his voice enter the room, soft and smooth, as he watched her return to the couch.

"The most critical aspect of my profession is my ability to stay alive. I do this by being aware of every tiny detail of my surroundings. Every person, every movement. If I lose this ability, I am a dead man."

He paused and smiled when he looked at her. "I must remember everything. Eye color. Hair color. Gait. Speech. Clothing. Shoes. Habits. At all costs, I must blend into the background. No flamboyant scarf, no expensive fedora, no Italian leather shoes. I must be commonplace, unremarkable. Then, when I must, I become a killer. A killer whose purpose is not only to kill, but to also kill efficiently.

"After I kill, I must escape. Escape is everything. It is in the middle of the night that I meticulously plan my escape. Escape is not random, it is designed." Gannon looked at the slim, long fingers that grasped the fur. "An escape designed as beautifully as your fur."

She stared at him for a long moment, then raised an eyebrow. "I can do all those things." Suddenly she stood, sweeping out into the room, the heavy fur trailing behind. When she turned, she flashed a smile at him. "Monsieur Gannon, I shall become a spy. An impeccable spy!"

CHAPTER NINE

Monsieur Bedeau's knock was gentle, a clandestine tap that whispered of intrigue. He opened the door and pushed a cart that held his lantern, bottles of wine, bread and the promised cheese, the stolen cheese that had so delighted him. His theft from the Germans had been a victory. A small victory, but, nonetheless, a victory. He eyed Gannon with a furtive glance. "I see you are still here, Monsieur Gannon."

With an acquired deftness, he uncorked the wine and poured not two, but three glasses. He passed them around as if he were a priest serving communion. From the cart, he pulled two apples and placed them on a piece of hand-painted Provencal crockery whose colors reminded one of a French meadow in full bloom. The cheese and bread followed, carefully aligned in a perfect row. With a flourish, he spread his arms, smiled and plopped himself into one of the King Henry XVI chairs, a perfect fit for his small, wiry frame.

The wine was very dry, perfect with the cheese and apple. No one spoke as the food disappeared and the candlelight dimmed. When Avery poured a second glass of wine, Monsieur Bedeau raised his eyebrows and smiled.

"Good wine. I brought two bottles." He reached over and

poured for Eléonore. His hands shook. The room had become even colder.

The old man cleared his throat. "Shall we discuss your escape, monsieur? The Gestapo? Your . . . shall we say . . . strategy to stay alive?"

Bedeau sat back, hands on his knees and gave Gannon a quizzical glance, an expression that seemed almost humorous. Gannon observed him carefully. How could this grandfatherly man be so adept at subterfuge? No one could imagine him as anything other than what he was. Old, somewhat feeble. Yet, his actions were that of an astute individual, an individual prone to decisive thinking, alert, with eyes that measured all they saw.

Gannon sipped his wine and felt it warm his cold body. He looked at his watch; an hour and ten minutes past midnight. Daylight was only hours away. When he last checked, the storm was still raging, but that would end soon. "I would consider any suggestions you may have."

Eléonore and Bedeau looked at each other and then back to Gannon. Eléonore spoke first. "Well, it is very clear to me what you must do."

Both men turned to Eléonore and waited.

"Ah, this is so simple I can't believe you have not thought of it." With the glee of a child, she laughed.

When she spoke, it was if she were in command of Paris, of all of France, of the entire world. She left the couch and circled the room like a prowling panther, her black coat following her like the wind of a great storm. She stopped and pointed a finger at Avery.

"My dear Englishman, it enchants me to savor you with the joys of becoming a woman. A Frenchwoman, no less. With red lips, beautiful long hair and glorious breasts!"

Avery stared, unblinking. She was mad, perhaps feverish and malnourished. Yes, her eyes shone with fever, perspiration slicked her skin. He looked at Bedeau, who abruptly lifted his hands and clapped wildly.

"Genius! Brilliant! Of course, a magnificent idea."

Avery stammered. "I don't understand."

"*Une évasion par un déguisement!*" Eléonore returned to the couch, triumphant as she waved her hands in the air. "Your identity must be changed. We shall disguise you as a woman,

Monsieur Gannon. Then, you shall escape to a safe house."

Avery stared at the woman who sat across from him, a flashing smile on her lovely face. Although her husband was dead, her beloved Paris stolen by the Germans, it seemed as though there was an awakening – the return of the life force needed to continue living. He lowered his gaze and said nothing. The candle flickered, burned to the end and sputtered.

From the blue and white chair, Monsieur Bedeau rose and lit a new candle, the smell of phosphorous strong as the match flared. He turned and picked up his lantern.

"I shall leave the details of your disguise to you. I must get some rest. I will return early in the morning, before daylight." He turned and looked at Gannon, then Eléonore, and smiled, his mustache lifting into his cheeks. "The snow is your ally. When it melts, there will be no place to hide."

CHAPTER TEN

They sat without speaking, a veil hanging between them. The spy's breathing was slow, a deliberate and calculated effort to quiet his mind. The woman had flustered him – Avery Gannon, a hardened spy. It was clear to him he could not succumb to the mercy of a beautiful woman. And, what about the old concierge who seemed to have no qualms concerning their plan to disguise him as a Frenchwoman, then thrust him into a German-filled city where his survival would, indeed, be questionable? Avery's strength lay in his instincts and now, as the night moved on, he had no intention of altering his means of survival. If he were to live, he must rely on himself. Forget the woman, the old man – his was a journey only he could make.

Her words came unexpectedly, soft and caring.

"Monsieur, let us rest for a few moments. Then, we shall begin your . . . shall we say, your transformation." In the candle-light, her smile was shadowed. She closed her eyes and pushed deeper in the fur.

Avery leaned his head back onto the couch and closed his eyes. *Transformation? How preposterous.* One thing he was sure of – he would never wear the breasts of a Frenchwoman.

The flame of the candle flickered and died, turning the room into a cold, dark cave.

From the fur, a soft whisper. "Edouard, I am thinking of you – wherever you are."

Avery shifted on the couch and stretched his legs across the blue silk. "Tell me about Edouard."

A long moment passed. "Ah, my darling Edouard. If it weren't for the war . . ."

He heard her sigh deeply. "When did you last hear from him?"

A rustling of fur. "A letter. A few weeks ago. Telling me he would meet me here at the Hotel de Crillon."

"How did you learn of his death?"

"A friend. Monsieur Plomion."

"Who is this Monsieur Plomion?"

Eléonore laughed softly. "Monsieur Gannon, you are a curious man." She waited a moment. "Monsieur Plomion is . . . was a close friend of my husband's. Though I am not sure, I feel he is involved in the *Résistance*."

"He came to the hotel?"

She paused. "Yes."

"What day?"

"I . . . I can't remember. Perhaps two days ago."

"What does Monsieur Plomion look like?"

Another soft laugh. "Like a Frenchman. Thin, a bony face. Large nose, black eyes. Why do you ask?"

In the dark, Avery patted his weapon. A reassuring gesture acquired over the years. "Just curious."

Her voice came through the cold darkness like the warm breath of an early spring. "What else would you like to know, Monsieur Gannon?"

Avery thought for a long moment. "Nothing more," he said.

"*Oui*. Then, I shall rest for a short while. We have lots to do." She paused. "Are you ready to dupe the Germans?"

Through the dark, his words were solemn. "Yes, I'm ready." In moments, he heard the soft whir of her breathing.

CHAPTER ELEVEN

Paris was a holy place. Its citizens, under demoralizing German rule, wanted to see the flag of France fly over Strasbourg and Metz' once more, to see the shame of the French defeat erased from their memories. They witnessed Germany's occupation of Paris and the demise of its society, a society that was indelibly marked by its history – artists, writers, its kings and queens. Sadly, Paris no longer belonged to the Parisians. The French flag was removed in less than an hour after the German army arrived on that June day in 1940. Now, the curfew required them to shutter their windows and wrap themselves in the gloom of oppression.

Behind the shuttered windows, there were those who defied the rules of the occupiers. They listened to the BBC in secret and talked of freedom. They also planned ways to kill more Germans.

At 12 Rue des Saussaies, the Hotel de L'Elysée remained dark. The snow fell in copious amounts, the temperature dropping to -5 degrees Celsius. The wind blew the snow into high drifts that obscured the façade of the streets and buildings and left a frozen, white, disoriented city that lay hushed and waiting. Dark, towering lampposts seemed ghost-like as they poked upward through the mounds of white, as if protesting the smothering snow and looking for air to breathe.

In Herr Krenz' office, dimly lit by candles, the zealous German had assembled his assistant and four officers whose specialties permitted a protracted search for the English spy. Once the storm had subsided, a manhunt would turn Paris upside down. At the helm would be the resolute head of the Gestapo's counterintelligence section.

Krenz paced in the shadowed room, disappearing into dark corners absent of flickering candlelight, then reappearing into the glow that spread like a spilled sunrise on a tiny section of the room. The Gestapo chief's uniform was custom made, every stitch, every button, every detail so meticulously assembled that one could imagine weary fingers working through the night to ensure its perfection. Perhaps even a Frenchman had made it – one of thousands sent to Germany to work in factories on behalf of the war effort. What a paradoxical task for the hands of the pompous, but pitiful, French.

The immaculate black boots that rose to the knee came from the shadows once more and stopped. Krenz ran his one good eye across his officers, then turned and faced the chalkboard. The four officers sat attentively, careful to focus their eyes on Krenz' one good eye. The chalkboard was marked with the last sightings of Gannon, a loose drawing covering a five-block area in every direction off the Champs-Élysées in the 8th arrondissement.

At 8:40 a.m. that morning, Gannon had been sighted on a footpath that ran parallel to the wide thoroughfare. Then, at 9:10, a man thought to be Gannon hurried along the Place de la Concorde. The man's coat was not the same coat as the earlier sighting, but his gait was similar. From 9:40 to 2:50 p.m., Gannon had disappeared. The men who pursued him backtracked and crisscrossed the entire area, only to resign themselves to the fact they had lost him, when a man was seen entering a church and then observed exiting the rear. Two dead soldiers were found in the church courtyard, guns drawn. A pursuit ensued but the man again disappeared.

A thorough search of the Hotel de Crillon, which was only a short distance from the church, turned up nothing. But, Herr Krenz prided himself on his instincts and instinct told him the spy had, indeed, been in the hotel.

"So," began Krenz, "the Hotel de Crillon. A perfect place to hide, wouldn't you say?"

He tapped the board where the hotel was denoted as a large square, a black check mark in the center of the block obviously indicating its importance.

"I have two men still out working surveillance, but I've not been in contact with them – obviously, because the weather has not permitted communication of any kind. For all I know, they could have frozen to death."

Krenz smiled, the right eye holding the attention of those who watched him, his left eye drifting off above their heads. "I am assuming the weather has also kept our spy in an unwanted captivity. He can hide, but he cannot run."

Uncharacteristically, Krenz laughed, his teeth large and slightly protruding. "Can you imagine," he stifled a chuckle, "the tell-tale footprints he would leave – like Hansel and Gretel's breadcrumbs." Then, a sudden grimness – he paused and shook his head up and down slowly. "We'll be waiting."

Krenz stretched his back, squared his shoulders and raised his voice. He pointed to Lieutenant Gerhart. "You, Herr Gerhart, will choose your best men to patrol the train stations, especially the *Gare de Lyon*. Yes, the trains are not moving, but they will be and we don't want Gannon to be on any of them."

"You, Corporal Braumen, have each and every soldier in Paris ask for papers from all male citizens. No exceptions. Cordon off at least ten square blocks around the hotel – no one gets past without inspection." Krenz turned toward the window and thoughtfully nodded his head.

"And you, Corporal Reichstugh, the electricity. As soon as you can move, inspect the generating stations and determine the status of all outages – when the power will be restored. Spread out your men so all stations can be inspected in a matter of hours after the storm ends. Also, get with the meteorologist for a full report."

He paused and looked around the room. "A meteorologist? Forgive me for my ridiculous request. We know very well what the weather is, don't we?" There was no smile.

Krenz began walking around the room, his head bowed. No one spoke or moved as they watched their leader pace back and forth in front of them. He stilled and turned to them once more. At first the left eye held them in its vision, then a quick shift to the right eye fell on the remaining officer.

"And you, Captain Linbaugh, I would like you to make your way to the hotel," he half smiled, "as soon as the weather permits, of course, and speak with the old gentleman – Herr Bedeau, I believe is his name, and see what more you can learn from him. Bring him here, if you must. Then, we will search the hotel again from top to bottom, every corner, and every square inch. If our spy is not there, then . . . Well, we'll have to see, won't we?"

Suddenly, as if Hitler himself had entered the room, Herr Krenz, in a stiff ramrod movement, extended his right arm, "Heil Hitler!"

CHAPTER TWELVE

At midnight, Herr Krenz left his office in the Hotel de L'Elysée and walked down a flight of stairs to the kitchens of the grand hotel. Famous French chefs no longer prepared luscious *gougères* and cocktails of *crème de cassis and white wine* in the pristine kitchens, where copper pots and silver tureens had lavished the shelves like gleaming jewels. With the Gestapo wielding a gray bleakness over the once-grand hotel, its corners lay dark and quiet.

By candlelight, Krenz poured coffee and brooded. He paced the large kitchen like an animal, his eyes searching the walls as though he were in prison and seeking escape. He turned the corner around a large table and stopped. Across from him, a large door, painted black, led to the outside. He stared at it with his right eye, his left eye cocked toward the massive gas stoves. On the other side of the black door, snow fell heavily.

He walked to the door and examined a primitive fastener, a crossbar permitting the door to be opened inward rather than outward. Mounted by a set of cleats, it allowed the board to slide past the frame to block or unblock the door. He reached out and slid the board through the cleats and pulled the door open. A gush of brutal cold swept past him, bringing large wet flakes into his face. Quickly, he pushed the door shut and slid the board back into place. He stood unmoving and cursed the cold.

He left the kitchen and walked up the stairs to the hallway that led to his makeshift office. From the middle drawer of the desk, he pulled Gannon's file once more and turned to the photograph of the Englishman.

Why did this man haunt him? In all his life, he had never feared anyone. Yet, as he studied the picture, he knew there was something different about this particular man. The photograph was small, a sepia cast to it. Krenz rubbed the surface with his thumb as if he were an exorcist, pulling the heart and mind of the man into his own, where he would dissect it like a laboratory specimen. He leaned back and pulled his gun, carefully checking the load. He was ready.

CHAPTER THIRTEEN

The cold that hit Avery Gannon was unlike anything he had ever felt. He pushed through the white drifts down the Place de la Concorde and realized immediately he must find the safe house and find it quickly or the snow would be his tomb. His bearings told him to move west, toward Avenue Gabriel where he would find the house as well as a route that would lead him away from the hotel. Unfortunately, it would lead him closer to 12 Rue Des Saussaies where the Gestapo waited out the storm. He pulled his fedora down farther onto his forehead and leaned into the wind, his legs thrashing into the snow, his shoulders hunched and stiffening by the minute.

He left the woman without the least bit of compunction. Had left her with no thoughts of what she would say or do when she awoke and found him gone. Why should he care; her plans for his escape were ludicrous and far removed from reality. Did she think the Gestapo was a special group of Germans whose job was to merely keep order in the occupied city? It was war. It was that simple. No more, no less. The life of an enemy was worthless as far as the Germans were concerned. After all, they were the conquerors, an army of murderers, thieves and rapists, who considered Paris and its citizens well-deserved bounty. If he got out alive, it would be his own doing, not that of a woman who lived her life in a cocoon of wealth and luxury.

Had he made a mistake? He cursed silently, his body temperature plummeting, his legs beginning to move in slow motion.

On Avenue Gabriel, he saw a small alcove nestled in a stone building and shoved himself inside, away from the wind. His breath came in shallow gasps as he peered into the night and wished for warmth.

While he rested, he scanned the avenue and the obscure facades of buildings that stood like white ghosts, frozen like the steep cliffs along the fjords. Oddly, in his small cave, the hush of snow seemed comforting, a quiet place that soothed him, promising a fleeting moment of reprieve. He closed his eyes and waited.

***

It was the noise of crunching snow that first alerted him. Boots, emitting sounds like the approach of a winter monster, moved closer, step-by-step, until they were a mere five meters away, only moments from Gannon's hide-away.

He moved his hand inside his coat and found his weapon. His hand shaking from cold, he released the safety, easing forward to see two figures coming toward him, each wearing a winter field hat, their bodies buffeted by the wind, their rifles hugged into their heavy coats. Were they following his trail through the snow? He watched and waited.

At three meters from Gannon's hiding place, the two men hesitated. Gannon gripped his gun tightly and watched as they huddled together and cupped their gloved hands around a cigarette. The match flame flickered only seconds. They were so close the smell of smoke drifted into the alcove. He would shoot the soldier on the right first, then the other. Only a few seconds between the shots.

His trigger finger throbbed in anticipation; his training ensuring calm. He aimed and stilled his heart. A full minute passed. His eyes burned, never leaving the soldier on his right.

If they continued in the same direction, they would fall right into his lap. If they changed course, perhaps he could escape. Escape without killing them. Finding two dead soldiers would mount a relentless search for their killer. As much as he would like to squeeze the trigger, he would rather diminish his chances for capture by remaining hidden. Patience. His profession had taught him patience.

It would not happen. The soldier on the left faced Gannon's hiding place and when he tossed the butt of his cigarette toward the alcove, his eyes followed. Gannon saw the instant his body language changed, the moment his eyes focused on the dark shape huddled in the recesses of the building.

It was only a split second, but seemed an eternity, as Gannon's finger pulled the trigger and watched as the impact twisted the soldier's body backwards. A second bullet struck the standing soldier, but the hit wasn't solid. A third bullet found his chest just as he lunged toward Gannon and fell into the snow.

Gannon did not move while he watched a thin blanket of snow cover their bodies. In an hour, there would be no sign of the soldiers, of their helmets, of their rifles. They would become frozen shapes in the snow. Young misguided men who had revered Hitler and proclaimed their loyalty to the Fatherland. How could they know their lives would end in a horrible war, never to dance the Blue Danube with a beautiful, plump girl with pigtails the color of fresh-cut hay?

Chapter Fourteen

The temperature dipped lower, minus eight degrees Celsius. Gannon pushed his way toward Rue du Faubourg Saint-Honoré where he knew he would find a haven. A haven not only from the wrath of the Germans, but also from the killer blizzard that swept him to his knees as he rounded the corner.

He pulled himself up and leaned on a stone fence and peered through the snow at a lone house that stood in a huddle of small snow-covered trees and shrubs. The safe house.

The windows were dark. No electricity, of course. He looked for the soft glow of a candle. Instead, the dark was like an abyss, promising no warmth, no reprieve from the cold.

His senses told him to wait and watch. A difficult thing to do when howling winds and biting snow threatened to take his last bit of body heat.

Again, he found a place to push his body out of the wind. This time it was against the fence, a fence with stones as cold as blocks of ice. He knew his energy was waning. He must get warm. Yet, approaching the house without some degree of observation was deadly. He waited a moment before deciding to move closer. Perhaps not as cautionary as he should be, but his circumstances were desperate; he could not last much longer.

Gannon left the fence and stumbled the few meters to the house where he pressed his body against the north wall and waited. Listening. Watching.

He cursed silently. A sign. That's all he needed. Something to tell him to go or stay. His eyes followed the line of the house, the roof, the yard, the stoop. Nothing. If someone had been there, snow would have covered their tracks. He had no choice. He must go inside or freeze to death. He pulled his gun and slid around the corner of the house to a lone door.

The doorknob seemed ominous to him, a last chance to turn around and leave. He stared at it for a long moment and reconsidered his plan. Gun drawn, he would bend low and step inside. Then, move immediately to his right and press his body against the wall. And wait.

It took three seconds to open the door, step inside and shove his body against the wall. The only sound was his own breathing, a slow deliberate breath that calmed him and kept him focused. He hated unknowns, yet he had, by his own admission, placed himself in a strange, dark house full of unknowns, depending only on luck and the skills of his trade to protect him. He lowered his pistol and relaxed his body.

He shouldn't have. The muzzle of the gun pressing into his temple was as cold and hard as the ice that gripped Paris.

"Ah, monsieur, your caution is good, but not good enough. I saw you at the fence. I almost heard you thinking - should I go or should I stay."

A low chuckle. "You Englishmen. You are so pompous. You think the world is made just for you. Did you really think I would just let you walk in here? You could be Hitler himself, eh? But, I smelled you first. You Englishmen have a certain . . . certain . . . odor. You know? Like boiled cabbage. I must introduce you to French perfumes. Perhaps then you would not be so offensive."

Laughter, like the devil himself, filled the room. In the darkness, Gannon shuddered and wished for light. *Who was this devil?* He waited a long moment before he spoke.

"I take it you are French with that surly accent of yours. Talk about pompous. And French perfumes? I would prefer to smell like boiled cabbage than smell like a fag in heat."

The gun pressed harder into Gannon's temple. "Englishman,

it would be to your advantage to be kind. You need a friend, not an enemy. Is that so?"

Gannon shook is head up and down. It was so.

"Let us go into the middle of the house so I may light a candle. We want no light showing in the windows." The man with the deep voice removed his gun from Gannon's temple and grasped his arm. "This way." He lit a match in the narrow hallway and Gannon followed.

Gannon was led through the house to a small, windowless bedroom. He heard the strike of another match, then saw light flicker from the wick of a candle. Quickly, he looked at the man who no longer held a weapon and felt a slight flicker of recognition. "Your name? It is Plomion. Am I correct?"

"Ha! You ask me my name? My friend, what is *your* name?" The man squared his shoulders and looked at Gannon, his eyes dark and curious. The light from the candle revealed deep vertical crevices along the edges of his mouth, a Frenchman's chin, narrow, almost feminine. But, his heavy day-old beard attested to his maleness. Black bushy eyebrows swept across his brow and lifted easily when he asked Gannon again, "Your name, monsieur?"

"You know very well who I am or you wouldn't have removed your pistol from my temple, sir."

The Frenchman laughed. "So, you are an intelligent Englishman. There are so few of them, you know."

He paused. "Yes, I know who you are, Monsieur Gannon. What I don't know is what we're going to do with you."

For the first time, Gannon relaxed his body. "What you're going to do with me? It is I who must decide what is to be done. Your assistance will be needed, of course. I say we consider all the options."

"Options? Monsieur, there *are* no options. Plain and simple, the Germans know you are still in Paris. As soon as the blizzard is over, they will come after you like a hungry pack of wolves."

Gannon studied the wool béret that fell forward on the low forehead of the Frenchman, almost touching his eyebrows. He seemed to be a man of no nonsense. Of course, he was. There was a war and French Résistance was written all over him.

He sighed heavily. Again, he had been taken from the safety of his own choices and decisions and thrust into someone else'. He felt himself become even more anxious as he looked at the Frenchman and raised his voice.

"Your escape routes, monsieur?" he asked.

The throaty laughter again filled the room. "My friend, there are none. That's what I'm here to tell you."

CHAPTER FIFTEEN

Eléonore stirred in the comfort of her bed, the black fur covering all but her nose. She lay quietly for a few moments, her body curled into a fetal position.

"Monsieur Gannon? You are here?" Her voice was small, questioning. She waited a few moments before she sat up and found matches on the bedside table and lit a candle, the flame sending soft light into the cold room and confirming the absence of Avery Gannon. She slowly moved her eyes around the room as if expecting him to momentarily evolve from a hidden corner, his deep voice telling her *'yes, I am here.'*

She waited, but there was no Englishman, no soothing voice floating through the shadows and to her bed. *So, he has left. What a foolish man. I am certain I could have saved his life. What a pity. The Gestapo will find him and that will be the end of the spy.*

Eléonore slipped her hand beneath the pillow and found a small photograph of Edouard. Handsome Edouard, his black eyes smiling. At her, she supposed. Everything he did was for her. But, if that was true, why did he leave her? Go to Turkey, to Greece? It seemed her entire marriage had been spent . . . waiting. Waiting for him to return to her. And now, there would be no more waiting. He would never return.

She trailed her finger along his jaw line. A French aristocrat. Born into a family of titles and positions that proclaimed his status, his nobility was not awarded by the French monarchy, but through heredity, an appendage of his family name. It was, however, the fact he was a *gentilhomme,* a gentleman, that was his greatest pride. The title *roturier*, commoner, could never be applied to Édouard Delafloté. *Count Édouard Delafloté.*

The image of the photograph blurred as Eléonore felt the hotness of tears. She pushed it back into its hiding place and buried herself deeper into the fur. *Thirty years old and I am a widow. Alone and without purpose.* For a fleeting moment, she thought about the pills.

She well knew she was no longer in the spring of her life, but in fading summer, a time that did not recognize the promise of a giddy youth, an age filled with carefree days and sweet dreams of summers on the beaches of Spain. Instead, her future seemed dark, groping for something to sustain her, to carry her through the long days that lay ahead without Édouard.

Who was she if she wasn't Édouard's wife? For a moment, she stilled. *Yes, who am I?* She sat up and felt a jolting of her heart, a pumping of her blood, a rising of her body heat.

Quickly, she gathered the fur around her, left the bed and crossed the room to the armoire, where her fingers grasped the pull and swung the doors wide, revealing a woman's wardrobe of luxurious capes lined with silk and bordered with mink, flirtatious hats with feathers and netting that swirled in the air and proclaimed its wearer a woman of fashion.

She slipped a long woolen dress over her head. Without a glance, she pushed her wardrobe aside and reached far back behind them and pulled out one of Edouard's suits. Wool, custom-tailored for his lean frame. She pressed the fabric to her face and smelled of him, a faint eau de Cologne, a citrus fragrance that he said reminded him of an Italian spring. *I am here, Eléonore.* Her heart stilled as she sank to the cold floor.

***

A soft tap at the door. The spy. He had returned. Perhaps he was smarter than she thought, had come back to beg her to assist him in escaping the Germans, had come to his senses, believing she was his only chance for survival. Another tap.

She stood and closed the doors of the armoire. "Yes?"

"It is I. Monsieur Bedeau. May I come in?"

"I'm coming." She crossed the room and opened the door to find a snow-encrusted Monsieur Bedeau. His bushy eyebrows held the wetness of melted snow, the fiber of his coat stiff with ice. His nose flushed red, almost comic, as she looked at his stern face. "Monsieur, you have been out in the awful blizzard! Come!" She pulled him inside, where he collapsed into a chair.

"Yes, how foolish of me. It is too cold for an old man such as I. I could have frozen to death or worse, been shot. The curfew, you know." He removed his wool hat and released wild tufts of stiff hair. "It was the Englishman, you see."

Eléonore's eyes widened. "The Englishman? What of the Englishman?"

"Madame, I am sure you have noticed he is not in your room." His words were impatient. "I saw him slipping through the lobby toward the rear of the hotel. I think he knew I was watching, but he ignored me. He had no intention of allowing us to help him escape. Not a single word of gratitude to you for saving his life nor to me for not turning him in to the Germans." The old concierge slapped his knee. "Let him save his own skin."

Eléonore sat on the small couch opposite the old man. What would she do if she were a spy trying to escape the Germans? It was simple to her – she would change her identity. If only Gannon had trusted her instincts that a new identity was his best chance to evade the Gestapo. "Why did you follow him?"

"I . . . don't quite know. I'm sure he is a capable man. But, the odds he will escape are not good. Perhaps I followed him in hopes I could talk with him. Convince him that his best chances were . . . "

"Were to stay here? Find a safe house?"

"A safe house most likely." The old man leaned his head on the back of the chair and closed his eyes. "Only problem is, there is no safe house. No escape routes. It is certain the Germans will not rest until they have the Englishman." Bedeau opened his eyes and leaned forward. "There is something I haven't told you."

Eléonore raised her eyebrows. "Oui, monsieur, I'm sure there are many things of which I am unaware." A wry smile. "Perhaps you'd like to tell me . . . everything you know."

The eyes of Monsieur Bedeau held Eléonore's for a long moment, perhaps contemplating his relationship with this woman, who, for the moment, seemed to know very well the difficulties they faced as well as the dangers in which they found themselves.

"I followed Gannon down Avenue Gabriel, where he stepped into the alcove of a building. I waited. It wasn't long before two German soldiers came from the direction of the Rue Boissy-d'Anglas and stopped mere meters from Gannon. I watched as he shot them. He waited in the alcove a few minutes and then continued toward Rue du Faubourg."

Bedeau stood and began pacing. "Can you imagine? Two German soldiers dead in the snow. When their bodies are found, the citizens of Paris will suffer at the hands of the Germans. No stone will be left unturned." Bedeau stopped his pacing and looked at Eléonore. "I fear for our lives, Madame. I am sure they know the Englishman was here at the hotel."

Eléonore stood abruptly. "Monsieur Bedeau," she said, an authoritative twist to her words, "we are citizens of Paris with no affiliation with anyone or anything that is anti-German. We have nothing to fear. They have no proof that the spy visited us. Only three of us knew of his presence and, certainly, *we* are not going to divulge that information to the Germans." She held Bedeau's gaze with such intensity that he looked away.

"And furthermore --"

The room stilled. Both Monsieur Bedeau and Madame Delafloté turned toward the door of the hotel suite and watched as the knob turned. They stood, not breathing, fear in their eyes. When the door pushed open, Avery Gannon stood stiff with cold, his gun in his hand. Behind him, the Frenchman, panting, leaned against the wall and whispered. "Have you some whiskey?"

CHAPTER SIXTEEN

Herr Horst Krenz, groggy with sleep, pulled himself up from the small cot in the dark corner of his room at the Hotel de L'Elysée. His watch read 5:10 a.m., two hours before the dim light of dawn revealed a snow-smothered Paris. *Still no electrical power*, he cursed as he stumbled from his bed and toward his desk. His position as head of the Paris Gestapo afforded him little sleep, especially now that a manhunt for the English spy consumed him.

He had even dreamed of him, the spy who seemed to vanish at every turn, disappear into a shroud of black air, a mocking laugh following him through the darkness. In the dream, Krenz had reached out and placed his Luger into the neck of the spy, twisting it until it was buried deep into Gannon's flesh.

He remembered the anticipation he felt in the dream, his heart rate rising as he pulled the trigger, the satisfaction of knowing the spy was dead. Yet, when he awoke, the barrel of the Luger had not been in the spy's neck, he had not pulled the trigger. Gannon was not dead.

At his desk, he lit a candle and pulled the Gannon file from the middle drawer once more, retrieved the magnifying glass and placed it over the small photograph.

If he could see his eyes, he would know the depth of his cunningness, the degree of his *mörderinstinke. Killer instincts.* He studied the information on Gannon for the hundredth time. On the first page, at the top of the sheet, the words: *Avery Gannon, Known Spy Since 1936, British Secret Intelligence Service.* Krenz picked up a pen and crossed through the word '*spy*' and above it, wrote "*meuchelmörder.*" *Assassin.*

The file on Gannon contained information dating back to 1936, yet he knew very little about *the man.* All he had was a photograph, a very small one with obscure features, more fedora and overcoat than anything else.

He knew there were two spies. Was it possible they were connected? Knew one another? The timing was interesting. Incongruously, he had no information on the man from Andorra, had no idea of his true identity. Had arrested him at a Paris train station simply because he appeared too casual, seeming unafraid of all that was taking place around him.

What man would behave in that manner when all of Paris reeked with Parisians whose fear of the Germans emanated from their pores and left them powerless?

He had looked into Andorra's eyes and seen no fear, but more of a mocking smugness that had riled him as he studied the face, then the papers he carried. The papers were forged, of course, stating he was a businessman from Andorra, a small landlocked country in the eastern part of the Pyrenees Mountains. Why would someone travel from the safety of a small neutral country to war-torn Paris, even for business with the Germans?

Had it not been for Andorra's eyes, Krenz would not have been so suspicious and perhaps let him go. But, again, his instincts had surfaced. He took him into Gestapo headquarters for further questioning. And as usual his favorite questioning tactics had been used. Much to the sorrow of the businessman from Andorra, the questioning yielded nothing, only a more intense desire by the Gestapo to learn his true identity.

Near death from endless torture, Andorra was shot and his body dumped into the River Seine.

Shooting him in front of the citizens of Paris had been a carefully designed act by Krenz. He so enjoyed keeping the spoils of war aware of the supremacy of their captors. In the end, he had learned nothing specific about Andorra. Yet, he knew he was involved with the Allies, a liaison perhaps, who carried secret information to the French Résistance. Ha, a liaison? A liaison was a spy.

Then, there was the clue. Overlooked by everyone but Krenz, it was so insignificant that Krenz did not notice its presence until Andorra was stripped naked and placed in a chair in the interrogation room at Headquarters.

A small wound near his armpit, a bullet wound. A scar that rippled the skin. Why would a businessman from Andorra have a bullet wound? When he asked Andorra to explain the wound, he saw an infinitesimal shift, a slight widening of his lids, then a veil that slid over his eyes.

He had circled Andorra's chair and looked at his back, where he saw a flushing of his skin, splotches of red. "Herr Businessman from Andorra, what is your real name?" he had asked.

"You have my papers."

"Of course, I have your papers. Forged as they are. You are not who you say you are." The German circled the chair again, a slow, menacing walk that allowed the sound of his boot heels to reverberate off the walls in the near empty room. What need did the room have for furniture? All that was needed was a single chair. A chair that had a simple use.

"The scar at the base of your right armpit? Explanation."

"A hunting accident when I was a boy."

A smooth utterance of words. But, again, too casual. Krenz' senses heightened. "A hunting accident? What were you hunting?"

"Rabbits."

"Where?"

"In the mountains of Andorra."

"What kind of gun?"

"A hunting rifle?"

"What kind of hunting rifle?"

A pause. "I was just a boy. I don't know what kind."

"Who shot you?"

"My cousin."

"What was his name?"

"Phillip."

"What happened after he shot you?"

"We ran for help?"

"Just the two of you?"

"Yes."

"How old were you?"

"Twelve."

"Two twelve year old boys, hunting alone?"

"That is correct."

Krenz paced while a heavy silence filled the room. "So your cousin mistook you for a rabbit?"

"No. The gun misfired."

Krenz stopped pacing and leaned toward the man from Andorra. His right eye studied the bullet wound, while his left eye wandered across the room. "The wound seems . . . new."

Again, a heavy silence, a silence that allowed the breathing of both men to be heard above the sound of Krenz's boot heels as he walked across the room and turned his back on Andorra. At last, the Gestapo chief stopped and stared at the naked man in the interrogation chair. "You're lying. The wound is new."

Again, the slightest shudder from the prisoner. Krenz's wayward left eye saw it. Such a small flicker of movement, but it was there. "My dear man, it seems we are at the end of this interrogation." A laugh, low in his throat, rose like a witch's brew.

The German meandered across the room and stood in front of Andorra.

"It baffles me that you continue to lie when you are certainly not who you say you are." Krenz waited a long moment as silence lingered between the two men. He walked to the door, hesitated and turned to stare at Andorra, a long calculating look as if making a decision. The Gestapo chief saw the veil that still covered his eyes. There would be no confession.

Krenz closed Gannon's file. Of course, Gannon knew Andorra. He also knew who had murdered him. Why else would he have remained in Paris?

CHAPTER SEVENTEEN

Eléonore watched as Gannon slid to the floor, his body rigid with cold, a moan escaping his chattering lips. He looked at Eléonore, his eyes pleading.

She crossed the room and knelt beside him. "Yes, I am here, Englishman."

When she touched his face, he closed his eyes, a hint of a smile at the corner of his lips. "It seems you are always saving me."

Eléonore said nothing as she stood and removed her fur, tossing it across Gannon. "It seems you continue to disregard my advice, Monsieur." She looked up at Monsieur Bedeau. "Please bring whiskey for these men. They are half-frozen."

"*Oui*, Madame."

Plomion lay only a few feet away, his eyes closed, breathing quietly. She glanced at Gannon. "You know Monsieur Plomion?"

Gannon opened his eyes, his lips beginning to turn pink. "We have not been formally introduced. Seems he knows me."

"How is it that you are together?"

Gannon remained quiet for a long moment. When he looked at Eléonore, he seemed hesitant. "I'm not sure."

"Do you think I am a fool?" The words fired across

Eléonore's tongue like bullets. "I assure you it is not so. I dare say you both are in this spy business. You treat me as though I am a happenstance in this . . . this grand scheme." Her voice rose. "By all means, Englishman, continue with your charade as you walk into the waiting arms of the Germans."

She stood as Monsieur Bedeau returned. She nodded to him and walked to the window. From the third floor, the room faced the Place de la Concorde. Only two hours before daylight. Now, as she pulled back the draperies, her thoughts were of Édouard. If only he were here, he would know what to do.

She watched as the night whispered of peril, of a day forthcoming that would be like no other day. She shivered and grasped the edge of the windowsill as if to stop time, to keep the inevitable from occurring.

When she turned toward the three men, her eyes were fierce, her jaw unrelenting. Gone was the wealthy, young widow, frightened and helpless, who had hidden herself in a dark fur and wished for death. She was replaced by a woman of indomitable strength, a woman who now marched across the room toward the three men like a soldier entering battle.

"Monsieurs, it seems you are in need of a woman."

The three men stared at Eléonore. *In need of a woman?*

The lovely black-haired widow returned to the armoire and pulled a custom-made suit Édouard had worn the last time they were together. A Chanel suit – chosen by Gabrielle "Coco" Chanel herself, long before she became a vocal supporter of the Vichy regime and fell out of favor with Parisians.

Eléonore turned slowly from the armoire, a slight smile creasing her face. "Monsieur Gannon, come here, please."

***

Gannon lay on the floor, the black fur a barrier between him and the woman who held her husband's clothing. He stared at her for one long, calculating moment, his mind sweeping the possibilities of its meaning. In a glimmer of tenderness, he felt his heart, not his cunning mind, consider the seemingly fragile woman who challenged him - who, with an abundance of naiveté, offered herself to him as the means to his survival.

It was an impossibility. Years in his clandestine career had taught him many things – especially the dangers of trusting anyone but himself. And, now, an alliance with a woman whose only life experiences had been cultivated inside sequined gowns and coalitions with French aristocrats. A husband who most likely protected her from the inequities of life and most assuredly the war. Could he survive if he succumbed to her salacious, but frivolous, instruction? Would it be foolish if he did as he was told?

"Madame, what is it that you expect of me?"

The smile on Eléonore's face widened. "Why, Englishman, your cooperation. Is that so difficult?"

"Difficult? Madame, we are in the throes of war. Could there be anything more difficult?"

"More difficult?" she asked, her smile fading, the jaw tightening.

Exasperation washed over Avery as his voice became hard. "More difficult than surviving this war?"

"Why, Englishman, you surprise me. That is what this is all about. Your survival. Do you find this discussion annoying? Would you rather discuss how beautiful the golden dome of Les Invalides is when the sun is shining? Or, the Place de La Concorde after a rain?"

She walked forward a few steps and looked down at him, her voice but a whisper. "Of course, it is possible you will not live to see either of those things." She stood without moving and stared into his eyes.

Avery felt a pounding in his ears. He looked at Monsieurs Bedeau and Plomion. Both men lifted their eyebrows in question. *Was the Englishman going to acquiesce to the French woman?*

***

Gannon pulled himself from the floor and faced the woman who commanded that he come to her. If he turned around, he could simply walk out the door, down the stairs and out into the streets of Paris, where he could hopefully hide from the enemy who searched for him. He hesitated with indecision, something unfamiliar to him. He must listen to his instincts if he were to survive. In the next moment, he felt himself move toward the woman. Could she save his life?

"Ah, Monsieur Gannon, your trust humbles me. Come." She

reached out her arm and waved her hand, the slim fingers beckoning him to continue toward her. Did she really have his trust? Her face was full of expectation, almost child-like with anticipation. Neither the inequities of life nor the horror of war had found their way into the luminous eyes. A sadness perhaps. But, that was expected. She had lost the man she loved.

He was closer now, could almost touch her extended hand. Behind him, he knew Bedeau and Plomion waited anxiously, perhaps wondering what the spy was thinking.

Gannon found he could not take her hand. Perhaps she didn't intend for him to do so. Yet, her hand lingered in the space between them, a bridge that he must cross. Again, he relied on his instincts. He touched her hand.

"Please remove your coat, Monsieur Gannon." Her eyes traveled the length of him as she slowly circled him. She stopped once to smooth her hands across the back of his shoulders, measuring him as her hands then slid to his waist.

It was the first time he had been deliberately touched by a woman since his arrival in Paris a year ago. He took a deep breath and felt himself relax. "Madame, would you be so kind as to explain what you have in mind?" He could feel her breath on the back of his neck when her hand pushed through his hair. From behind him, he heard her sigh.

"Monsieur, we must cut your hair." She turned and addressed Monsieur Bedeau. "Scissors, Monsieur Bedeau?"

A quizzical look washed the face of the old concierge. "Scissors?"

"Yes, scissors. At once!"

Gannon stiffened. "Again, Madame, you must explain."

She turned and faced him. "But, of course. You are to be my husband, Monsieur Gannon. My darling, handsome husband. It delights me so. But, we have work to do. Undress, please."

"Undress?"

"Again, the language problem?" The young widow seemed irritated as she returned to the armoire and pulled more of her dead husband's clothing from the cloth-lined hangers. She laid them on a chair, unbuttoned a shirt the color of fresh fallen snow, threw a red silk tie across her shoulder, then scooped a pair of cufflinks from an ornate wooden box. When she looked up, Gannon was undressed except for a pair of shapeless under shorts that hung too large on his lean body.

Eléonore walked to the middle of the room where Gannon stood and examined him carefully. She did not fail to notice the swell beneath the threadbare shorts that draped his slim hips.

CHAPTER EIGHTEEN

Herr Krenz watched as the dim light of morning crept across the rooftops of the city. No sun. The day would remain dismal, but at least it had stopped snowing. The cold would keep the monstrous drifts in place for days, the sidewalks and streets lost under the tons of snow that obscured familiar landmarks. Perhaps the passing of night would reveal the hiding place of the English spy, the assassin who had kept the City of Light on high alert for months.

He called for his aide. "Corporal Bauer, arrange transportation to the Hotel de Crillon. We leave in one hour." He turned back toward the window. He had advised Captain Linbaugh that he no longer wanted him to interrogate Monsieur Bedeau. He decided he himself would do the questioning. The old concierge knew something. He was sure of it. He would question him in a civil manner in the beginning. If he did not cooperate, there would be no leniency, no softness for the citizen of Paris.

"Also, Herr Bauer, have Lieutenant Vogel come to my office at once.

Lieutenant Paul Vogel. His loyalties to the Third Reich ran through his blood as powerful as the armies that had crushed France. Krenz heard the click of Vogel's heels and turned from the window. "Herr Vogel. I trust you slept well."

"Yes. Thank you, Herr Krenz." Vogel's back stiffened. It was obvious he considered a meeting with Krenz stressful, never without a certain amount of trepidation that made one shake with anxiety. Perhaps it was the wayward eye that caused the unrest, confusion as to where to catch the gaze from the German. He waited and focused his attention on the right eye.

"Herr Vogel, while I am visiting the Hotel de Crillon, I would like your assessment of Herr Gannon's file. Perhaps you can gain insight into how such a successful operation by the British occurred. And the French. I'm beginning to think the English spy has worked with the French more than once thought. If that is the case, our visit from our dear art collector Hermann Göring might be . . . shall we say . . . somewhat precarious."

Herr Vogel lifted his eyebrows. "Göring?"

A curt nod. "Yes. He arrives the day after tomorrow. When I return from Monsieur Bedeau's interrogation, I would like to assemble my staff and organize a plan of safe passage for him. His visit is only twenty-four hours. But, it must be a safe twenty-four hours." Krenz paused and watched the face of his subordinate. "You seem surprised Göring is visiting this lovely city. You are aware this will be his fifth visit since the summer of '40?"

The younger man, Krenz' best strategist, looked confused. "What about Herr Göring's own bodyguards? Surely, they are sufficient to ensure his safety."

"Do you really think so? For the past three months, we have done nothing but bury the bodies of our superior officers while their killer dances in the streets of Paris." *If Göring falls prey to a bullet, I am a dead man.* His face flushed. "We'll provide our own security for his visit." He turned and again walked to the window. "Of course, it goes without saying; we'll capture the spy before his arrival."

Krenz' shoulders sagged slightly. He heard an almost imperceptible tremor in his words. *Capture the spy?* All the Germans in Paris had been trying to do that for quite some time.

CHAPTER NINETEEN

The distance from Gestapo Headquarters to the Hotel de Crillon was one kilometer, down the Rue des Saussaies to Rue du Fauboure Saint Honoré and finally the Place de la Concorde, where Napoleon's hearse had proceeded from the Arc de Triomphe down Champs-Élysées, across the Place de la Concorde to the *Esplanade des Invalides*.

Krenz' entire adult life had been spent studying Napoleon, marveling at his extraordinary abilities in espionage and deception, a mastermind for winning battle after battle across Europe. He considered Napoleon the epitome of the Romantic hero, the persecuted, lonely man with a flawed genius.

He had paralleled himself with the Imperial Monarch of France. Had it not been for his flaw, he felt he could have led Germany's armies much like Napoleon had led the French. Even so, his genius was not wasted. As head of the Paris Gestapo, he fulfilled his dreams of power, of dominion over the weak. And, now, as he thought of the arrival of Göring, he smiled to himself. He would hand Göring the head of the English spy.

Krenz cursed as his motorcar slid into an embankment and its motor stalled. His soldiers immediately pushed the car back into the roadway and proceeded toward the de Crillon. Krenz reached inside his coat and felt for the Luger he had treasured since Hitler called for the youth of Germany to believe as he believed.

Along the avenue, Parisians slipped from their shops and pushed the snow to the street with their makeshift shovels, planks that two men could maneuver like a small bulldozer. From the windows, faces peered out into the morning, relieved the blizzard had moved on, had found another place to ravage its winds and cold.

The Hotel de Crillon seemed inviting. Snow had been brushed from the entryway, the smell of coffee drifting from the kitchens where a woman peeled potatoes.

Monsieur Claude Bedeau, dressed in his worn woolen hotel uniform, pulled on his gloves and watched the street from his post inside the lobby. His old eyes were keen enough to see a German staff car travel slowly up the Place de la Concorde, the Nazi swastika emblazoned on the motorcar flags, which snapped loudly in the early morning, an ominous announcement of the arrival of the Germans.

He remained still. He wondered how he knew they would come. Perhaps it was the German colonel who had burst into the hotel looking for the English spy. He squinted his eyes. Yes, it was the colonel with the crooked eye who had sniffed and smelled the hotel like a bloodhound, who had seared the rooms with his one good eye like a pre-historic monster looking for prey.

Bedeau placed his hat carefully over his head of chaotic hair, took a deep breath and pushed open the heavy door of the hotel, a grand show of fictitious welcome for his portentous visitor. He was a good citizen of Paris.

"Herr Bedeau. I see you survived this foul weather."

"Indeed, Colonel Krenz. As have you." Bedeau's words were smooth, low, like a rumbling from a dark cave. Deep and controlled, they held no fear.

"Do I smell coffee, Herr Bedeau?" A sly smile revealing large teeth crossed the face of the German and fell upon a waiting Bedeau.

How wolf-like he looked, thought Bedeau, as he nodded

slightly. "Not true coffee. More or less, a mixture of ground acorns and roasted potato peelings," he said casually as he held the eyes of the German. "There's been no coffee since June 1940."

Bedeau knew the statement did not go unnoticed by Krenz as it referenced a well-known date: the month Germans marched into Paris and destroyed the French flag. Krenz ignored Bedeau's subtle lack of respect. "Acorns and potato peelings. How ingenious. I think I should like to have a cup, Herr Bedeau."

Bedeau played the game. "By all means, come." Krenz walked past him and instead of seating himself in the hotel dining room, walked the hall to the massive kitchens and pushed open the door. He stood in his inglorious uniform and waited until Bedeau walked past him into the cavernous room, finding the stove and the gleaming pot.

Madame Lefèbvre, the cook, sat nearby with a large bowl of potatoes in her lap. At seeing Krenz, her expression did not change; her face was always contemptuous when she was in the presence of Germans.

Krenz called across the kitchen, "I'll serve myself if you don't mind."

Bedeau gestured with an open hand to the stove and pot. He then glanced at Madame Lefèbvre, who peeled potatoes while sending furtive glances at the German.

With a show of feigned enthusiasm, Krenz poured coffee into a large ceramic cup he had pulled from the shelving above the stove.

"I am curious, Herr Bedeau." He returned the pot to the stove and shifted his body to lean against the large wooden table that housed a myriad of spices and utensils. "I am curious about your guests at the hotel. Would I find them acceptable?" Krenz turned his face and his left eye found Bedeau.

Bedeau raised his bushy eyebrows slightly, but his eyes did not waver. He held them steady and replied. "Acceptable? And what would you perceive as an acceptable guest, Colonel Krenz?"

Krenz smiled and sipped his coffee, a long, slow sip, while he contemplated the question from the stoic concierge. Then, the smile faded, revealing an expression that sent a chill into the room. "It occurs to me, Herr Bedeau, that your question reveals a certain . . . shall we say . . . ignorance."

He placed his cup on the wooden table and walked a step closer to Bedeau. "If you are ignorant of the wishes of the Third Reich as regards who you should or should not house, then I must conclude just anyone could be residing at your hotel. Am I correct?"

Bedeau smiled. "Your conclusion that I am ignorant is incorrect, Colonel Krenz. Your conclusion that just anyone could be residing at this hotel is correct." He paused. "The guests at this hotel are just that – guests. I portend you will adhere to the wishes of the Third Reich as you look at the guest registry and determine if there is anyone who . . . shall we say . . . does not . . . "

"Enough! I take offense at your blatant disregard of proclamations placed on the City of Paris and its citizens." Krenz placed his hand near his Luger. "It is well known who can or cannot reside at your hotel. Indeed, I will look at your registry as well as every square inch of this hotel." Krenz moved toward the doorway. "I suggest you advise your guests that there will be an inspection of their rooms . . . as well as they themselves."

Krenz burst through the doorway, barked at his soldiers. "Place men at the front and rear of the hotel. Watch the roof, the windows. No one enters or leaves this hotel."

Bedeau looked at Madame Lefèbvre. The knife in her hand stilled as she returned his stare. "Madame Lefèbvre, I am thinking you should peel extra potatoes."

CHAPTER TWENTY

In Room 308, Avery Gannon and Eléonore Delafloté were alone. Plomion had left with Bedeau. There were things they had to do. Gannon stood before a mahogany cheval mirror, surprised he hardly recognized himself. His hair was no longer disheveled, but had been neatly trimmed, combed in the fashionable style found in the most elite establishments in Paris.

In amazement, he had watched as Madame Delafloté brushed black shoe polish into his hair, transforming his light gray to the color of coal. Even his eyebrows glistened with dark highlights, all due to shoe polish.

She had even shaved him. What a traumatic occurrence when he kept still and watched the sharp blade of a razor skim past his quivering cheek and down his jaw. Never in his life had he trusted anyone, with such trepidation.

His eyes left the face he saw in the mirror and traveled over his custom suit, where shoulder pads and a tapered waist smoothed his body into a man who reeked of wealth and position. His cuff links were gold and pearl encrusted, his champlevé tie clip encasing a silk tie the color of a blood orange. The woman who had even commanded he wear a pair of silk underwear had overlooked no detail.

When her work was complete, she simply looked at him and said, "Edouard, darling, please have a glass of Cognac with me."

It was at that moment that he knew the transformation had been successful. Her words had snared him like a wire noose. There was no escaping the fact her plan had been brilliant. She had all the tools, her dead husband's identification, his clothes.

Now, with Édouard's imposter, she had a husband and Gannon had a wife; a beautiful woman whose skin glistened, whose lashes flashed black, whose lips gleamed red and who, at this moment, caused a stirring within him. That not only surprised him, it astounded him.

"Cognac?"

She smiled. "You cannot continue to flounder over the French language. You speak perfect French, yet you question most everything I say."

A frustrated Gannon shook his head. "Madame – "

"You must call me Eléonore."

He hesitated while his eyes swept her face. "Eléonore, it is not the language that is troublesome to me. I understand perfectly what you are saying. The problem seems to be *what* you are saying."

"And what is so troublesome about having a glass of Cognac with me, I ask you?" Her indignant tone did not go unnoticed.

He wanted to laugh. When had he lost control? The moment he entered her hotel room for the first time? The instant she had informed him she wanted to become a spy? The second she had inflicted upon him her idea of disguising him in order to elude the Germans?

How did any of this relate to his position as master spy for the British Secret Intelligence Service? It all came back to one thing: he wanted to survive. And, right now, all he had was clothing from a dead man, shoe polish in his hair and a passport in the name of Édouard Delafloté.

"The Cognac?" he heard her say. He looked up from the wing-tipped spectators in which he had placed his feet only moments before and caught her eyebrow lifting in question.

"I think there are more important things to do than drink a glass of Cognac . . . Eléonore."

"And what would they be?"

"If I am impersonating another person, namely Édouard

Delafloté, I would think it beneficial to know a little bit about him. Don't you think?" He paused. "And, by the way, it pleases me if I had to change my identity that I am not a buxom French-woman as you first proposed."

"Actually, it wasn't such a bad idea. You would have made a lovely Frenchwoman, I assure you."

***

Eléonore stared at the handsome Englishman who had so adroitly emerged into an aristocratic Frenchman. His resemblance to Édouard was striking. She felt herself wanting to touch him, to embrace him, to touch her lips to his warm cheek, then tell him she loved him. She felt a surge in her heart rate, a washing of tears in her eyes. She blinked and felt the hurt in her chest grow deeper. She wanted to speak, but could not.

Finally, she walked to the credenza and placed two glasses on a small silver tray. The Cognac bottle was full, a gift from Édouard. When she opened it, she thought she heard him laughing behind her. But, it wasn't Édouard; it was the Englishman. She poured the Cognac and turned toward him.

"My darling," she said. "Do you remember the time we were in Vienna? The time you told me I was your only love, that you could never love another?" She handed Avery the glass and smiled at him.

"Englishman, please remember that I am your wife now and that you love me very much." She tipped her glass toward him. "To your survival."

CHAPTER TWENTY-ONE

Herr Krenz pushed the guest registry aside. "Only fifteen residents at this time? I will assume you know who they are and where they're from."

"They are paying guests in the hotel. I know their names, but that is all," said Bedeau.

"You have no curiosity about them other than their names?"

"No. What would be the purpose?"

Krenz tapped the small book with his forefinger. "Herr Bedeau, just because you know no more than their name does not mean you are innocent of harboring an enemy of the Third Reich." He lifted his chin. "Am I clear?"

Bedeau felt a creeping up his spine, a small movement of skin that found his neck and caused a slight shudder within him. The German was quite clear. Why didn't he just say it: *Are there any Jews at your hotel? Are you hiding an enemy of Germany?*

He found himself wanting to look at the German's wayward eye, the one that moved on its own, away from its brother. An odd thought. Did each eye reveal a different man, one a superior individual who reveled in his powerful role in the Third Reich; the other, a man who was not whole, but merely a semblance of someone who did not meet the standards of the Aryan race of perfect humans? Did the two eyes struggle with each other, confront each other, the right asking the left why are you an imperfection in my almost perfect self?

"Very clear, Colonel Krenz. There are no enemies of the Third Reich in this hotel." Bedeau's words were precise, lacking incongruity.

Hesitating a moment, Krenz walked into the lobby and to the front entryway where his soldiers guarded the hotel. With his back to Bedeau, he said, "There's something else I would like to know, Herr Bedeau."

Bedeau waited and felt his left eyebrow twitch. It had been a signal to him all his life, a twitching eyebrow meant danger, a warning. It twitched again.

"Before the storm, we searched your hotel for an English spy. Was he hiding in your hotel?"

Bedeau hesitated a moment. "You searched the hotel and did not find a spy, Colonel Krenz."

Krenz walked slowly back to the registry desk where Bedeau stood. As if it were a gunshot, Krenz slapped the face of the old man with such force that Bedeau's glasses flew from his face to the floor, blood spurted from his nose and his eyes watered with pain.

"Answer my question, you fool! Or, you will be shot!"

Bedeau reached up and wiped the blood from his nose with a worn handkerchief, never taking his eyes from the German. "There was no spy hiding in the hotel."

In a voice just above a whisper, Krenz spoke, "I trust you are telling the truth, because if I find you are not, I shall enjoy placing you in front of a firing squad. Perhaps in the lobby of your very fine hotel."

"Come!" yelled Krenz, pointing to his guards. "You, too, Herr Bedeau!" Ignoring the waiting elevator, Krenz bounded up the stairs to the second floor, where a search began for the English spy he knew full well had been in the hotel only twenty-four hours earlier.

CHAPTER TWENTY-TWO

"Tell me about Édouard if I am to be Édouard." Gannon crossed his arms and waited.

Eléonore slowly twirled the Cognac in her glass. "A fine, fine man," she said softly, as though to herself. When she looked up, her eyes seemed wistful, a misting that shone in the light.

"More." Avery said. The conversation was necessary, a prelude to action, a reconnoitering with a subordinate prior to entry into a dangerous mission. Despite his impersonation of Édouard, he became the spymaster he was. He had no choice if he was to survive.

"More, of course," she said. Her gaze wandered as she searched for words. "Édouard was quite intelligent, a deep thinker, I would say. Always contemplating situations and finding solutions to problems rather quickly. I guess that is why he rose to such high ranks in the Legion. A leader of men. Decisive." She turned to Avery and looked at him with her luminous eyes, a hesitation as she seemed to study him intently. "Like you."

Avery held her gaze, then. "This French Foreign Legion? Why would a man of his wealth and position fight wars?"

"Oh, that was Édouard. A principled man. A believer in

freedom and democracy." She brushed her hand across her hair. A small gesture of nervousness. Perhaps it was difficult to talk about her dead husband. Had she been able to grieve?

"How often did you see him?"

A wry smile, "Not often enough. He called when he could. Was never able to really tell me where he was or what he was doing. It was all so secretive." She looked at him. "Secretive . . . like your work." She stared a long time, her eyes never leaving his.

"Like my work?"

She nodded slowly. "Yes, like your work. Came and went in the middle of the night. Always seemed rushed."

"What was he wearing when you saw him?"

She frowned. "Wearing?" She thought a moment. "Never a uniform. You know, like a military uniform. I always wondered about that. Wondered why someone of rank in the French Foreign Legion would wear non-descript clothing."

"When did he join the Legion?"

She lifted her chin and looked toward the ceiling, studied the chandelier as if counting the bulbs. "In January of '40. Just before the invasion."

"What did he talk about when you saw him?"

She dipped her chin when she looked at him. A mischievous smile crossed her lips. "I assure you, Monsieur Gannon, there was not much talking when my Édouard came to me." She paused and looked sadly into her empty glass. "He was a tender lover." She sighed. "I shall never forget his touch."

Avery stood and walked to the credenza where the bottle of Cognac sat half empty. He poured a small amount into her glass, then his. "So he never talked about the Legion?"

"No. I wondered why he didn't. Oh, occasionally, he'd say something, but it was cryptic to me." She looked at him. "Was it so horrible that he couldn't discuss it? So secretive that it was too dangerous to talk about?" She wrinkled her brow. "Do you ever talk about your work?"

"No. I do not."

"Even with your lover?"

"My lover? I assure you . . . Eléonore . . . I have no time for lovers." He closed his eyes for a long moment. "That's not to say I haven't had lovers." *Why did I say that to her?*

Eleonore smiled. "Indeed, Monsieur Gannon, I assure you my intuition tells me you have had many lovers." She continued smiling until he turned away. "Too personal a conversation? I saw you in your underwear – we're practically *married*." She laughed out loud. Too much Cognac.

The knock at the door was followed by a rush of soldiers into the room. Behind the soldiers, Colonel Horst Krenz entered, his right eye aimed directly at Avery Gannon.

CHAPTER TWENTY-THREE

"What is the meaning of this? Have you no manners?" Eléonore Delafloté, no longer the frail widow, stormed across the room. "Édouard, speak to these men, whoever they are, and tell them I am offended at their lack of consideration."

Avery Gannon placed his glass on the credenza and faced Krenz. He recognized his rank, the Gestapo uniform, the killer of one of Britain's most revered agents, his friend, his compatriot. "May I introduce myself? I am Édouard Delafloté. This is my wife, Madame Delafloté. How may we help you?" Avery relaxed his stance and smiled inquisitively at Krenz. He placed his arm on Eléonore's shoulder and pulled her gently into him.

"Édouard Delafloté. I saw your name on the hotel registry. What is your business in Paris, this hotel?" Krenz lifted his chin, careful to keep his right eye squarely on Gannon.

"But, of course. I have just returned from Greece. An expedition, you see. There is need of medical supplies."

Krenz extended his hand. "Your identification papers."

"Gladly." Gannon reached inside his coat and pulled Édouard Delafloté's passport as well as citizenship certificate from the document pocket. When he handed them to Krenz, he noticed a slight tremor in the German's hand.

The Gestapo chief studied the papers without speaking, a long minute. When he looked up, he studied Gannon's face. "Your hair is darker than the picture on your passport." A non-emotional voice, almost robotic.

"Is it? Let me see?" Gannon leaned forward and glanced at the picture. "Ah, a summertime picture after holiday on the Spanish coast. Such carefree days." He looked up at Krenz and smiled. "Oh, to be there again and away from this awful weather we're having."

"Your visit to Greece. Who sent you?"

"Totally a philanthropic endeavor. I saw a need and, with my own funds, traveled there to converse with the people who could provide medical supplies. A very successful mission, I must add."

"Where are the supplies?"

"They are to be shipped in April."

Krenz nodded, his right eye never wavering. "I was here in this room in the last forty-eight hours. I did not see you."

"Oh? When were you here?"

Krenz stepped forward slightly and looked at Eléonore. "I was here when your wife was ill."

"Ah, but of course I was in the city looking for medications for her. A terrible cough, you see. Turns out the best thing for her was a warm glass of Cognac. As you can see, she has improved greatly." Eléonore stared stoically at Krenz.

Krenz' gaze left Gannon and traveled over the room, where he saw the black fur draped across a small couch, the same fur that covered the Frenchwoman when he had searched her room. When his gaze returned to Gannon, he seemed curious. "Why are you and your wife staying at the hotel?"

Gannon smiled, "A second honeymoon. Our tenth." He squeezed Eléonore to him and looked down at her. When he saw her eyes, they were full of fright. He reached up and brushed a piece of hair from her brow. Then, grazed her head with his lips.

"Where do you live when you're not at the hotel?"

Gannon froze. *Where did they live?*

Eléonore offered a slight smile. "My family's estate is in Senlis, near the Chantilly forest. Only sixty kilometers from Paris." A pause. "On the banks of the River Nonette."

"When do you plan to return home?"

Gannon shook his head. "As soon as this horrendous weather passes and the roads are passable. Probably a day or two."

"I see." Krenz glanced around the room once more. "Do not leave without advising my office," he said.

From behind Krenz, Bedeau stepped forward slightly. "Madame Lefèbvre has prepared breakfast if you would like some sent to your room."

Gannon saw the dried blood around Bedeau's nose, the broken glasses. "Thank you, Monsieur Bedeau. That would be lovely."

Krenz left the room, followed by his soldiers and a stooped Monsieur Bedeau, who looked over his shoulder at Gannon. A smile hovered at the corners of his mouth. They had fooled the bastards he seemed to be saying.

CHAPTER TWENTY-FOUR

Gannon watched the back of Colonel Krenz as he left Room 308. At last, a face-to-face meeting with the man he intended to kill. He found he was sweating under Édouard Delafloté's jacket, not perspiration from fear, but from eagerness. He anticipated the German's death like a child anticipating Christmas, a new toy, a piece of candy. He knew exactly how he would kill him. Slowly.

He felt a stirring beside him and realized his arm still held Eléonore Delafloté. When he looked down, he caught a hint of fragrance, a soft cloud of sweetness, a clean soap. She looked up at him, as if just realizing his presence, his arm around her shoulder. She moved away and found her empty glass. She said nothing as she poured another sip of Cognac.

He watched her quietly and wondered what she was thinking. Perhaps she was contemplating the wisdom of harboring an enemy agent, of aiding someone whose only mission was to thwart the enemy by whatever means possible. She could not know his mission in Paris had been to assassinate high-ranking Germans, whether military or otherwise. She could not know what pleasure it was to kill a Nazi. She could not know he planned to continue his mission as long as he was alive. She could not know he never intended to utilize the escape routes offered by the French Résistance. What he had needed from the French was a safe house. What he got was a new identity from a dead Frenchman and a haven in his widow's hotel room.

"Madame, breakfast will be coming shortly."

She seemed not to hear him. Her back to him, he saw her arm rise to lift the glass. How thin she was.

"Breakfast?"

"Yes. Monsieur Bedeau is having breakfast prepared for us."

Finally, she turned and looked at him. He was surprised to see her smiling, a gleam in her eyes. A raised eyebrow. "I see you are not a perfect spy."

He looked at her and accepted the challenge. "I will agree."

She seemed disappointed in his answer. "But, of course, you could be." Her long legs moved her toward the window, where she looked up into the Paris sky. When she turned back to him, the smile was gone. "If you are to be Édouard, you must know all about him. Colonel Krenz does not appear to be a man who overlooks the slightest inconsistencies in one's conversations." She paused and studied his face. "Would you agree?"

He found her stare unsettling, as if suddenly she knew what he was thinking, knew that he would leave the moment he felt it safe to do so, that he would go into hiding to continue his role as an SIS assassin. He cleared his throat. "I agree."

She was right. If he were to survive in a city where thirty thousand German troops occupied the streets, he must acknowledge his vulnerabilities. At this moment, as he looked at her, he realized that she could be his most precarious vulnerability.

She moved closer to him. "Then, shall we discuss my late husband?"

She said it gently; unhinged from the pain she must have felt at his death, the loss of his love, his touch. Gannon felt himself waver. How could she possibly be capable of doing what would be asked of her?

"Yes. Let us discuss your husband . . . whenever you're ready. It's important for me to know as much as possible."

The knock at the door was barely heard, a tap.

Avery looked at Eléonore, who shrugged her shoulders.

"Come in," called Avery.

The door opened and Monsieur Bedeau entered, a cart

rolling in front of him. "Ah, at last, some food for my friends." He smiled as he removed his hat, the wayward hair jumping up in glorious tufts.

"Monsieur Bedeau, you have saved us from starvation!" Avery crossed the room to the cart and stood in front of the old concierge. His eyes scanned the Frenchman. The blood had been washed away, the eyeglasses repaired with a scrap of wire. He held Bedeau's eyes for a moment. He saw resignation. The head of the Gestapo would never intimidate such a man, resolute, loyal to the French flag, a patriot.

"Of course. It is mostly potatoes, compliments of Madame Lefèbvre. Some toast. Coffee is ground acorns and roasted potato peelings, of course. A genius of a woman in the kitchen. I think I shall run away with her and we shall make passionate love." A small chuckle accompanied his flushed face.

"My dear man, you are amazing." Avery lifted a piece of the fresh toasted bread. "Tell me about Krenz. From the beginning."

Bedeau glanced at Eléonore, then back to Avery. "A dangerous man. You fooled him once, but I'm not so sure you can do it again."

Avery nodded. "I will take your words seriously, Monsieur Bedeau."

"That would be wise, Monsieur Gannon. That would be wise." He turned and walked slowly to the door. "I must go." He hesitated and looked back at Gannon. "I have been summoned to Gestapo Headquarters. It seems Colonel Krenz' failure to find the spy has prompted him to question me further." Bedeau shook his head slowly. "As if I could hand him the spy."

CHAPTER TWENTY-FIVE

Colonel Horst Krenz slammed the door to his office, a fierce anger pushing him again to the file that lay in the drawer of his desk. How many times had he read it? How many times had he cursed the name Avery Gannon?

His second search of the Hotel de Crillon ended in failure, just like the first. Every room had been scoured without restraint. All residents of the hotel had been interrogated. *No, there is no spy here.*

The old man. The old man knew something. He was sure of it. All he had to do was convince him to talk.

"Herr Bauer," he yelled. "I would like my staff in here in thirty minutes. Everyone. And most certainly Herr Vogel."

He opened the file once more and placed the magnifying glass over the face of Avery Gannon. "Highly intelligent," he said. *What could this man do that I couldn't?* He leaned back in his chair. If he was unable to capture the spy before the arrival of Göring, his future was uncertain and he'd be replaced as head of the Paris Gestapo. How humiliating. Everyone would think he most certainly failed because . . . because of his wayward eye. No, he would find Gannon. He would have every single German in Paris looking for him. And, when he found him, he would

delight in watching him hang. Or, possibly, shot. Or, maybe even
. . . tortured to death. Suddenly, Krenz was happy. The mere
thought of the spy dangling from a rope was euphoric. He left
his chair and walked to the window. Clouds raced west under a
dark sky. He watched the street below, his right eye scanning the
buildings, the piled snow and the men clearing the streets.
Gannon was out there somewhere. When Monsieur Bedeau
arrived for questioning, he would find out exactly where.

Krenz heard a commotion behind him. He turned and saw
his staff assembling in their usual places. He lifted his chin while
he scanned the room. "Let us continue with our little . . . shall we
say . . . our little project of the day." The five men stared at Krenz
and waited. The project was not a *little* project; each of them
would participate in a fierce manhunt for the English assassin,
who it seemed had outsmarted them at every turn.

"Herr Gerhart, what about the train stations?"

Gerhart jumped to attention. "Every train station has two
patrols guarding the platforms and trains. Of course, no trains
are moving at this time."

"No suspicious sightings?"

"None."

"Herr Braumen, you have enacted your plan to screen all
males on the streets? Asked for their identification papers?"

Braumen took a deep breath. "Yes, Colonel Krenz. The
streets at this time have few citizens out and about because of
the blizzard. We are, however, prepared to approach all males
and ask for identification."

"If anyone is the least bit suspicious, bring them in and question them further. I want a report at the end of the day. Am I
clear?"

"Perfectly."

Krenz left the group for a moment and walked to the
window, where he again studied the streets, almost willing the
spy to expose himself. When he returned to his staff, he seemed
thoughtful.

"Herr Reichstugh, I do not intend for Paris to spend another
night in darkness. What do you have to report on the electrical
outages?"

Reichstugh stood at attention. He was a slight man, intense,
a high voice that became shrill if he was stressed in any way.

Today, his voice was quite shrill. "Colonel Krenz, the high winds during the storm have caused extensive damage. It is our hope to have the generating stations operating within the next twenty-four hours." He caught his breath. "The north and south grids were less damaged. It is the east and west grids that suffered the most."

Krenz stared at Reichstugh. Another black night would further hinder their search for Gannon. Reichstugh squirmed before him. "Herr Reichstugh, I am out of candles. Tonight, I would like to dine in a manner that I can see what I am eating. I encourage you to increase the work crews so that I will be successful in doing so." He turned his head and the left eye settled on Reichstugh. "Need I say more?"

"No. No, I fully understand your instructions." Reichstugh sat back down and calmed his beating heart.

Krenz turned around and began writing on the chalkboard.

Arrival Hermann Göring via Asien 10:10 a.m. January 23

Without turning, he said. "Herr Vogel, it is my wish that you provide a security plan by this afternoon, at which time you and I will determine exactly how we are going to protect Herr Göring." He continued writing.

Gannon. Capture by midnight.

"Questions?" he asked as he placed the chalk in its tray. When he glanced at his staff, his face seemed slightly contorted, as if the ghosts of failure had seeped into his bones.

"None? Good." He looked at Corporal Bauer. "Corporal, bring my car."

CHAPTER TWENTY-SIX

Krenz left Gestapo Headquarters without his driver and turned his car toward the Rue de Surene. Piles of snow had been pushed along the curbs and sat waiting for their eventual demise. Despite the lack of electricity, the shops along the avenue were open. *So what there is no electricity? That is the least of their problems. Let them drink and be merry. Let them ignore the Germans.*

He crossed Rue d'Anjou and continued over Boulevard Malesherbes. In a short distance, he parked his car in a deserted alley where only a skinny cat rummaged for food. He watched for a moment, then looked up to a small third floor window, where a faded yellow curtain covered the glass. Krenz stared a long moment, his breathing slow and steady, while beneath his heavy coat he felt the tremblings of desire. The cat ducked under a pile of scrap lumber. Krenz could still see his protruding tail. He smiled. *No one can really hide.*

The stairs were narrow, snake-like, with twists and turns that led to doorway after doorway. Arriving on the third floor, Krenz smelled soap, a pure, clean smell, like fresh mown grass. He paused. *Did she know he was coming?*

When he came to her door, he hesitated. Always before, he

had burst in with such hunger that she cowered in a corner of the room, her large dark eyes wide and still. He would turn his back to her as he removed his clothes. When he turned around to face her, his erection lumbered in front of him, red and bulbous, the tight skin glistening and searching for her. He would wait while she stood and removed her clothes, her eyes never leaving his. Naked, she lay on the bed and spread her legs for him. Without fail, the first thing he saw was the shimmering wet of her pubic hair and a tip of pink protruding from it. At that moment, he would fall to his knees at the bedside and bury his face into her. He rejoiced in the taste and smell of her. He rejoiced that she could not see his left eye.

Somehow, today was different. He slowly pushed open the door and stepped inside. She was at the window. She had seen him arrive, perhaps had heard his car. He knew she heard him, but she remained still, facing the window. "Mademoiselle, I am here."

When she turned, he was once again aware of how beautiful she was. Young, probably twenty-five. He had first seen her at a café during his first week in Paris and had been drawn to her, perhaps because she never seemed to notice his eye. She spoke to him in a shy manner, but friendly. Of course, she was friendly. He was the Gestapo.

He returned week after week just to see her, watch her and, finally, follow her home. As she parked her bicycle, she saw him. At first, she seemed alarmed, but then lifted her chin and smiled. Did she smile because she was afraid of him? No words were spoken as he followed her inside. In the dark hallway, she turned and looked at him. He leaned over and lifted her skirt and his fingers pushed deep inside her. She cried out, whimpering as he thrust himself into her.

Krenz removed his coat and sat in a chair near the window.

"Some tea?" she asked.

"Yes, that would be nice."

He watched as she placed two cups on the table. He found her body seductive. He knew she felt herself a typical Frenchwoman, a little too plump. Her skin was smooth and pale, inviting the touch of a man. He felt himself grow hard. It was so easy with her.

She handed him his tea and sat in a chair across from him.

"Are you staying warm?"

"*Oui*," she said. "There is plenty of coal here."

He knew there was. He had personally seen to it.

"Food?"

"Of course. The cheeses and bread you send are wonderful."
She smiled.

He liked her teeth. He smiled back as he lifted his hand and
motioned her to his chair. She walked across the floor and sat in
his lap, cocooned like a child. He smelled her freshness.

"I have missed you, Célina," he whispered.

She nuzzled his neck with her face.

He had realized some while back that he no longer felt
uncomfortable around her with his wayward eye. He rubbed her
arm and fleetingly wondered what it would be like to have a
child with her. Impossible, of course.

He enjoyed their sex play. Now, as she sat on his lap, he
reached down and kissed her breast, tasted the fabric of her
blouse, then saw the wet spot where his mouth had found her
nipple. When he reached under her skirt, he heard a sharp
intake of her breath.

"*Mon chéri,*" she whispered and slowly removed her blouse.
She turned around and straddled him, her breasts shiny globes,
their areolas surrounding hard nipples. When she looked down
at him, he felt king-like, that he had the most beautiful princess
in the land. He gently lifted her hips, pushed himself inside and
felt the rhythm of her body move against him.

CHAPTER TWENTY-SEVEN

Avery Gannon stepped out onto the Place de la Concorde.
Behind him a step or two, Eléonore Delafloté pulled on her
gloves and braced herself for the cold. The winter wind had less-
ened somewhat, but occasionally swept the avenue with arctic-
like gusts. The streets were oddly empty of cars, reminiscent of
the arrival of the Germans. The conquerors of France had not
marched into Paris with banners flying and bands playing on
that day in June 1940, but in a heavy, monotonous manner.
There had been little actual resistance in the French capital.
Amazingly, there was not the "Bolshevik" mentality in the troops
that marched by the closed shops and houses, their faces
unsmiling. The Parisians had collaborated or compromised, ten-
dentious in what they did not show, coping as best they could.
Three million had coped by fleeing south.

Avery felt a peculiar air of normalcy as he looked down the
long street, a sense of life going on. He had hidden in the house
of an old Frenchman on the day Paris fell and recalled not a cry
was uttered, only the cadence of marching men and horses. If he
closed his eyes, he could see the faces of shocked Parisians, their
city no longer belonging to them.

He took Eléonore's arm as they turned onto the Champs-

Élysées. To their right, an old woman, bundled in wool, sat on a bench in a winter garden, her hands flying back and forth with long knitting needles. They walked a few moments before entering the Café di Roma where well-dressed Parisians enjoyed their aperitifs, a hint of gaiety in the air, the winter storm over. A smell of fresh baked bread hung in the air.

They seated themselves near the windows that faced the avenue, a clear view of the entryway. Avery habitually scanned the patrons. He noticed they watched the beautiful woman who sat with him. Eléonore was oblivious, her attention on the wine list. It was if her beauty and wealth were secondary to her status as a widow, a young widow who craved the comfort of her loving husband.

All she had now was an imposter, a man who was not interested in comforting her, a man who, in essence, was using her. Perhaps she knew this and accepted the irony of it. She could not have forgotten that only a mere forty-eight hours earlier, she had tried to take her life.

Avery studied her profile and wondered if she could actually become a spy, a woman who was able to carry out the requirements of the British Secret Intelligence Service? She seemed to think so. He turned away for a moment and when he found her again, he was surprised she was looking at him.

"Édouard, have you decided what you would like to drink? There are two wines that look exceptionally good. A Riesling. Ha, such a travesty, a German wine while we watch the Nazis devour our city."

She paused. "Then, there is a Bordeaux, full-bodied, from our vineyards south of here. What do you think?"

When she closed the wine list, she looked at him, her eyebrows raised, her lips parted. When he realized he wanted to touch her, he quickly looked away. What was happening to him? It was like falling down a well, nothing to hold on to, only a feeling that at any moment he would feel his body hit the bottom and then a desperate attempt to keep his head above water. He calmed his heart.

"I'd like the Bordeaux. Enough of the Germans . . . my . . . darling."

She laughed, "The Bordeaux it is." She continued watching him, seeming to study the lines around his eyes, the tenseness in his jaw. "You are a handsome man, Édouard. Rugged." She paused. "Desirable."

He ignored her and watched as two German officers entered the café and sat only a few meters from them. His eyes took in their shiny boots, the pistols in their holsters. For some reason, he wondered if the shoe polish in his hair was obvious. He squirmed slightly and felt for his identity papers.

One of the soldiers looked their way, a quizzical look on his face. The German's eyes ran over him as though he were suspect, settling on his shoes. Why the shoes? His shoes were fashionable, but not pretentious. To distract the Germans, he reached over and kissed Eléonore on the cheek and spoke into her ear.

"Are you watching the German officers across from us?" he whispered.

Eléonore smiled as if her lover had said "I want to make love to you" and shook her head.

Avery placed his finger on her chin. They were lovers, of course. The Germans would not think anything else. Would not think that one of Germany's most hunted enemies sat across from them, would soon push his weapon into the skull of Paris' Gestapo chief. When he leaned in to kiss Eléonore on the mouth, he felt a small quiver in his stomach. What would His Majesty's Secret Service think of their spy now? *Kissing in the line of duty,* that's what they'd think.

Eléonore returned his kiss, soft, wet and long. He drew back and looked at her. She was doing quite well in her role as a spy for the Allies.

***

They left the café and walked into a bright sun that glinted off the snow-covered streets of Paris, toward 12 Rue des Saussaies, the Hotel de l'Elysee, where Colonel Horst Krenz, the self-proclaimed avenger of misdeeds to the German people, sat throne-like in his office and thought of nothing else but apprehending the English spy. In the hotel room of the de Crillon, Avery had felt the intensity with which Krenz had questioned him, his one good eye boring in on him as though in a trance, locked in a vice-like hold that promised no reprieves.

Avery had felt no fear. His decisions had been made. He

would find the right moment, the right place to confront Krenz. It would be his choosing, not Krenz'. He felt a shudder from Eléonore, who walked beside him. "Where are we going?" she asked.

"A little stroll. We've been inside too long. Time for fresh air."

"The fresh air is good."

He looked down at her and saw a soft pink in her cheeks, almost childlike. Yet, he knew there was quiet determination in this fragile woman. He knew at any moment she would again insist he teach her the art of spying. He smiled to himself. How could he teach her what had taken him years in the classroom to learn, then many years of honing that knowledge into what he was today, a respectable British SIS agent? He must stick to his plan, the plan he had formulated only moments after the death of his fellow spy.

He heard her voice float up to him. "Monsieur, the kiss? The kiss in the café? Was that necessary?"

Avery stopped walking and looked at her. He stumbled somewhat before his reply. "That's what is called a diversionary tactic. Quite necessary." His expression was serious, his voice calm.

Eléonore contemplated his answer for a few moments. "A diversionary tactic, you say."

"Yes, I would rather have the German officers observe us kissing than the shoe polish in my hair."

She laughed. "Is this my first lesson in espionage? This diversionary tactic?"

He became the stoic professor. "A diversionary tactic is a vital tool in staying alive."

She was quiet for a while. "I am wondering how often you will use a kiss as a diversionary tactic."

When he looked at her, she was smiling. He was not. "Madame, our lives are in an inordinate amount of danger. I will use whatever means necessary to ensure we are able to survive another day."

He took her arm and crossed the street, one more block closer to Gestapo Headquarters. A German car passed in front of them. The ashen face of Monsieur Bedeau peered out. After a slight nod, he faced forward, stiff with resolve.

CHAPTER TWENTY-EIGHT

The interrogation room at Gestapo headquarters was an old storage room on the basement floor of the quaint hotel. Dark and windowless, it had been cleaned out of broken furniture, worn and tattered linens, a collection of old dishes, all things not fine enough for the prestigious guests who once considered the Hotel de l'Elysée one of the finest hotels in Paris. The Germans, precise and methodical, had transformed Paris into a German city. Organized and structured, it was like a cultural Berlin; only the citizens were French speaking and lived under duress.

The small room rang of ghosts, perhaps of lovers who hid away amongst the discarded, once-noble pieces of dilapidated Louis XVI furniture and touched each other in the dark, made love standing against a neo-classical armoire. Ghosts who knew the secrets of the hotel, the long ago dalliances of its famous guests. Now, with the smell of Nazis in the air, the apparitions seemed always in chaos, running in wild refrains down the halls and into rooms as if they, too, were intent on escaping the Germans.

When the Gestapo chief's soldiers pushed Bedeau into the dank room and closed the door, he fell onto the cold floor, his small frame hitting the hardness with such force, he moaned, then cursed. "Fucking Germans," he said, immediately regretting his words. His wife, Hélène, would admonish him severely if she had heard him speak with such anger and use such despicable language.

Bedeau pulled himself from the floor into the darkness. Any moment, he would be at the mercy of one of the most feared members of Germany's secret police. It was clear Colonel Krenz believed the spy had sought refuge in the de Crillon. He also believed Bedeau had arranged for the spy's safe passage, most likely aided by the French Résistance.

When he heard footsteps in the hallway, he turned toward the door and took a deep breath. He would not succumb to the Germans, would not give them one tiny bit of information that would result in the capture of the spy. He was an obstinate man, sixty-seven years old, a Frenchman, a proud Frenchman with no intention of relinquishing a sliver of intelligence to the Germans.

The door opened and light flooded the room. In their inglorious uniforms, four German soldiers entered the room, followed by Krenz, whose face resembled a flesh-eating piranha intent on devouring whatever lay in his path. The crooked left eye gazed at the ceiling, while the right eye found the Frenchman. Bedeau recoiled. Oddly, he wished he had a cyanide capsule.

The ceiling bulb cast a wan, sinister light over the room. On his left, Bedeau saw thick metal rings mounted on the walls where prisoners had been chained. The windows were barred; no one escaped this room.

"Ah, Monsieur Bedeau, my gratitude for your presence." Krenz walked around the room as if on a Sunday stroll, finally ending up in front of Bedeau, his hands placed casually on his hips. "Shall we have a nice little chat?"

The smallness of Bedeau's frame seemed hopelessly vulnerable, its slightly hunched-over shape exuding a softness, a softness susceptible to the whims of someone who delighted in the delivery of pain.

The interrogation began pleasantly, almost like a meeting of two men whose intellect hovered on the brink of genius, a discussion of philosophies, doctrines and ideologies that placed them in the world's classification of philosophers who changed the thinking of ordinary men. It was evident that Krenz seemed to savor the conversation as though it were an aphrodisiac, a stimulant that brought him closer to the god he thought he was, much like a lover who has discovered the joys of orgasm. Was that possible? Bedeau saw Krenz as a man who danced in the moonlight carrying a blood-soaked bayonet and proclaiming he was the deliverer of the pure and innocent?

"Ah, you Parisians. You love your country like a man loves a woman. Yet, you did not protect her. You shrugged your shoulders as if our arrival was a passing fancy, an afternoon of Champagne on the Champs L'Elysée. What a dishonor to your friend Napoleon." Krenz raised his eyebrows and, when Bedeau did not respond, he continued to pace the room.

"So," he began again, his grin wide and engaging, the large teeth predatory, the lines of his smiling eyes stretching out to his hairline, "is this not the most incredible thing? A missing Englishman." He laughed. "Can you imagine, in all of Paris, he has found the perfect hiding place?" He shook his head. "I am just absolutely astounded." He paused and looked intently at Bedeau. "Aren't you?"

"Paris is a large city," he replied. Bedeau stared into the space in front of him, the blue right eye of the German watching him, the left eye hovering above Bedeau's right shoulder. If he reached out, could he straighten the eye, push it into its proper place, a simple twist of the eyeball? He felt his fingers twitch.

"That is true. The British spy, however, was spotted only meters from your hotel. Then, he vanished? Can you explain that?" Krenz motioned for Bedeau to sit in a wooden chair, while he himself pulled a metal chair from a desk that was pushed against the wall.

Bedeau hesitated. A wooden chair. A torture chair? If he sat in the chair, would his life end there? He looked at Krenz, who sat waiting, the perpetual smile of the piranha lifting his cheeks. Slowly, he sat in the chair and felt the hard, cold wood press against his back. He gripped the smooth arms with his hands and, with a quiet indifference, replied. "It seems the spy is quite intelligent."

Krenz stiffened. His right eye left the face of Bedeau and found the soldier who stood at attention at the door. The message was clear.

"My dear Monsieur Bedeau, it seems your propensity for providing obscure answers to my questions is quite adept." Krenz closed his eyes for a long moment. When he opened them, his anger was evident. "I do not believe I asked you whether or not the spy was intelligent."

Bedeau pressed his back into the chair. The breath of Krenz was hot, the breath of a devil lurking within and waiting to expel a putrid poison. "Colonel Krenz, the location of the spy is not known to me."

"Ah, but I do not believe you, Monsieur Bedeau. And, since I do not believe you, I must insist you . . . shall we say . . . come clean."

The strap came from behind, a thick binding that pressed Bedeau's body into the chair. The arm straps followed, bound so tightly, his arms numbed immediately. When he turned his head to look behind him, a hand shot out and slapped him so hard he felt his neck crack, his ears ring. He watched as his glasses sailed across the room. The interrogation had begun.

CHAPTER TWENTY-NINE

From the outside, the Hotel de L'Eysée seemed a peaceful respite. The ancient building had known old world grace and beauty, a beauty now tarnished by the blood of war, by the presence of the Germans. The elite Secret Police of Germany occupied its rooms and dispensed the decrees of Hitler himself, the little corporal who rose to power in a mere blink of history's eye.

Bedeau's body lay in a heap outside the side door of the north side of the hotel. Barely breathing, he opened his eyes and looked into skies whose clouds swept past the cold city, toward the sea. He did not feel the cold nor the blood that dripped from his nose into the white snow beneath his face.

Oddly, he smiled, revealing a hole where a tooth had been. Had he had the strength, he would have bellowed a guttural laugh, a laugh coming from the depths of his weakened lungs. But, his strength was gone, left in the interrogation room where he imagined his missing tooth still lay.

How he loved being a Frenchman, a charming, old Frenchman who spat in the eyes of a German and, hopefully, would live to tell about it. He lifted his head, then his shoulders, and sat upright. Just then, the sun escaped the shade of the building, its rays spreading across his face. "Merci," he said to himself, to the sky, to the Paris afternoon.

CHAPTER THIRTY

A very studied The Hotel L'Elysée with a discerning eye. It was the last place he had seen his fellow spy, a man he had simply referred to as *Frenchie*. Not a demeaning reference by any means, simply convenient, an obscure codeword, which is what MI6 required. He had met him soon after parachuting from an RAF Halifax into the hills near a small farming village southeast of Paris. Under a December half-moon, he quickly melted into the French underground. The British had arranged a rendezvous: "Go to the Tuileries Gardens and look for a lean Frenchman, dark hair. He'll be wearing a beret, black. Oh, and by the way, the two of you will assassinate Herr Ernst Wilhelm Bohle, SS Lt. General. He's due to arrive in Paris on the 8th of January on the 10:10 a.m. train from Berlin."

Indeed, they planned to assassinate the German. Though, not at the train station. *Frenchie* had better ideas, always risky, but successful. At least, until the last one. The last one had gotten him killed.

Avery pulled gently on Eléonore's arm. "Here. Sit down a moment." He brushed the snow from the bench. "I'll be back in a moment."

From the bench, he walked across the street and the few

meters to the front of the hotel where two German soldiers watched him with caution. He ignored them and continued down the sidewalk where a statue stood black and cold, past a row of leafless trees and then around the corner where he could not be observed.

He leaned against the fence and removed his gloves. His eyes followed the façade of the hotel. Only five stories. Tall, narrow windows on every wall. Stone. Ridges along the wall dividing the stories. Black ornate ironwork running the length of each exterior floor. Not smooth, but rough and . . . climbable. Climbable? Who was he kidding? He had never climbed ten feet. He knew Krenz' office was on the 2nd floor. Plomion had told him so. Plomion knew everything.

From the stone fence, Avery studied the back of the hotel, the entryways, the guards. No guards on the back. Only the front. Interesting. Then, he saw the door. A lone wooden door. Actually, a double door. The kitchen? Perhaps for deliveries. He waited, hoping someone would exit. No one did and he left his vantage point and headed to the front of the hotel.

When he glanced across the street, he saw Elèonore watching him. What would he do with the woman? Nothing. He would do nothing. He would leave her at an opportune moment. His only purpose to remain in the city was Krenz.

He crossed the street to the bench, smiling as he approached Eléonore. He wondered if she knew how beautiful she was. Beautiful, but a problem. He must remove himself from her. But, how could he? He was Édouard Delafloté, her husband. He carried Édouard Delafloté's identity papers, wore his clothing. Without them, he was a dead man. Sooner or later, they would save his life. But, until then, he would think only of Krenz.

"I am cold," she said.

"Of course. Let us return to the hotel." He reached out to take her arm and heard a voice behind him.

A hobbling Monsieur Bedeau walked toward them. Hatless, he smiled and lifted his arm. "Madame. Monsieur. We must talk. There is something you must know."

***

Avery listened carefully to Monsieur Bedeau while Eléonore gently wiped the dried blood from his face and ears.

"So, you see, the crooked-eye German thought I was uncon-scious. What an imbecile! I heard every word spoken to his staff."

Bedeau coughed, then winced as though pain shot through his body.

"Did you know that Hermann Göring will arrive by train in Paris in just a few days? It seems Colonel Krenz has been assigned the task of protecting the Reichsmarschall."

A wide grin creased the battered face. "Monsieur Gannon, it would delight the citizens of Paris if you were to . . . shall we say . . . contribute to the demise of this monster, Göring."

Avery paused. It was well known in the French Underground that he was one of Britain's most efficient assassins. How did Bedeau know this? Perhaps Bedeau was more entrenched in the Résistance than he realized.

Bedeau knew Plomion. Plomion, the tenacious Frenchman who was a close collaborator of the Free French both in and out of the Résistance. Plomion, a compatriot of his fellow spy known by his code-name, *Frenchie*. Frenchie, who was now dead. Gannon glanced at Eléonore. Should she be listening to this conversation?

"I have received no orders from Britain regarding Göring." Gannon turned away.

"Orders? Who needs orders to kill a Nazi? Especially this Nazi."

Avery saw the fierceness in the old man's eyes. Bedeau had been through too many wars to follow protocol, sneering at the absurdity of rules in wartime. One did what one must do. Wait for orders from Britain? Bedeau would not consider such a thing. No, give him a good rifle and he would kill Göring himself.

When Gannon looked at Eléonore, she was resolute. "Why not kill the Nazi?" she asked.

"At the moment, my priority is to stay alive as long as the Germans search for me. I must maintain a semblance of nor-malcy as the husband of Madame Delafloté. Assassinating Göring or any other German will take extraordinary work, meticulous planning involving others."

Gannon looked toward Gestapo Headquarters where shadows had placed a heavy fog across the cold stone. Krenz. It was all about Krenz.

Bedeau looked at Gannon, his eyes slitted to a menacing stare.

"My friend, do not underestimate the loyalty of the French. We love our country, our flag. Whatever you need, it will be yours."

Bedeau then closed his eyes and sighed deeply. When he opened them again, Gannon saw his blue eyes were sharp, alive. Bedeau wanted to live to see France liberated.

"Madame, let us accompany Monsieur Bedeau back to the hotel. The temperature is dropping."

From the Hotel L'Elysée, they made their way back to the Hotel de Crillon, where they would continue their façade as Monsieur and Madame Delafloté, where Monsieur Bedeau would again place his concierge hat upon his frazzled head and dream of killing Nazis.

CHAPTER THIRTY-ONE

Colonel Krenz left the interrogation room, perspiration darkening the back of his shirt, his lips as thin as a knife blade, and walked the stairs to his office. The cadence of his steps was military, an attempt to control his anger, to sedate himself after an unsuccessful questioning of Monsieur Bedeau. The old man was tough, the demeanor of someone who had nothing to lose, even if his skull had been crushed, his tongue cut out, his eyes gouged. Nothing to lose but his life. And, he was certainly willing to give that up for his beloved France. Had he been a young man, perhaps he would have talked immediately, given up information that, hopefully, would let him live. A young man had something to live for - a night at a café with a beautiful woman, then, making love to her at sunrise. No, a young man would not want to die at the hands of the Germans for just a little information.

He should have killed Bedeau. He was, however, the only link to Gannon. If he had killed him, the trail would turn cold. Yes, he would kill him eventually and his instincts told him Bedeau would make a mistake. One small mistake that would lead him to Gannon.

Krenz walked the hall to his office, where he found his waiting assistant. "Corporal Bauer, let Herr Vogel know I have returned."

***

Hermann Göring's arrival in Paris would be via his special train, the *Asien,* the purpose of his visit having nothing to do with his position in the Third Reich as head of Germany's Luftwaffe. His position as primary looter of France's art treasures was the reason for his visit to the cultural city. The *Masters*, Degas, Cézanne, Monet, Renoir, hung on his walls at Carinhall, his large estate near Berlin. Göring was nothing more than a thief, a sly procurer of some of the rarest art treasures in the world. He deemed they belonged to him, at least half of them anyway. The other half he would share with Hitler.

Göring was a buffoon of a man who cared only for personal gain, not the success of Germany's siege of Europe nor the extension of the land masses for the rise of the Great Race. Krenz bristled. He had no respect for the man and, now, as word came from Berlin that he would arrive on Thursday on his personal train, Krenz felt an even greater loathing for him.

The fact he would be in charge of protecting Göring while he ravaged the cultural jewels of Paris was unacceptable. He felt his priority was not protecting Göring, but the capture of the spy; the man Krenz knew would not leave France until he had settled a score with him.

Krenz heard the click of heels behind him and turned to see Lieutenant Vogel, a sheath of papers in his hands, the security plan to protect Göring during his stay in Paris.

The lieutenant was a serious man, not much younger than Krenz. Two good eyes that bored into Krenz' right eye. Vogel's face was flushed, a glistening of perspiration across his forehead indicating a nervousness.

It seemed most everyone became nervous around Krenz, a fear perhaps of his fanatical military mind, a mind that missed nothing. Vogel had better have orchestrated a brilliant security plan. Krenz gave him a slight smile, saw a relaxing of his shoulders, his face smoothing across his forehead.

"Lieutenant Vogel, I have anticipated this meeting all morning. What have you brought me?" The lieutenant moved forward a few steps and Krenz could see the anxiety in his eyes, pupils very small, a nervous blink.

"Colonel Krenz, it pleases me to provide an excellent plan of security for the safety of Herr Göring."

"By all means, come sit and let's hear it." Krenz seemed almost jovial. It was his way of putting someone at ease. *Do not be afraid of me. Yes, I am your superior officer, but you may trust me.*

Vogel opened his file and picked up a sheet of paper. "Herr Göring will travel with his personal bodyguards. Five of them. They have been with him since 1939 and are trusted. The "Asien" has an engine and fifteen wagons. The fifth car is Herr Göring's lounge. That's where he spends most of his time. From the information we have received from Berlin, he is not traveling with his wife." Vogel paused. "Nor his mistress."

The last car travels with four soldiers who carry Gewehr 43 rifles. The top of the first and last car carries two soldiers, each manning a Maschinengewehr." Vogel looked up from his paper to Krenz. "It is my understanding the engine holds the engineer and two more soldiers."

Krenz nodded. "What is your assessment of the security they are bringing in?"

Vogel hesitated. "Ah, from a numbers point of view, the security is adequate. Of course, the experience of his soldiers is another factor. I cannot imagine Herr Göring traveling from Berlin without a very experienced group of guards."

Krenz looked away and seemed thoughtful. "Yes, I agree."

Vogel cleared his throat. "If I had a concern, it would be from the air."

"From the air?" Krenz raised his eyebrows.

"Yes. Should the Allies cross over France, perhaps on their way to Algiers or Egypt, they would have prime access to Herr Göring's train. They would most certainly take advantage of the target. Of course, they would not know it is Herr Göring's train, but that it is simply an enemy target that is presenting itself. Who knows the outcome?"

"There is no way to protect a train from an Allied bombing. Correct?"

"Correct. It is safe to say that most transports across France are not in danger from the Allies, especially on the route from Berlin. Germany's *Luftwaffe* is too powerful. And, after all, Göring is head of the *Luftwaffe*. I feel what we must worry about is the French, their guerrilla tactics pose the most danger."

Krenz contemplated the validity of Vogel's words. Most likely, Göring will arrive without incident. Arrive with his entourage of bodyguards and soldiers. There was, however, still a possibility the French Résistance would learn of Göring's arrival, then plot to assassinate him.

"Now that we know the extent of their security, how do you propose we contribute to that security?" The demeanor of Krenz changed, his face hard, his lips a grim line, the right eye non-blinking, fixed on the face of Vogel.

Vogel seemed to shudder. He gripped the papers in his hand, perhaps fearful that somehow his gaze might wander to the crooked left eye, the eye that stared into space. Krenz smiled slightly as if he knew Vogel's body had grown cold from fear, could see that his hands strangely atrophied into themselves as if he must protect himself from a violent seizure. He imagined Vogel's voice had strangled, his throat muscles tightening into hard knots.

Krenz waited for him to recover, struggle to present his meticulous security plan with the confidence and assurance required by his superior.

Finally, Vogel shifted in his chair and began.

"This plan proposes we clear the area of civilians a day prior to Herr Göring's arrival. The only personnel allowed would be the stationmasters who regulate the trains. They will be thoroughly screened. All entrances and exits to the *Gare de Lyon* will be guarded, four guards each location. When the Asien reaches a distance of one mile from the station, a platoon of fifty soldiers will guard the remainder of the tracks en route into the station. Snipers will be placed at various points around the station, with instructions to shoot anyone who is not in a German uniform."

Lieutenant Vogel paused, his mouth void of saliva, and looked up at Krenz. When Krenz did not comment, he continued.

"Once Herr Göring disembarks the train, he will be escorted to the hotel by his body guards as well as his soldiers. We will provide appropriate transportation. On the outer perimeter of his entourage, our soldiers will be at every point that we think is logistically beneficial."

Krenz held up his hand. Then, rubbed his chin while Vogel waited. "It seems you have planned Herr Göring's protection as if there has been a pointed threat against him. Is that so?"

Vogel stammered. "I . . . I am unaware of any specific threat against the Reichsmarschall, but . . ."

Krenz stood and began to pace the room, the only light from the window that faced north, the winter nightfall only hours away. In the shadows, he appeared almost ghost-like, an apparition whose feet did not touch the floor, instead hovered on small clouds of black. He circled the room twice, ending up at the lone window where the dim light illuminated his face. He spoke without turning.

"Lieutenant Vogel, I am impressed with your efficiency." The words were spoken slowly, barely audible, but finding the waiting ears of Vogel. When he finally turned, his face darkened.

"If Herr Göring is assassinated while he is in Paris . . .well, need I say it, we're dead men."

CHAPTER THIRTY-TWO

Temperatures dropped quickly as charcoal clouds dimmed the City of Light, snow remaining on the roofs of grand buildings, along pathways, atop limbs of hemlock where one was careful to avoid the sporadic plunge of snow from above. Avery pulled on the arm of Eléonore and led her across the Place de la Concorde toward the Crillon. Behind them, a limping Monsieur Bedeau boisterously sang *Guand Madelon,* a song about soldiers flirting with a lovely young waitress in a country tavern. Avery had heard Marlene Dietrich sing the poignant song in 1939, in Paris, only a year before the Nazi's arrived and hung their humiliating flag from the Eiffel Tower. He could hear her throaty voice as though she presently stood before him, her cigarette smoldering, her sad eyes searching the faces in the room, faces that would soon become German.

Gannon looked back at Bedeau. Odd that he could sing after being tortured by the Gestapo. The old man had proved himself a staunch Frenchman, a Frenchman not diluted by the façade of the reigning German regime nor by collaborators for the Germans, but a man who acknowledged his duty to his country.

Inside the hotel, though battered, Bedeau resumed his position as concierge, found his wool hat, replaced his coat and stood at attention inside the doorway. The resolute expression on his face seemed to be saying: *I have survived one more day with the Germans.*

Eléonore placed her hand on Bedeau's shoulder. "Monsieur Bedeau, you must let me make you tea."

She reached up and straightened his hat, tugged a wisp of his hair and pushed it under the rim. She smiled and leaned in closer so he could hear her whispered words, "*Monsieur, vous êtes mon héros.*"

Bedeau smiled, a gaping hole where a tooth had been, blood still smeared on his gums.

"Ah, Madame Delafloté, a hero? You give me such happiness." His eyes swept her face as though reminding himself of her loveliness.

Eléonore said nothing as she turned and walked with Avery to the elevator. Before the doors closed, Monsieur Bedeau rushed forward, a bottle in his hands.

"More Cognac. You will need it." He paused, a cunning expression, as he glanced behind him. "Do not ask where I got it."

On the third floor of the de Crillon, Avery opened the door to 308 and quickly scanned the room, moving his hand near his gun. The draperies opened into the early evening light and filtered across the room, the bed, the lounge and finally to the face of the young widow who stood beside him. His eyes ran the length of her profile, noticing the curve of her neck, her small ears. A feeling of uneasiness crept up his spine. When he left her, he did not want any harm to come to her. After all, she had saved his life.

"We must open the Cognac," she said as she crossed the room, removing her coat.

The black fur that had provided a haven for both of them, their salvation. Had it not been for the fur, Gannon knew he would be in a cold grave somewhere, dirt piled on top of him so shallow the animals would have found him in hours.

He watched as she moved to the credenza, chose two tulip glasses, poured and lifted one to her chin. She swirled the glass slowly and waited. When she turned to him, she was holding out the glass, a smile on her lips.

"*Napoleon,* a fine Cognac, from Poilou-Charentes perhaps."

Avery walked to where she stood and took the glass. When he glanced at her, he hoped she would sip it and not drink it quickly as she had previously done. She was too fragile to engage in too much Cognac, too much war and too many thoughts of her dead husband.

"Monsieur Gannon . . . I shall call you by your proper name . . . for what reason did you visit Gestapo Headquarters today?"

Gannon studied the woman, a woman whose face seemed innocent and naïve, yet somehow was expert at honing in on others' motives and agendas. She appeared aloof, obscure for a certain amount of time. Then, when it suited her, she became inquisitive, probing.

At the moment, he felt almost defensive as he contemplated her question. Her eyes were intense, non-blinking. From his training, he had learned to watch the eyes, the size of the pupils, and the length of time between blinks, telltale signs that would indicate a person's honesty or lack of.

He slowly glanced around the room, the window where the last of daylight withered away. The woman baffled him.

"Madame, I do not believe I visited the Gestapo." He raised his eyebrows.

Eleonore sipped her Cognac. Twice. She waited a long moment, watching him all the while.

"Oh? Then, it was just happenstance that we were in front of the most powerful building in Paris? A building where men decide who live or die? How amusing you are, monsieur. Perhaps you meant to go to the Arc de Triomphe or the Grand Palais?" A small laugh escaped her whiskey-ladened lips.

Avery held her gaze. Why did he vacillate in his trust of her, even his opinion of her? It seemed one moment she was an austere Frenchwoman who had succumbed to the tragedy of war. Then, in a whirl of mystique, she became a wealthy young widow who plied the moments of conversations with innuendos that seemed foolish.

"I assume you consider our time on the bench in front of Gestapo Headquarters as a "visit?" He was not kind, his words biting. Damn if he would play her game.

His words did not affect her. She simply moved her glass to her lips and sipped.

After a long moment, she returned to the credenza and refilled her glass. Her back still to him, she spoke, harshness in her words.

"I see, Monsieur Gannon, you still resist me. Still consider me a . . . shall we say . . . an inconvenience. This woman who allowed you to push your body into hers while the Gestapo searched her room. At any point, I could have exposed you as the enemy spy you are."

"Exposed me? Madame, you were in the throes of a deep, almost permanent sleep. You were incapable of doing anything. Do you think I did not know what you had done?"

He caught his breath. "It was quite obvious to me simply by your breathing that you were on the brink of never waking up. And, now you intimate to me that you could have alerted the Gestapo as they searched your room?"

Gannon paused, realized his voice had risen. He spoke again, his words resigned.

"I understand your needs, Madame. A reason to live. Am I correct?"

He waited. When she finally looked at him, he saw the wetness of tears on her cheeks, a quiver in her voice.

"A reason to live? What do *you* think? My Édouard in some unknown grave somewhere. Never a chance to say goodbye. Nothing left of him but his clothing, his jewelry."

She looked at him through half-closed eyes. "Clothing and jewelry you now wear in your role as his imposter, to escape the Germans. What if I had not given you his passport? What if your resemblance to him had not been so uncanny?"

He watched as she refilled her glass once more. When she spoke, her words were bitter.

"Yes, English spy, you are correct." Her shoulders slumped as she remained facing the credenza, her silhouette showing the graceful lines of her body, the nape of her neck where her hair swirled in soft waves, pinned underneath a large comb. He felt a stirring within him. Pity? Remorse? Troubled, he shrank back into the lounge and struggled to calm his thoughts.

***

Gannon said nothing as he watched her light a candle, its soft light soothing. She remained still, a slow sipping from her glass.

Above all, he must not let the woman get in the way of his mission, the revenge for the death of his fellow spy. If he wavered, he was a dead man. And dead men did nothing to kill the enemy, win battles or liberate the victims of war.

He stilled as her voice floated toward him. Like a lullaby, soft and searching, an ethereal melody that fell balm-like on his ears, made him catch his breath, caress his heart. "Édouard, please make love to me."

She turned and even in the dim light of the room, he saw her flushed face, the yearning in her eyes, the tenuous smile on her lips as she walked toward him. *The Cognac. The damned Cognac.*

Calmly, he said. "I am not Édouard."

She hesitated only a moment, then laughed softly. "Oh, how you tease me, Édouard. I know very well who you are. My husband. My lover." She moved closer.

Avery stood from the lounge and stepped toward her, his words spoken with heart-felt softness, "I can see why you are confused. I am wearing Édouard's clothing."

"I am not confused. I know exactly who you are. Do you think I cannot recognize my own husband? Why do you torture me so, Édouard?"

She was smiling, her words somewhat slurred, a slight weave in her movements. When she reached him, she placed her hand on his cheek. "It has been so long since we've made love. I have missed you so."

When she kissed him, he felt a slow devouring of his lips, felt unmovable, cast under a spell. It had been two years since he'd made love to a woman and, if he was to make love again, he knew without a shadow of a doubt it could *not* be this woman.

"Do you remember the last time we made love?" She kissed him again and he felt her tongue brush his lips.

"Madame, we have never made love."

She ignored him. "Please." Her body pushed into his and, in one swift moment, he felt his legs weaken, his breath catch.

Her soft laughter became sensuous, captivating like the strains of a beautiful aria, with no possibility of his escape. He did not know the moment he reached out and unbuttoned her dress and removed her underclothing. He just knew she stood before him in exquisite nakedness, her small breasts tilting upward, their nipples erect and beckoning. He also knew he wanted her long, curvaceous legs wrapped around him.

He would make love to her. There were no barriers, no moments of indecision. He lifted her and was amazed at her thinness as he laid her gently on the bed. He looked down at her, her sensuality embracing him. There was no turning back.

"Édouard," she whispered. "I want you to make love to me like you did in Italy, in Salerno, the Mediterranean."

"Italy?"

"Yes, Italy? You do remember, don't you?" she whispered.

Avery leaned over, kissed her breast and heard her gasp. "Remind me," he said, playfully.

He heard a low rumble from her throat, an animal-like sexuality. "My darling, let me have your hand." Slowly, she moved his hand below her naval. "Here," she said. "Here."

When he kissed the smooth skin of her stomach, he felt her hips rise and his tongue find exactly where she wanted it to be.

CHAPTER THIRTY-THREE

Daylight crept into the room from the east window, a soft yellow that seemed reminiscent of spring, an oddity in the deep crevasses of the winter that currently blanketed the city. Avery leaned on the window frame and watched the street below. Across from him, the shops were deserted, funeral like. Too early for Parisians to stroll the sidewalks and the cafés, their bicycles unable to traverse the snow that preempted the normalcy of their day. Strangely, he thought he heard music from Puccini's aria, "*Nessun Dorma.*" *Nobody shall sleep, nobody shall sleep, even you, o Princess, in your cold room. Watch the stars that tremble with love and hope.* He had seen the opera *Turandot* when he was young and impressionable, full of hope. A sadness overcame him, perhaps a yearning to return to his youth, innocence. As he watched the sunrise, he quietly succumbed to his duty to fight an enemy, to fulfill his role as a self-proclaimed patriot. He sighed heavily. He acknowledged that the filth of war and the death that accompanied it did not preclude him from desiring beauty, a serenity in his life, the love of a woman.

Below, on the Place de la Concorde, an old man shuffled toward the Avenue Montaigne. *The Parisians.* After nearly a year of German occupation, they were either collaborative or compromising, whatever suited their lives. Their brazen attitudes toward the Nazis were reserved for the darkened rooms of their homes, a hidden corner in a café on a secluded street.

He considered the French weak, their politicians caring only that their names were listed in the history books as the saviors of France. Their pomposity shaped their decisions, their alliances. Just once he would like to see the French government cohesive, not torn by the backbiting and bickering that incessantly plagued them.

In London, De Gaulle lambasted the interim government of the French, while its citizens were at the mercy of not only the Germans, but the titular French government as well. *Se débrouiller.* They coped as best they could.

Another thing bothered him about the French. They hated the English.

***

Avery glanced at a shadowed corner of the room where the Louis XVI bed held the black fur, the body of Madame Delafloté beneath its warm softness. She slept soundly, an occasional whimper, much like a kitten that has been separated from its mother. He had made love to her as she wished. Whether she thought he was Édouard or not, her passion was unchecked. She screamed at him, bit him and, finally spent, she sobbed late into the night. There had been tender moments, moments where she caressed him, smoothed his lips with hers, played with his hair, all the while whispering, *"mon cherie, je t'aime."*

He, too, uncovered his passion. He found it in the woman who had consumed his strength, had begged him to enter her, and had deceived him with a supposedly frail body that was not so frail after all.

The absence of women in his life had been depressing at times, laden with a fear of attachment. How could he love a woman as she should be loved when the necessity of fighting the war was constantly chasing him?

The covert life he led as a spy was not conducive to long, loving relationships. He felt his throat tighten. For an instant, he thought he would give it all up, embrace the Frenchwoman and take her far away. But, spycraft would never allow it. What would his grandmother say? He had committed the sins she had warned him about. *Sins of the flesh.*

He moved to the bed where, at his feet, he saw a small photograph. When he picked it up, he studied the picture of a handsome man looking into the camera, his eyes dark and intense, a hint of a flirtatious smile on his lips. Avery flinched, a rare thing for the stalwart spy. Looking at him from the photograph was *Frenchie.*

CHAPTER THIRTY-FOUR

The heavily-guarded Reichsmarschall left Berlin on January 22, with crisp blue skies following him south, then east to Frankfort. The eight-hundred mile journey would take three days, through Luxembourg, then across France to Paris. Traveling in opulent comfort in his fifteen-wagon train, the *Asien*, Göring lavished himself with caviar from the Caspian Sea, the beluga sturgeon providing the most sought after delicacy in the world. History decreed caviar was reserved only for royalty. The arrogant man had no problem seeing himself as royalty; he felt the title of King of Germany would suit him quite well. Seeping with self-importance, he was also crude and vulgar, the myriad of medals on his chest in no way diminishing that he was an ambitious buffoon. Intelligent, but a buffoon nonetheless.

Following the engine of the *Asien*, a flak wagon stretched long and ominous as it chased the powerful locomotive. Almost completely enclosed, the car carried machine guns on the wagon top at each end, their barrels continually searching for the enemy.

The wagons were comprised primarily of utility, service and luggage wagons. The fifth car was Göring's personal wagon, where he monitored the cables brought to him from the communications car. He frequented the dining wagon often, his eyes piggish as he satisfied himself with whatever he desired. At the end of the train, another flak car, sprouting the ever-present machine guns, stood ready to protect Germany's Luftwaffe Commander.

The face of Hermann Göring was large, moon-shaped, with small eyes. A pompous man, he did not walk; strutted instead, while the copious amount of medals on his chest added another few pounds to his beefy body. His self-importance dominated his life in such a way that even Hitler found time with the commander of Germany's Luftwaffe mind numbing. He told his staff to limit Göring's visits to fifteen minutes at the most. Göring never suspected that his ostentatious behavior was anything but befitting his coveted position in the hierarchy of the Third Reich.

***

"Herr Göring , a cable has just arrived from Berlin." Hesitantly, his valet, Robert, placed the paper in Göring's hand. Göring puffed from his long tobacco pipe for a few moments, then read the communiqué.

"Ah, one more threat of assassination, Robert. How many does that make now? Fifteen? Twenty? When will they realize how impenetrable we are?"

His large chest rumbled with laughter. "The superiority of the Germany army will assure my safety.

"I am also sure Colonel Krenz will provide a superb security plan upon my arrival."

Göring stood. "Robert, send a cable to Colonel Krenz. Let's advise him our estimated arrival time as well as this new assassination threat."

Göring yawned as he walked from the car, speaking over his shoulder. "These French. They are idiots."

Chapter Thirty-Five

Avery Gannon slipped the small photograph into his pocket and returned to the window and the emerging dawn. It seemed he could not get enough breath. The ringing in his ears had become so loud he felt he would never hear again. His heart hammered in his chest while his hands grasped the windowsill to steady himself. *Édouard Delafloté was Frenchie. He had made love to Frenchie's widow. Frenchie, his fellow spy, who was murdered while he helplessly watched.*

He heard a rustling from the bed and turned to see Eléonore push herself deeper into the warmth of the fur. How ironic. His grandmother had been right all along. The sins of the flesh were more than they appeared, touched much deeper than the physical aspects of the sexual act. It had just been proven to him. In all its complexity, he understood perfectly. *Nothing was pure if you took it illicitly.* The coldness wrapped him like death's hands, touching him as though to take him to another place. He faltered, felt sorrow envelop him. He had loved Frenchie like a brother. Could he have saved him? *Frenchie, I didn't know. I didn't know.*

A creak in the hallway, a soft rushing of air beneath the door, a hesitant knock. "Gannon."

Avery pulled his gun and walked quickly across the room. "Oui?"

"It is I. Plomion." The door pushed open and Plomion entered the room. "We must talk."

"The woman is still asleep." Avery pointed to the hallway.

Plomion leaned himself into a corner of the dark hallway and grasped Avery's shoulder.

"I have some very interesting information." The Frenchman, whose two-day-old beard darkened his already cragged face, licked his lips in excitement. "We have received intelligence that our dear, dear friend Göring will be visiting our lovely city tomorrow." Plomion grinned. "What an opportunity for us, *oui?*"

Avery saw the glint in Plomion's eyes, knew the Résistance fighter would make the most of any opportunity to kill a German, especially one so close to Adolf Hitler. "Go on."

"He is coming, of course, to load his train with more loot from the museums. The theft of French treasures must be stopped." Spittle escaped Plomion's mouth as he snarled the words and clenched his jaw.

"But, of course." Avery raised his eyebrows. "Why are you telling me this?"

Plomion smiled. "Monsieur, you are the finest assassin in this war. It is your duty to kill the German."

"Duty?" Avery looked at the Frenchman for a long moment. His words were slow and deliberate, resolute. "Killing Göring is not in my plans."

Plomion's eyes widened. "Not in your plans? Surely, you are not serious. We have very good intelligence that puts Göring at the Gare de L'est tomorrow. It's an opportunity we must not ignore. I beg you to reconsider."

Avery turned from Plomion and walked the dark hall to the top of the stairs. The chances of killing Göring in the midst of his elite security were almost non-existent. The Germans would close the station to civilians, post guards at every point between the station and Göring's hotel. Any plan the French devised would be flawed. True, his skill as an assassin seemed almost magical to those who knew of him. *Get the British spy; he will put the fat German in his sites and fire away.* Not an unpleasant thought.

"I no longer have my rifle," he said as he walked back to the Frenchman.

Plomion seemed surprised. "Your weapon? Where is your weapon?"

Avery seemed irritated. "I was lucky to escape from the Germans with my life, much less the tools of my trade." His eyes watched the top of the steps. "My weapon is at the bottom of the Seine. What else could I do with Germans on my tail?"

A low rumble eased from Plomion's chest. "Britain's most revered assassin has no weapon?" The laughter came in short spurts. "I can't believe it. An Englishman who is not perfect? My friend, I thought I would die before I would ever see such a thing."

Avery glared at Plomion until the man backed quietly into the dark corner, his smile fading. "My apologies, monsieur. Of course, the most important thing was escaping the Germans . . . not the care of your weapon."

Neither man spoke for a few moments. Avery jumped when Plomion clapped his hands together. "Monsieur, our worries are over. I have one of the most extraordinary assassin's rifles ever made."

Avery narrowed his eyes. What could it be? One of the rifles the French used in World War I? The French had been slow in upgrading their armor, their weaponry. Even their fighting tactics left much to be desired, archaic strategies that had put them in harm's way when Germany began its quest to conquer the world. They had not been prepared for the Germans and their modern war machinery.

Avery bit. His role as an assassin for the British had instilled in him an almost fanatical thirst for sharpening his skill. "Who makes it?"

The wide grin on Plomion's face lifted his ears and exposed his unusually long teeth. The ends of his mustache pushed into his cheeks where a rosy glow emanated, the result of an early morning entry into his whiskey flask.

"Ah, monsieur, I knew you could not resist." Plomion shivered with anticipation; an opportunity for a Frenchman to instruct an Englishman was indeed rare. "A MAS 36." He paused, his face posed in reverie. His eyes glistened. "French made."

Gannon rolled his eyes. "I know who makes the MAS 36." A rare bolt-action rifle recalibrated in 22LR, an efficient take-down version. "You've added a scope?"

Plomion gleamed. "But, of course. A beautiful kill at 200 meters."

That's all the distance he would need. The gun offered an excellent balance of strength, rugged, reliable, lightweight. Gannon nodded his head, a rifle with superior accuracy. "Where is it?"

"Ah, monsieur, do not worry. I have it in my possession, ready for firing."

"And the cartridges?"

Plomion spoke with smugness, an air of superiority so reminiscent of the French. He walked in a small circle in the shadowed hallway, rubbing his chin, then swiping the ends of his mustache. "Gevelot." His eyes narrowed when he grinned at Gannon. "Grande Precision."

Avery nodded. They would more than do the job. He could fire from 150 meters with ease and expect an exact hit. The weapon's cartridges were powerful, a high-velocity, with less bullet drop and wind drift, allowing for greater accuracy at greater distances. Best of all, the weapon was highly concealable, could be assembled in seconds, yet would offer a stable firing platform.

Avery deliberated while Plomion drank from his flask. The cartridges were realistically capable of making a lethal headshot. Yet, it wasn't the weapon or the cartridges that concerned him. It could have been the most accurate weapon in the world, but the execution of the plan was the most crucial. If he didn't have the perfect opportunity to fire the rifle, then what did it matter?

"We don't have enough time to perfect the plan."

Plomion gritted his teeth. "You Englishmen, you are too cautious with your plans. Just shoot the son-of-a-bitch!"

What a pleasure that would be. Line the bastard up in his sights and fire. A headshot? Of course, right between the eyes. How could he not seize the opportunity to assassinate Hermann Göring? Avery stilled. He may be able to assassinate Göring, but in doing so he would certainly lose his own life.

Avery turned away from the Frenchman and pushed open the door to Room 308. He heard Plomion open his flask again and looked over his shoulder. "We will talk later. Do what you can regarding the logistics."

The rising sun had lightened the room, but not the despair that had found its way into Avery Gannon. He had broken spycraft's number one rule: the mission is your number one priority. In fact, he had broken many of His Majesty's Secret Service rules. He shook his head. He had also broken his grandmother's rules.

When he looked up, he saw a sleepy-eyed Eléonore watching him, her hair in wild disarray. She was beautiful.

CHAPTER THIRTY-SIX

Colonel Horst Krenz read Göring's cable a second time. *Ensure Security Adequate.* Göring had made it clear whose responsibility his safety fell to – not his own elite guards, but the Paris Gestapo, specifically Krenz. It was madness to think otherwise. Krenz felt perspiration wet his upper lip, a rage simmering in his bowels. It was the following words that squeezed his throat tightly, caused his heart rate to skyrocket. *Assassination Threat. Assume the French.*

Assume the French? He's fucking right it's the French. Who else could it be? Little trolls that guard the Arc de Triomphe? Krenz shoved the cable into his pocket and began to pace the small room. At the window, he slammed his fist into the wall. *Fucking bastards.* The prissy little men who served wine by day in the elegant cafés on the Champ-Élysées and made bombs at night. They were invisible, cloaked in the guise of subservient Frenchmen. Of course, they were subservient, especially when they had a Karabiner 98 shoved up their noses.

Krenz paced down one wall, another wall, ending up in a square. Then, back again. A nervous, agitated step that pronounced his heightened anger. It was the Englishman. *He knew it.* Knew as long as the Englishman was alive, there would be more assassinations. *Less than forty-eight hours to find him*. He passed the single window and stopped, his hands clasped tightly behind him. *He must find the Englishman.*

"Herr Bauer!" Krenz' voice elevated to a shrill scream, manic and devoid of human qualities. "Come at once!"

He closed his eyes and waited, his thoughts oddly running to the Greek historian, Thucydides, and his accounting of the war between Sparta and Athens. He had studied the writings of the historian in military college, had marveled at his strict standards of evidence gathering, his analysis in terms of cause and effect, all without a reference to intervention by the Gods. But, it was his role as the father of political realism that had made an indelible impression on Krenz' young mind.

He saw his professor standing before him, his face full of wisdom, a teacher who had reached into the minds of his students and dispensed knowledge as though it were life-sustaining food. *Thucydides viewed relations between nations as based on might, not right.*

Yes, Krenz thought, somewhat pacified, it is Germany's might that will establish a new order, a culmination of our Aryan society, the *master race*. Krenz smiled and opened his eyes. Everything was so clear now.

"Herr Bauer, please summon Herr Vogel immediately."

***

"Colonel Krenz, I am at your service." The young lieutenant saluted smartly.

Krenz turned from the window and studied the face of Vogel. *Yes, you are at my service.* You must serve me well for it is I who will lead you, show you that war is a violent teacher, that you must not take lightly the perils of battle. He walked the length of the room and found the chair of his desk. "Sit, please."

Vogel quickly pulled a chair and sat across from his commanding officer.

"I have received a cable from Herr Göring." Krenz spoke with a controlled anger. "He arrives Thursday as we calculated. Approximately 10:00 a.m."

Vogel said nothing. There was more.

Krenz leaned back in his chair and placed his thin legs across the edge of his desk. His eyes were closed. Some moments passed before he opened them and found Vogel. A slight snort from his twisted mouth, "Surprise, surprise. Another assassination threat."

Vogel pushed his chair closer to the desk. "Yes, Colonel Krenz."

The room seemed to have darkened. Still no electricity, despite promises the Parisian skyline would, indeed, become The City of Light in only a few hours. Krenz vowed to shoot the power station engineers if he dined by candlelight another night.

"I received a cable a short while ago from Göring. Seems he has received word from Berlin that rumors of an assassination attempt against him have surfaced."

Krenz shook his head. "It baffles me where they get their information. I have no information that indicates a specific threat. Of course, we are prepared for anything."

He glanced at Vogel, a message. "At least we'd better be. Herr Göring expects *adequate* security. Says he suspects the French are responsible for this last threat . . . as the last dozen times."

Krenz removed his feet from the desk and pulled Gannon's file from the desk drawer.

"Our culprit is the same, Herr Vogel. The English spy. Perhaps he is addicted to killing Germans. Especially high-ranking Germans."

He opened the file and his eye once more fell to the initials "HI" written in the margin, felt a surge of anger. From the file, he pulled the small, faded photograph and placed the magnifying glass near the surface, stared so long his eyes blurred. He shifted his head and used his wayward left eye to scrutinize the photograph as if it were a specimen under a microscope, a moving, living organism that needed identification. "Interesting," he said in a whispered hush.

There was an odd contortion of Krenz' head, the slightly globular eyeball sweeping slowly across the photograph, machine-like, only inches away from the sepia surface.

Krenz lifted his head and rubbed his eyes, a slight smile hovering on his lips. "Well, Lieutenant Vogel, I do believe our Englishman is fond of Melachrino cigarettes."

How extraordinary. His flawed left eye had seen what his supposedly perfect right eye had not. Excitement surged through Krenz' body, an exhilaration that surpassed anything he had ever felt. For the first time in his life, he felt absolved of any inadequacy, any limitation. No longer was he deficient, but rather like a savant, someone with a gift, a talent. His amazing left eye, a human magnifying glass, saw what his right eye could not.

The cigarette in Gannon's hand at first seemed non-descript, unremarkable, a trail of wispy smoke exiting the tip, rising upward slightly. Above the forefinger that held the cigarette, an emblem, red, a regal shape. Melachrino. One of London's finest Egyptian cigarettes.

Krenz looked up. The ceiling light crackled and buzzed. Electricity. At last, after two long days, light fell across the City of Paris. He closed the file and looked at Vogel.

"Let us pay Monsieur Bedeau a little visit."

CHAPTER THIRTY-SEVEN

"*Quand puis-je attendre vous me faire un café, monsieur?*"
Her words stilled the morning with their sweetness, a
cajoling, like angels whispering.

"Your coffee?" He looked across the room at the smiling
woman, imagined her a princess of long ago, with handmaidens
brushing her hair, dressing her. "Madame, I would be delighted
to bring you coffee." He took a step toward her, could not help
himself.

"Monsieur Gannon, it is my desire that you bring us both
coffee. I should also like to have a croissant."

Gannon saw the brightness in her eyes, like a woman who
had been kissed, who had begged for more. "But, of course," he
said

He saw her cock her head, hold up her fingers, crook them to
summon him, as if he were a servant. No chance he would dis-
obey her. He walked across the room and found the edge of the
bed. Her ivory skin flushed pink, the lids of her eyes swollen
with sleep. He noticed her lips were also puffed, kissed endlessly
by a lover who fervently desired her. He felt himself falter. She
could have anything she wanted from him.

Eléonore said nothing as she reached out and touched his

cheek. Her eyes roamed his face, her fingers felt his beard, brushed his lips with her thumb. He thought he saw a glistening of tears.

"Monsieur Gannon, it is true we have crossed some boundaries?"

Her question fell heavily upon Avery, a resounding truth. It was a simple truth, but laden with far-reaching complexities. His crossing of boundaries had not only jeopardized him, but most certainly her. Whitehall had taught him to curb his passions or emotions. He looked at her a long moment, took her hand, felt its softness and thought, *I will never be able to turn loose of her hand.*

He found the courage to speak, a far away voice found somewhere in his heart. "That is true, Eléonore." He paused. "I have no regrets."

"Nor I."

He felt the significance of the moment, a letting go, and then a grasping of a riveting reality. He would have to leave her, one way or the other, most likely by a German bullet.

"We must talk, Eléonore."

She pulled the fur around her shoulders, plumped her pillows and leaned back into their softness. A slight frown creased her forehead, her eyes searching his, waiting.

"I have placed you in grave danger, my presence in your room, my guise as your husband. Against my better judgment, you have become involved in my life, my work as a British agent. This was not supposed to happen; yet it has. I feel a need to undo it all, to free you from any harm." He paused, tightness in his throat. An unusual vulnerability washed over him. "Yet . . . yet, I feel I may not have the strength to do so."

Eléonore reached out and touched his hand, said nothing.

"My instincts tell me to leave. And I must. Your survival, my survival depends on it." When he looked at her, the pain in her eyes was so great that he turned away. He stood and moved to the small lounge that faced the bed. "We must work cautiously and – "

"Is it your wish to leave me, leave me after the boundaries we have crossed?"

"I do not wish to leave you. I wish to protect you."

Her gaze was steady, a challenge. "You confuse me, Monsieur

Gannon. One moment you cannot leave me, the next you are leaving me. Tell me . . . is it the language again, the French you speak very well, but have difficulty translating?" Her words were unforgiving, perhaps meant to prod him into her reality.

Avery looked to the window where bright sun had slipped past the draperies and warmed the walls, the rugs, with a yellow as soft as young buttercups. It was near 10:00 a.m., a morning where no plans had been made, where Plomion had insisted he commit to a mission involving an assassination. He closed his eyes. He saw Krenz, his menacing Gestapo uniform and the grim set of his jaw. *Monsieur Delafloté, come by Gestapo Headquarters before you leave town.* He saw Krenz arresting Frenchie.

He turned back to Eléonore. "Madame, what is it you would have me to do?"

She stared at him for a long moment. Her words were as cold as the Paris snow. "I would simply have you do what I asked of you in the beginning." Her eyes turned a smoky black, held his a moment longer.

"And that is?"

CHAPTER THIRTY-EIGHT

The Hotel de Crillon was a hotel of history. In 1758, when King Louis XV asked Ange-Jacques Gabriel to build Place Louis XV, he decreed: *I want two palaces, equally beautiful, in the center of Paris. From my rooms I want to see the entire city in its golden splendor.*

The Louis XV suite on the top floor, graced with a terrace, overlooked Paris and the Place de la Concorde, the pillared façade of the exterior walls portraying the lavishness of the French and their love of excess. In the distance, the Eiffel Tower rose like a cultural icon as the tallest structure in Paris, a great pylon that proclaimed to the world the beauty of the City of Light. History found its way into the grand lobby in 1778 when the French-American treaty was signed, recognizing the Act of Independence of the United States, a breathtaking event given the fact that the United States had become the most powerful nation on earth.

It was only befitting that the Reichsmarschall of Germany, Hermann Göring, would find residence in Louis XV's majestic suite. After all, he considered himself sovereign and a representative of the people of Germany; of the Third Reich and its supreme hierarchy in the world. Never mind that his suite was only a breath away from Monsieur and Madame Delafloté's quarters, only a short walk across the landing of the 3rd Floor. Monsieur Plomion would be pleased to know that the British spy could merely walk down the hall with a bottle of A. de Fussigny Cognac and present it to the German along with a shot in the gut. What a fantasy for the Frenchman; for the British spy, it would be suicide.

***

Monsieur Claude Bedeau knew nothing of the arrival of Herr Göring. To his credit, the Louis XV suite remained in pristine condition at all times. Who knew when a monarch's entourage would arrive expecting the luxurious rooms to be available at a moment's notice.

Erect in his hotel uniform, he stood outside the entrance of the hotel and watched the slow drip of icicles that lined the edge of the roof on the building across the street. The temperatures had warmed, but only slightly. Parisians leaned into the wind as they sought a warm café, a liqueur perhaps, a Chambord that smelled of raspberries.

Bedeau pulled his watch from his pocket and studied the time. Still early. Just as he turned to enter the hotel, he saw the black staff car of Colonel Horst Krenz round the corner onto the Place de la Concorde. A chill greater than the Paris cold traveled up his spine. His eyebrow twitched. He made no movement as he watched the car slide to a stop in front of him. The driver quickly emerged and opened the rear door for its passenger.

"Monsieur Bedeau, you look very well." A smiling Krenz pulled off his gloves. "Come, let us go inside. I have been yearning for a cup of coffee made with ground acorns and roasted potato peelings."

His words seemed sincere, but Bedeau knew better. He said nothing as he followed Krenz into the hotel, noting his stiff walk, erect back and the ever-present black knee-high boots that were perhaps once worn by the devil.

Krenz found his way to the doorway of the massive hotel kitchens and paused. "The hotel is cold, Monsieur Bedeau. I'm sure your guests must complain." Again, the knowing smile. The Germans had confiscated France' entire coal supply.

"Indeed, it is cold and no, our guests do not complain,

Colonel Krenz. A pity."

Krenz entered the kitchen and found the coffee urn. "A pity? Why is that?"

"Our guests deserve a warm hotel."

Krenz nodded and poured coffee. "A cup for you?"

"No. But, thank you." Bedeau felt his eyebrow twitch again and waited. He knew the purpose of Krenz' visit was forthcoming. He watched as he slowly paced the kitchen, seemingly interested in the great stoves that lined the walls.

He stopped abruptly and turned toward Bedeau. "Ah, how could I not tell you the news, Monsieur Bedeau? You are to have a guest, a very important guest."

Bedeau lifted his eyebrows, a curiosity claiming his thoughts. An important guest? A German, of course. But, what German and for how long? Then, he became alarmed; a German and a British spy in the same hotel. He felt a coldness travel his body and settle in his chest.

"The Hotel de Crillon would welcome a guest, Colonel Krenz," he said smoothly.

Laughter erupted from the Gestapo chief. "Perhaps, Monsieur Bedeau. Perhaps."

He left the end of the kitchen and walked to where Bedeau stood. "You may expect the arrival of Reichsmarschall Hermann Göring within forty-eight hours."

His smile widened. "Of course, you must ensure the hotel is comfortably . . . warm . . . for our important guest. He is known for his . . . shall we say . . . his irritability if things are not to his liking."

"Comfortable? There is no coal to heat the hotel. We have barely enough food to feed our present guests. You ask something of me that I cannot provide."

Krenz cocked his head in confusion. "I am surprised to hear you say that, Monsieur Bedeau. The Hotel de Crillon is famed for its amenities. How could you make such statements?" The right eye bore into Bedeau, a challenge searing the face of the old concierge.

The room stilled, an ominous quiet that threatened any semblance of control that Bedeau might have possessed. He stood facing Krenz while he let any thoughts of survival fade away with his next words. "It is my opinion that we must join together in the quest to ensure the Reichsmarschall is comfortable during his stay at the de Crillon. You will provide coal and food or Herr Göring will most definitely be . . . irritable." He lifted the heels of his shoes and stared into the face of Krenz.

Long moments passed and neither man moved. Outside the kitchen, notes from a grand Bosendorfer piano floated across the lobby – *Rêverie* by Debussy. How fitting, a French composer whose music stroked the City of Light like the touch of an angel's wing.

A short laugh from Krenz, stifled intentionally, phony. "My, my Monsieur Bedeau. Your audacity amazes me. I . . . I don't know whether to shoot you or applaud you."

He eyed him with a long hard stare, through stiff lips, said, "You shall have your coal and food."

He smiled warmly, as an afterthought. "I would like to arrange a reception for Herr Göring. Tomorrow evening here at the hotel." He narrowed his eyes. "I will have Corporal Bauer contact you. He will provide you with everything that is necessary to ensure the Reichsmarshall is . . . content."

Bedeau watched the German in his ominous black boots circle the long table and stop. Krenz' words echoed across the kitchen.

"I'll arrange a guest list. I'm thinking I should like to invite Monsieur and Madame Delafloté."

A long, slow walk to the exit of the kitchen, then a turn so orchestrated one would assume it was a movement from a ballet.

"Oh, another bit of news." The right eye found the waiting Monsieur Bedeau. "I had a lovely chat with Madame Bedeau only a short while ago. An absolutely delightful woman." He waited while Bedeau absorbed the words. "Seems she adores you. Let's see . . . married forty-three years? Am I correct?"

Bedeau was statue still, the foot of an elephant on his chest, his breathing so shallow he felt faint. "That is correct," he whispered.

"Ah, I thought so." A large, toothy grin. "And when is your forty-fourth anniversary?"

"September."

"September. I *love* September, especially in Paris." He turned and without looking back, said ever so softly. "The Eng-

lish spy, Monsieur Bedeau. I expect you will reveal his whereabouts very soon. Say before Herr Göring arrives? Say by
midnight tonight."

Bedeau did not answer. He thought of his beautiful Hélène.

***

Krenz tapped his driver on the shoulder. "Rue Lavoisier." He
had been thinking of Célina for most of the day. He found most
of his days were filled with thoughts of her, even thoughts he
may love her. A German in love with a Frenchwoman. That
would not be to the liking of Herr Hitler. I am a good German,
thought Krenz, as he felt the hardness rise in his trousers.

Chapter Thirty-Nine

"What a pity, Monsieur Gannon, that your memory is so poor." Eléonore clucked her tongue. "So many flaws you Englishmen have. Your difficulty with the French language the most obvious." She sent him a sly look. "Do you not remember our discussion of yesterday?"

"We talked of many things."

"Yes, we did."

Avery became irritated, felt an urgency to resolve any issues regarding Eléonore. Yes, he had made love to her, but her safety was foremost. "I do not enjoy these games when our lives are in such danger. *What is it that you wish of me?*"

She rose from the bed and stood before him, the fur wrapped tightly around her. "It is my wish to become a spy, monsieur."

He looked into her pleading eyes. "Madame, please forgive me, but that is impossible."

Gannon watched as the woman in the fur coat moved across the room and stood at the window. The early morning sun seemed almost touchable as its rays spread across her face and bathed her hair in golden light. She turned and looked at him. "I wonder . . ." She paused and turned back to the window, her words dreamlike. "I wonder the purpose of our survival. Your escape from the Gestapo, my awakening from a desire to take my own life." When she looked at him, her eyes were large and luminous, glistening with tears. "Surely, there is a reason for our prolonged breath in this putrid Nazi air." She raised her eyebrows. "Would you agree there is a rationale of sorts in our continued existence?"

Gannon contemplated her question. She had become philosophical in her quest to understand their current predicament. Her answer to the reality in which they found themselves was to acknowledge that their survival served a greater good, one that would anchor them both in a world that had been drenched in the blood of war.

His answer was more complex, a more direct approach to what he considered his duty as a spy. *His duty as a spy?* He felt a hardness surround his heart, a malevolence enter his brain; not a mindless malevolence, but a calculated, anticipated hatred of his enemies. *He was an assassin.*

"Perhaps, Madame. But, let me assure you, it is I who must continue my work on behalf of His Majesty's Secret Service as a lone assassin, without a hindrance of any kind. I must leave here and regain what I have lost in these past few days. You, as a Parisian, must stay within the limitations that have been imposed upon you by the Germans. Your survival depends on it."

He paused. "My survival depends on my autonomous performance as an Allied spy."

Gannon cleared his throat. "I must leave."

***

The knock at the door was loud, an intrusion of the uncertainties that lay between the occupants of the room. "Yes," Gannon called. He wanted to pull his weapon, but, at the moment, he was Édouard Delafloté, not the spy.

Again, a knock. Gannon walked across the room and opened the door to a young German soldier. "Yes. What is it you want?"

The soldier clicked his heels together and stood at stiff attention while he handed Gannon a small, cream-colored envelope. "From Colonel Krenz, Herr Delafloté." The young man turned quickly and disappeared down the hall.

From Krenz? A summons? On the front of the envelope: *Monsieur and Madame Delafloté.* Slowly, Gannon opened the envelope.

COLONEL HORST KRENZ
THIRD REICH, GESTAPO COUNTER-INTELLIGENCE OFFICER
REQUESTS THE HONOR OF YOUR PRESENCE AT A RECEPTION
TO WELCOME
REICHSMARSCHALL HERMANN GÖRING
THURSDAY, JANUARY 25
AT 7:00 O'CLOCK IN THE EVENING
AT THE HOTEL DE CRILLON
10 PLACE DE LA CONCORDE

Gannon could hear Plomion's laughter as if he sat atop his shoulder, like a parrot whose endless chatter caused one to emit a bewildering sigh. *In the same room, the spy, Germany's Reichsmarschall and the Gestapo.*

Despite the quickening of his heart, he turned and looked at Eléonore. "It seems, Madame, we shall be together a while longer."

A weak smile formed on his lips. "We have been invited to a reception, a reception full of Germans."

PART II

CHAPTER FORTY

Plomion's face flushed with excitement. "*Oui*, this is the most astounding news I have heard since the beginning of the war. Hermann Göring! In the palm of our hands!" The Frenchman danced around Room 308 while Avery Gannon and Eléonore Delafloté watched silently. "I can see it now, the fat bastard lavished with French wines and cheeses while the starving citizens of Paris cringe in his shadow. No more! We will poke him with a pitchfork and watch him implode!" Plomion's throaty, diabolical laughter filled the room.

Gannon stood from the small couch and eyed Plomion with mounting trepidation. Plomion's flair for orchestrating the demise of Germans was unparalleled. He had earned his reputation as a result of his proclivity to build bombs, bombs that destroyed bridges, communication towers, anything the Germans used to fight their misguided war.

Had Plomion not had poor eyesight at long distances, he could have also been the Résistance's star assassin. Even a powerful scope precluded him from obliterating his targets with one carefully placed shot. As it was, his bomb-making abilities had caused the Germans incredible losses in and around Paris, where the exuberant man had been able to exploit his talents to their utmost efficiency.

Gannon became uneasy. While he had no problem working with the Résistance, in the end it was his own judgment that gave him the sense of control that he needed to do his work. Plomion, as a citizen of France, had witnessed the rape of his country, had lived the humiliation of Germany's rule and, therefore, had no hesitation in his pursuit of killing them. Gannon felt his own tactics were more restrained, with a greater need for planning and organization that would result in a successfully executed mission.

He knew his collaboration with Plomion was necessary, a reliance on his knowledge of the City, but mostly the invaluable support of the Résistance as a whole. His Majesty's Secret Service had sent him to France to support the Résistance, not run it. Yet, he doubted he could succumb to a complete capitulation to Plomion in any situation that would require relinquishing his own judgment.

He did not consider Plomion a hothead, by any means. But, one thing was sure: the man was capable of a frenzied approach when it came to killing Germans.

He kept his words non-committal. "I agree the arrival of Göring is an opportunity for us. What is it you have in mind?"

Plomion stopped his pacing and looked at the ceiling, a careful examination of the chandelier, an occasional glance at the tall windows. The Frenchman had a lean, wiry frame that emitted a hard, intense power and when he looked at Gannon, his eyes were coal-dust black, almost smoldering.

"What I have in mind is to ensure our dear fat German never returns to Germany." He grinned. "And, if he does, it will be on a funeral train."

"Go on." Gannon cleared his throat, anxious for Plomion to reveal his plans.

"It seems we have two opportunities to kill the German. The train station or right here in this glorious hotel while he sips wine and boasts of his many accomplishments on behalf of the Third Reich. It is my – "

"Here at the hotel?"

"But, of course. What better location to place a bomb?" Plomion's voice rose. "We know where he will sleep, we know where he will eat. And what about this ridiculous reception?

Every German officer within thirty kilometers of Paris will be here in just a matter of hours." Plomion clapped his hands together, a prelude to an astonishing epiphany that promised to be earth shattering. He licked his lips, brushed his mustache and leaned closer to Gannon.

A whisper, "Monsieur, it is my desire to make the evening of the reception quite memorable."

Gannon felt himself searching for air. "Is it possible you have forgotten that Madame Delafloté and I will be attending the reception?"

A small pause by the Frenchman. "Monsieur, this is war. We must do what we must to ensure the reemergence of France, to save Her. Surely, you must know that. I suggest you find an excuse not to attend the reception if you feel your life will be in danger."

Gannon's anger flared. "Monsieur, I do not *feel* our lives will be endangered. I *know* it. Since when do we not do what the Germans tell us to do? The Madame and I have been *summoned* to attend the reception for Göring by Colonel Krenz. We have no choice in the matter."

Across from Gannon, Eléonore returned to the couch. When she looked at Gannon, her expression was placid. He studied her for a long moment, convinced her look held a distinct message of a laissez faire attitude toward what was being discussed in the room.

 Gannon spoke to her. "Madame, I am curious. Would you like to attend a reception full of Germans who may possibly be blown to hell and you along with them?"

Eléonore smiled. "My dear Englishman, where is your trust? Do you not consider Monsieur Plomion the *élite* of those who would free France from the Germans? If you have no trust, then I must state my disappointment in you."

She looked at Plomion and with a voice that held an inordinate amount of strength, said, "If you would, enlighten me of your strategy to . . . shall we say . . . to contribute to the demise of the Germans." She turned and looked at Gannon. "And, of course, your plans to exclude Monsieur Gannon and I from the . . . how do you say it . . . *the énorme détonation.*"

"Your naiveté amazes me, Madame," said Gannon. "Perhaps you should return to Senlis and continue your life in the wealth and safety of your family. There is no place for you here."

Gannon was not prepared for the anger unleashed by the frail widow. She snarled at him.

"But, of course, Monsieur Gannon, you have put me in my place, labeled me an insignificant woman who has known only a lifestyle of wealth and comfort."

She caught her breath. "The war has not touched me?" she screamed. "My dead husband's heart is still beating somewhere? He will come and hold me and tell me he loves me?"

Spittle flew from her heated words. "How dare you diminish my place in this war, keep me from the hatred I feel, the revenge I desire."

He remained still as Eléonore came closer, so close, he felt her breath on his face, her words barely audible. "You have denied me what is mine and I shall not forgive you for that."

She turned from him and looked at Plomion. "Monsieur Plomion, I will do whatever is required of me." A slight smile graced her lips. "At present, my only dilemma is what I shall wear to the reception."

Plomion bowed slightly. "My gratitude to you, Madame."

***

The occupants of the room fell into a thoughtful quiet. From the couch, Gannon spoke, "What of the train station?"

"Ah, so glad you asked." Plomion walked quickly to the door and opened it. When he returned he was holding a customized sniper version of an MAS 36 rifle, scoped and deadly.

Gannon said nothing as he took the gun from Plomion and rubbed his fingertips along the short barrel, looked through the scope, felt the weapon's balance. He touched the forward position bolt and mentally thanked the French for their thoughtful design.

A rare version of the rifle, it had been recalibrated into 22LR. A take down in two pieces, he would use it at a mere one hundred meters. Close and amazingly accurate. Instantly, he knew the rifle would become the path to his waning chances of survival. The train station? He would have little time or opportunity to escape after the trigger was pulled.

"A fine rifle," he said quietly, noticing the position of the scope.

"Monsieur Gannon, I assure you the weapon will perform as you require. The head of Herr Göring is a perfect target, *oui*?" Plomion reached inside his coat. "Here are your cartridges."

Gannon took the small box. *Gevelot 22LR Grande Precision.* He opened the box and saw it was full, 50 rounds, more than enough cartridges. He slipped the box into his pocket and looked at Plomion. "I will need three men at the train station."

"You shall have them." Plomion nodded and turned to Eléonore. "Good evening, Madame Delafloté. We shall talk again."

Gannon watched as the Frenchman left the room. As much as he despised Reichsmarschall Hermann Göring, the bullets he carried in his pocket were for Colonel Horst Krenz, Paris' illustrious Gestapo chief, the murderer of his fellow spy. Perhaps, if he had time, he would also use the French weapon on Herr Göring.

***

Plomion eased quietly through the darkened hallway. From the corner to his left, he heard movement. Monsieur Bedeau stumbled forward, his face pale. "Monsieur Plomion, I must talk with you," he whispered.

"*Oui*, what is it?"

"My Hélène."

"I don't understand."

"If I do not reveal the whereabouts of Monsieur Gannon to Colonel Krenz by midnight tonight, my Hélène will die."

CHAPTER FORTY-ONE

Colonel Horst Krenz felt he was very well suited for his work, found it exhilarating, thought of the accolades he would receive from Herr Göring when the English spy was finally captured, the assassin who had terrorized Germans in the City of Light for so many months.

Fresh air bathed his face as his Horch 852 roadster traveled along the streets of Paris. Snow piled high along the roadways, workers clearing the streets and removing debris tossed by the winter winds that had blown incessantly for over forty-eight hours.

He had enjoyed his visit with Bedeau, the little lying man who knew exactly where the British spy was hiding, had known all along that the Résistance had either provided a safe house or, as Krenz suspected, the spy had taken refuge in the Crillon.

The sighting of the spy just one block from the hotel and then his subsequent disappearance left no doubt that he had found refuge in the hotel. How he could escape two thorough searches of the hotel was a mystery, a mystery in which Bedeau was involved. Krenz smiled to himself. Mrs. Bedeau had been the answer all along. So simple. The thought of her in the interrogation chair was all Bedeau needed to *inspire* him to reveal the whereabouts of the spy. The old Frenchman had less than twenty-four hours to expose Gannon, who, as far as Krenz was concerned, was only hours away from capture . . . and death.

"Driver," he called from his leather-clad seat. "I wish to go to the train station."

It was there that Göring would arrive on Thursday morning on his train, the *Asien*, scheduled to arrive at 10:10 a.m. Göring had begun his journey from Berlin the day before and would arrive in Paris to find soldiers standing on high alert, prepared to protect the Reichsmarschall with their lives.

Krenz smiled to himself. He had known for a long time that Göring was addicted to morphine, could not stray away from a ready supply, which, of course, his personal physician provided.

For a man who was held in high esteem by Hitler, Göring had many flaws. His arrogance was unparalleled, driven by his elitist attitude as the founder of the Gestapo, his role as Wehrmacht Commander over the united armed forces of Germany and, most importantly, his position as Commander in Chief of the Luftwaffe. The generals who ran the armies of Germany, especially Rommel, despised him, could not bear his boasting of the grand accomplishments of the Luftwaffe, of his endless victories.

***

At the *Gare de l'Est*, Krenz leaned forward and tapped his driver on the shoulder, "Stop here."

Krenz's black boots found the pavement, cleared of snow, and stood stiff and waiting, his attention focused on the many soldiers who patrolled the station.

He envisioned the arrival of Göring, his entourage, his bodyguards, the flair with which the Reichsmarschall would descend his train. Then, oddly, he imagined a bullet entering the skull of Göring, an explosion of blood and tissue. Suddenly, Krenz caught his breath and swept his right eye around the station, the shops, the cafes, the soldiers who stood at attention. Krenz was well aware Göring was next in command should anything happen to the Führer and that knowledge caused within him a sudden fear. At all costs, he must ensure the safety of Göring.

"You! You there!" Krenz beckoned a group of SS troopers who stood at the entrance of the station, their rifles pressed against their chests. "Come! Come at once!"

The soldiers seemed confused. Their lieutenant, a thin, gaunt-faced man, walked toward Krenz. "Colonel?" Only six feet away, he stopped and, through hardened, weary eyes, looked at Krenz's uniform, clearly Gestapo, clearly the Chief of Gestapo. His eyes fell to the ashen color of Krenz' uniform, the right side collar patch black and without insignia.

"Your name?" asked Krenz.

The soldier stood ramrod straight and saluted in military fashion. "Lieutenant Martin Fischer."

Krenz studied the officer's uniform. An experienced soldier, obviously a veteran member of the German army. He saw an awareness in his eyes, a knowing that Krenz realized as a quiet intelligence.

"Lt. Fischer, what is the status of security at this moment?" Krenz acknowledged to himself that his voice was shrill, a combination of stress and anxiety. He was well aware that the unknown whereabouts of the spy and the arrival of Göring were cataclysmic circumstances that threatened to unravel any semblance of control he had over the safety of Hitler's designated replacement should Hitler's life end abruptly.

"At full alert, Colonel. There are four patrols that guard all the entrances to the train station as well as intermittently along the perimeter of the tracks. Snipers are in place at various high-points around the station."

He paused and lifted his arm to indicate the vantage point from which most all areas of the station could be seen.

"I would estimate a total of one hundred men guard this station." His statement was concluded with a terse nod toward Krenz.

Krenz nodded his head slowly. He looked up and his right eye caught a glint from a sniper's weapon from one hundred meters away. *If I were a sniper, where would I hide?* He felt himself become a would-be sniper, a stealth operative who moved like a fluid drop of mercury and melted into the curve of a tree, a rooftop, a building. He knew instantly if Gannon were able to infiltrate the train station, he would get off a shot, despite the fact there would be no escaping once that shot was fired.

He shuddered as he envisioned a cable from Berlin: *Report*

to Berlin at once to submit the details of Göring's death.

"Thank you, Lt. Fischer. Should the time of Herr Göring's arrival change, I will advise you. Meantime, I want every part of this train station covered at all times." He looked hard into the lieutenant's eyes. "Report to me immediately if there are any suspicious activities during the next twenty-four hours."

"Yes, Colonel." He thrust his arm forward. "Heil, Hitler."

Krenz returned to his car and motioned the driver forward. He remained thoughtful on his return to headquarters. Monsieur Bedeau would most certainly deliver the Englishman. If not, he would be a widower by midnight. No more time for chats in the Crillon's kitchen. Poor Mrs. Bedeau.

***

He was met at Gestapo headquarters by Corporal Bauer. "Colonel Krenz," he called from the top of the steps. "There has been a cable from Berlin. The Reichsmarschall has fallen ill. It seems his trip has been cancelled."

"Cancelled?" A sudden relief spread over Krenz. A reprieve. Now, his only concern was the capture of the spy.

"That is correct, Colonel. However, the cable states Herr Heinrich Müller will arrive in his stead."

Müller? Gestapo Müller? Krenz felt the ground shake beneath him, a cold hand grip his throat. *Herr Heinrich Müller,* Chief of Gestapo for all of Germany. Ruthless, Müller would tear Paris apart as well as Krenz in order to stop the assassin.

Krenz gasped for air. Herr Müller was not known for his lieniency.

CHAPTER FORTY-TWO

Gannon left Room 308 and found himself in the opulent lobby of the Crillon, a travesty if one chose to acknowledge the pretense in which Paris and its citizens lived. He scanned the lobby, a habit, of course. Where was the danger? Who stood in the shadows and waited for the unsuspecting to expose themselves and the secrets they may or may not be hiding?

From the bottom of the stairwell, he saw Monsieur Bedeau at the concierge station, a studious expression on his face, as if the outcome of his tasks was the difference between life and death. Bedeau was a simple man without a pretentious persona that caused one to guess his intent, a subtle openness that belied his judicious ability to perceive the thoughts and intents of others. Bedeau was his ally.

"Monsieur Bedeau, your devotion to your work is inspiring. Have you had a meal today?"

The old man, his skin pale, a corpse not in a casket, a cadaver not yet autopsied, turned from his task and looked at Gannon, "Monsieur Gannon, your concern touches me. No, I have not eaten."

Gannon studied Bedeau's face, noticed the weakness of his words, the breath that was shallow and empty of life. His blue eyes seemed clouded, unseeing. He knew instinctively that the Frenchman was in a precarious place, a place of never-ending fear. Gannon recognized fear. It was such a prevalent occurrence in his life, he could smell it, taste it. "Monsieur Bedeau, it troubles me that you seem distraught."

Bedeau turned away, found another small task so that his nimble fingers lifted, moved and set in a non-descript place things that meant nothing more than a mere need to remain occupied.

A deep sigh from his old lungs. "Ah, it is unthinkable that the Germans will be here tomorrow night. A reception! Can you believe it? A reception for an illustrious German. Caviar! Wine! The thought of it when we seem to have faded away, seemed to have become a passive, submissive people who have ignored our dignity, our place in the world. And, now, here we are catering to the Germans. It is not my choice, I assure you." The lips of the old man fell into a hard line, his jaw rigid.

Gannon studied Bedeau as he nervously pushed papers from corner to corner of his desk. "Is that all that troubles you today, my friend?"

Bedeau stilled the twitter of his hands, the jerk of his body and looked at Gannon. "My life is not in your hands, Monsieur Gannon. You must understand that."

It was a cryptic statement. Gannon's eyes fell to the silent hands, thin and suspended over a myriad of documents, saw veins that traveled blue and red down the transparent skin. When his eyes found Bedeau's, he felt an overwhelming need to submerge himself into the needs of the Frenchman. "What are you saying, Monsieur Bedeau?"

Bedeau's clouded gaze swept the lobby of the Crillon, the high ceilings where chandeliers hung in magnificent brilliance, the light promising a new tomorrow, a new Paris where music and laughter prevailed, where the presence of Germans was a mere memory.

When his eyes found Gannon, there was clarity. "I am a Frenchman," he said. "I will die as a Frenchman."

The finality of Bedeau's words settled on Gannon with alarming resonance. He leaned closer, as if to better grasp the essence of their meaning, to clarify what he suspected was a chilling prophecy. He whispered and touched Bedeau's shoulder, the ruse of a confidant, a snare that enticed truth. "Again, what is it that troubles you?"

Bedeau smiled, the tips of his mustache reaching into his weary cheeks. "I shall say no more, Monsieur Gannon."

***

Gannon left the Hotel de la Crillon and stepped into radiant sunlight, into crisp air ladened with the smell of winter, a biting cold that traveled deep in his lungs when he breathed. His footsteps fell in with a group of Parisian women who chattered their way into a café on the Place de la Concorde, leaving the fragrance of their perfumes wafting into the Paris morning.

He walked toward the Rue Royale, which would eventually take him to the *Gare de l'Est*. Only two kilometers away, a brisk walk would put him at the train station in forty-five minutes, a walk he hoped would clear his mind. His encounter with Bedeau had been unsettling. There was evidence of stress in the old man's appearance, a trauma of some kind. Yet, Bedeau had not been willing to discuss it with him.

Even more troubling was Madame Delafloté's insistence that they cooperate with Plomion. Though he trusted the Frenchman, he did not want Plomion to take the lead in planning the German's assassination.

As experienced as he was, Plomion's approach to an actual kill was quite different than Gannon's. Gannon possessed a methodical, cautious view of any mission in which he participated. He had a hard time giving up control of the smallest detail. He was even apprehensive about the weapon Plomion had given him. He had not test fired it, had not broken it down. Had not become comfortable with its weight, its . . . *feel.*

Clearly agitated, Gannon walked faster. At the train station, he would purchase tickets for himself and Eléonore to travel to Senlis on Friday. A pretext, of course. His plans were to send her to her estate near the picturesque village and then, at some point, leave the train and escape through the French countryside.

But, it wasn't the purchase of tickets that propelled him faster along the avenues. It was the opportunity to observe the train station, assess the strength of the German guards. And, most important, choose his kill spot. He shivered inside. Always before a kill, his adrenalin pumped ferociously, dried the saliva in his mouth, tensed his muscles.

As he turned on Rue Royale, he heard footsteps behind him, a quickening of feet, an anxious "Pssssssst." He glanced to his right where shop windows reflected not only him, but also a man scurrying behind him. *Plomion.* So identifiable by his limber, wiry body. He slowed and eased to the wall of a stone fence where graffiti demanded the Germans go home. *Rentrez chez vous sales boches! Go home German bastards.*

"Plomion, it is dangerous for you." Urgent words prompted by the German patrols that scavenged the cold streets.

"*Oui*, monsieur," he said, "but I must talk with you."

"Why didn't you catch me at the hotel?"

"I tried, but you had already left. Come," he motioned, "there is a place we can go."

Gannon, dressed in Édouard Delafloté's fine clothes and formal fedora, the embodiment of French nobility, walked casually after Plomion. Such an energetic man, ferocious like a mad mongoose with snarling teeth and quick movements, Plomion hurried into an alley that lined the rear of cafés that emitted fragrances of yeast and cardamom. The snow remained in piles along the narrow passage, walking paths that remained like a frozen luge for anyone who risked its slippery surface.

Crates and boxes formed walls of small, room-like hiding places where clandestine conversations would go unnoticed and it was here that Plomion finally stopped and pushed himself into a hidden crevice.

It was an unusual place for someone dressed like Gannon to bury himself, but he seemed quite at home in the confines of such an unrefined environment, obviously not the first time he had done so. For an instant, he recalled the back entry alcove of the Hotel de Crillon where he had crouched among rotten potatoes and eluded the Germans, planning for his survival within its walls.

Plomion's breath poked the air with white cloud-like puffs as he settled into the small space.

"Monsieur, there is much to tell you."

"I'm listening."

"The most important thing is Bedeau."

"Bedeau? What of Bedeau?" Of course, it had to be Bedeau.

Bedeau's demeanor earlier in the morning had alerted Gannon to a premonition of looming disaster.

Nervously, Plomion pulled his ever-present flask from his coat pocket. With a dramatic swirl, he unfastened the top and drank long. When he finished, he motioned the flask toward Gannon. Gannon shook his head and waited.

"Bedeau is in big trouble." He shook his head vigorously. "Big trouble."

Gannon became impatient. "Get on with it, Plomion."

"His life has been threatened."

"Threatened? By whom?"

"Who do you think? Krenz, of course."

Gannon nodded. "Of course."

"When I left your room earlier, Bedeau was waiting in the hall. Very distressed. Krenz told him to turn over the English spy by midnight tonight, or he would have his wife murdered."

"Bedeau's wife?"

"That's right. Krenz knows where Bedeau's weaknesses lie. Bedeau would give up his life in a second, but his wife is another story."

Gannon felt the cruel reach of the German's malice, the tenacity of the evil that pumped through his body and came out at moments of his choosing. Krenz would not stop until he had captured the one man who had caused so much peril on the streets of Paris for the past year.

The French widow as well as Bedeau had saved his life. At any point, Bedeau could have revealed Gannon's hiding place, but he chose instead to retain the integrity of his position as a loyal Frenchman. Gannon knew Krenz would make good on his threat to kill Bedeau and his wife. There was only one thing to do.

"We must remove Bedeau and his wife to safety. And now."

Plomion's black eyes widened. "And how do you propose we do that? You know he is being watched. Not only on the streets, but also most certainly inside the hotel. It would be almost impossible to –"

"Impossible to what?" Annoyed, Gannon removed a pack of cigarettes from his pocket. He had not smoked for a while. He lit the cigarette with vengeance, pulled harshly on the tobacco and exhaled in obvious frustration. "I do not want to hear it. No harm will come to Bedeau and his wife. We will do what we have to do. You cannot tell me the Résistance will be unable to take them to safety." He looked at Plomion and spoke with heated words. "I will do it. I refuse to let one old man and his wife die because of me."

Plomion lifted his flask and looked at Gannon. "And?"

Gannon replaced his Fedora. "As I said, I will do it."

"How?"

"I don't know." Again, the need to methodically plan a mission took over and Gannon closed his eyes in thought. He felt the cold of the snow seeping through his shoes and stamped his feet.

Plomion snorted. "Ah, you *rosbiffs!* Your bravado is quite inflated." He emptied his flask and checked the alley. "I shall work with you on any plan you may come up with. Meantime, I will keep an eye on Bedeau and his wife. But, we must act quickly. The German is a very impatient man."

"There is not a lot of time," agreed Gannon. "What else?"

"Ah, I thought you had forgotten. Göring. We have learned he is ill and will not make the trip to Paris. His train has been rerouted to return to Berlin." Plomion smiled at Gannon. "There is, however, someone else who will come."

"Who?" asked Gannon, his curiosity heightened.

"Heinrich Müller."

"Müller?" Gannon stared without blinking. He knew exactly who Heinrich Müller was. Had read his file while in London two years prior. Müller, known as Gestapo Müller in some circles, was a man who demanded one's attention, especially if he was your enemy. And, Avery Gannon considered Müller one of his most ardent enemies.

"Yes, Müller. Arrives by train at 1:19 tomorrow afternoon. The reception will take place as planned. Only our special guest will be Müller instead of Göring."

"How nice. It seems we have gone from bad to worse." Gannon's thoughts ran rampant. The thought of assassinating Müller was as tempting as killing Göring. Both men were optimum targets. How pleasurable it would be to see the headlines in the London Times – "*Gestapo Chief Heinrich Müller Assassinated in Paris.*" Most likely, the Nazis' editorially- controlled newspapers would parlay the murder into some absurd drama that strayed significantly from the actual event.

Joseph Goebbels' newspaper *"Der Angriff"* or the *"Der Sturmer"* had the capabilities of the pervasive use of propaganda that was a crucial instrument in painting the war in the colors he chose. And, what about the daily radio broadcast by the *Wehrmachtbericht*? Gannon smiled to himself. The words rang out in dramatic prose: *Gestapo Chief Heinrich Müller has traveled to the mountains of Bavaria for a few days of respite.* Ha! Few days? When Gannon fired the Mauser 36, Müller's respite would be permanent.

Both men stilled when they heard the approach of footsteps. They began a conversation of food and wine, a project of shoveling snow. Laughter from Plomion. "Ah, my friend, let us find a good table inside. This weather is – "

"Du da! Ihre papiere!" Two soldiers thrust their rifles from their chests. Their noses red from cold, their eyes brightly alert. "Your papers," they repeated as their eyes scanned the small alcove and the two men who huddled inside.

Casually, Plomion offered the soldiers a cigarette. With a harsh shake of their heads, the soldiers held out their hands. "Papers."

Gannon pulled aside the rich wool of his coat and reached inside his pocket. Again, he was asked to prove he was Édouard Delafloté. The first time had been in Room 308 of the Crillon when Colonel Horst Krenz had burst into the room, his hand extended, and asked for identification. When Krenz had commented on the lightness of the color of his hair in the passport picture, Gannon had responded in a light-hearted way. "Ah, the summer sun."

Now, he watched closely as the German soldier studied his papers. Twice, the soldier lifted his eyes and looked at Gannon and then returned to the document. *He is considering. Is the man in the photograph the same man who stood before him?*

"What are you doing in this alley?" he asked, still holding the papers.

"Having a smoke with my friend. We are trying to decide where to eat breakfast."

Gannon glanced at Plomion. *Don't explain too much.* He noticed the coal black eyes of the Frenchman, could tell he did not like to be this close to Germans. For an instant, Gannon thought Plomion might pull a knife or small handgun strapped to his leg and fight his way out of the confines of the hole they had put themselves in. He saw the dark skin flush, his mouth harden. *Don't do it, Plomion. You are such a hothead.*

The second soldier backed away a foot or two, alert and stiff, and observed while the lead soldier made inquiries. He turned to Plomion, his hand extended. "Your papers?"

Plomion did not move for a few agonizing seconds. Then, with menacing, deliberate slowness, he extinguished his cigarette on the side of a nearby crate and found the pocket in his coat that held his papers.

In an act of sheer provocation, he pulled out a key and laid it on top of the crate next to him. He then laid a few francs along with a folded newspaper clipping on top of the key. He shuffled his hand inside his pocket and decided it was empty. His hand went to his other pocket and felt around for long moments for the contents. At last, in slow motion, he extended his papers to the German, who snatched the documents and flipped them open.

Gannon watched the face of the German. If he found fault with Plomion, he would also find fault with him. What a risk Plomion was taking when it wasn't necessary. Another good reason to bypass him when making any assassination plans. Gannon controlled his breathing and lit another cigarette.

"Olivier Plomion," stated the soldier. "Your profession?"

Plomion smiled. "At the moment, I am not employed. I am living with a beautiful woman who cares for me . . . and what I give her in return."

The soldier stared without speaking. He glanced at Gannon and seemed to notice the difference in the clothing each man wore. What would be the reason for that he seemed to be thinking. Once again, he looked at Plomion's papers. "The address is the woman's?"

"No. That is my family's address. When I am not with the woman, I am with my mother. I sometimes cook and clean for her. She is quite elderly."

"Where does the woman live?"

"On Rue Royale. In a small apartment above the café."

"If we were to go there now, she would substantiate your information?"

Plomion did not hesitate. "But, of course. She knows me very well." He paused. "Very well."

The soldier turned to Gannon. "What business do you have with this man?" He nodded toward Plomion and turned back to Gannon. From any perspective, Gannon and Plomion were a motley pair.

Gannon smiled. "Monsieur Plomion has been a friend of my family for years. On occasion, a handy-man of sorts at my estate in Senlis."

"You do not live in Paris?"

"No. Just visiting."

"Where are you staying?"

"The Hotel de Crillon."

"What is the purpose of your visit?"

Gannon became uneasy, but kept a slight smile. The German was becoming too familiar, too close. "I'm on a holiday with my wife." Gannon slowly pulled a cigarette and held it suspended as if to distract the German. Next to him, Plomion struck a match, reached out and lit it.

The soldier, still holding Gannon's papers, looked down and studied the photograph, pulled it a little closer. Gannon could see his eyes boring into the picture.

He looked up quickly. "Be on your way." He turned and proceeded down the alley, turning once to look back at Gannon, a perplexed look on his face. He was still thinking.

Gannon turned to Plomion. He was angry. "Please do not do that to me again! There is no need to incite in the Germans some form of harassment. Your hostile demeanor will get us into trouble. Had you not been with me, I think there would have been problems. They would have hauled you to Gestapo head-quarters."

Plomion eyes became slits. "Monsieur, rest assured, had I not been with you, the two soldiers would be lying in their own blood."

He lifted the heels of his shoes and pushed himself closer to Gannon.

"It offends me that you Englishmen seem to insist on doing things your way. I am Olivier Plomion, a Frenchman. A loyal Frenchman who, at the present time, has an enemy on my home soil. It does not make me very friendly or cooperative when I have to prove who I am to my enemy. It would please me, Monsieur Gannon, if you would refrain from criticism when it is *you* who are currently a foreigner on French soil."

Gannon nodded slowly as he looked into the blazing eyes of Plomion. "I apologize if I have offended you, Olivier."

"I accept your apology, my friend. Now, let us continue discussing our problems."

"Shall I begin?"

Plomion bowed slightly. "But, of course," he said, a smile lingering on his lips, his words as soft as a woman's silk stockings.

CHAPTER FORTY-THREE

Eléonore Delafloté stood at the east window of Suite 308 and watched as Parisians traversed the piles of snow that remained along the Place de la Concorde. She lifted her eyes and found the sky cloudless, a pure blue that seemed almost transparent, as if on the other side of it there floated a shimmering mountain of white diamonds, rendering one into blindness.

Her heart, skipping to a flurry of quick beats, felt a release of warm tears. In a matter of days, she had become a widow, cheated death and now, as she gazed at the Paris skyline, she felt a strength she had not felt in some time. She strived to understand the circumstances that led her to this moment, this place. Who guided these events and placed her in the middle of them? Were they a test of her fortitude, her courage?

She left the window and found the lounge in the sitting room. She pulled the black fur around her thin shoulders and leaned back. The Englishman. Her breath caught as if his warm lips were resting on her neck.

Her memories of the night before were anything but vague. True, she had had too much Cognac, had floated in her body as she sought some semblance of reality. But, there he was. Not Édouard, as she had called him. But, the Englishman. The

Englishman, whose warm body had soothed her, had given her more than physical love. He had avowed in her what she already knew: she wanted to live.

She smiled. *There are two of me.* Madame Delafloté, a widow who knows too well the tragedy of death and war. And, Eléonore, a woman who has, through bizarre circumstances, decided she is not ready to fade away into the frailties of her existence. Had she been unfaithful to Édouard's memory? She closed her eyes. Édouard - tender, kind, loving. Her first love. She would always love him.

She stood, walked to the bed, slipped her hand beneath the pillow and searched for the photograph of her dead husband.

CHAPTER FORTY-FOUR

At the *Gare de l'Est*, Gannon saw nothing but German soldiers. At every turn, field green tunics with their Waffen SS insignia dressed young men who had left their farms in Germany, their schools in Berlin, and followed the cry of Adolf Hitler. *Er allein die Jugend, wem erhält die Zukunft. He alone, who owns the youth, gains the future.*

At the entrance gate, Gannon pulled his identification papers from his coat and handed them to the guard. The stoic young man took them without comment, read them carefully and looked up at Gannon. "Your purpose here today?"

"To purchase railway tickets?"

"May I see your travel papers?"

"Travel papers?"

The guard seemed surprised. "All travel must be approved by Gestapo Headquarters."

Gannon smiled. "I was unaware. I shall get approval at once." He hesitated and looked across the way. "I am craving one of the delicious croissants from La Petite Boulangerie over there." Gannon pointed to the small café that was surrounded by small outdoor tables and chairs, then rubbed his stomach in an animated gesture.

The German glanced at the small bakery. "Since your identification papers are in order, you may." He stepped aside and allowed Gannon to pass.

"Thank you," said Gannon. "Shall I bring one for you?"

The German shook his head. When he did, Gannon saw the Nazi swastika embedded on the side of his field cap. Gannon felt a cold chill run the length of his body. A premonition, maybe. He walked slowly into the train station, his eyes, like tiny cameras, scanned everything, registering details as quickly as stars fell from the sky. He counted the number of soldiers in the immediate area. Thirty-three. Then, he knew. There was a manhunt and he was the hunted.

CHAPTER FORTY-FIVE

At Gestapo headquarters, Colonel Horst Krenz closed the door to this office and sat in the hard wooden chair at his desk. When he closed his eyes, he had a vision of Heinrich Müller. Dressed in his Gestapo uniform, Müller seemed almost handsome, a handsomeness that belied his skill as one of the most treacherous men in all of Germany. Hitler had chosen him well. In fact, he had chosen someone to head the Gestapo who was much like himself, someone driven by a fanatical force that transcended all reason, a force that defied the fundamental, innate elements that created a human being, a human being who . . . who felt love, compassion.

Krenz could have handled Göring. He would have flattered him, catered to him, brought him the finest wines, the most desirable cheeses. Perhaps even a beautiful French woman. But, Müller was a different story. Müller was unapproachable. There was no weakness in his armor. He was as hard and untouchable as a moving bullet.

Krenz left his chair and walked to the window. Below him, the same cat he had seen at the beginning of the snowstorm lay sunning on top of a stone fence, its black fur sparkling in the bright sun. The stone fence ran perpendicular to a row of trees that bordered a small courtyard. Within the courtyard, squirrels skittered from one tree to the other.

"I am doomed," said Krenz out loud. There would be no excuses when Müller arrived. *"Tell me how many fine Germans have been assassinated by this Englishman."* And, Krenz would reply: *"Twenty-seven."* Then, it would begin. Merciless questions by Germany's most proficient interrogator. There would be no lying. No apologies.

His only hope was Bedeau and his knowledge of the spy. With Bedeau, he would survive Müller. Without Bedeau, he was a dead man.

CHAPTER FORTY-SIX

G annon arrived back at the Crillon in the early afternoon, his face grim. He had come to several conclusions that pushed him further toward a decision regarding Bedeau and his wife. His refusal to put them in harm's way was steadfast. When he walked through the entrance of the hotel, he saw Bedeau in the same place he had left him, at the concierge, long-faced and brooding.

"Monsieur Bedeau, I wish to speak with you," he called across the lobby, loud enough for all to hear, especially the two men who sat in chairs along the wall that faced the Place de la Concorde. When Gannon leaned into Bedeau, his words were barely audible.

Bedeau lifted his eyes and stared at Gannon.

CHAPTER FORTY-SEVEN

The afternoon sun had eased above the buildings across the Place de la Concorde and filled Room 308 with soft light. When Gannon knocked lightly, he heard a rustling inside, the sound of small feet crossing the elegant flooring, a small "*Oui?*"

"Gannon," he said softly.

The door opened slowly and Eléonore's dark eyes peered up at him. "Monsieur Gannon," she said, her voice soft, whispery. She moved aside.

Gannon stepped into the room, smelled perfume, a mixture of rose and jasmine. Most assuredly French. He heard the door close behind him and turned to Eleonore. Her words to him earlier in the morning had been harsh, critical that he had placed her in a non-relevant role in helping free France from the wrath of the Nazis. She stood steadfast in her conviction that she was capable of performing as well as anyone in the position of patriot. She did not seem to be concerned that she had been cocooned in wealth and privilege her entire life, having no experiences that would have prepared her for the hardships of war, much less the extreme danger of a being a member of a group as subversive as the French Résistance.

Her dead husband had been a brilliant spy. Gannon's relationship with him had been a phenomenal blending of two men who worked together like one. His death had affected Gannon greatly and, now, as he looked at his widow, it was almost as if Frenchie were in the room. As if somehow he had embodied himself in his widow, had left with her his own sense of duty, of integrity. Could that be possible? Could Eléonore grasp the meaning of all that was? He looked at her intently. Somehow, he must tell her of Frenchie and his life as a spy.

"Madame," he said quietly. "Have you had lunch?"

"*Oui*, Monsieur Bedeau brought a small plate of fruit and cheese. No wine." She smiled and sat on the lounge. Her face revealed an expectancy, as if he were to tell her something interesting.

Where should he begin? He must not continue his exclusion of her. "There is much to discuss." He sat opposite her in a Louis XVI chair whose large stripes seemed like bars on a jail."

"But, of course. Do begin."

"I went to the *Gare de l'Est* for our railway tickets to Senlis, but I was unsuccessful. It seems the Gestapo must approve all travel."

"I knew that. I'm sorry I did not think to mention it to you."

"No harm done. I plan to visit them shortly."

Gannon paused. He was about to admit her to his dangerous world of spycraft and her entrance into it would forever change her life. Did he have a choice? What would Frenchie say? Frenchie would say *no! Do not endanger this precious creature with the horrors of war.* But, Frenchie was dead and, amazingly, his widow wanted to take his place.

He began lightly. His smile was teasing. "May I assume you have found something lovely to wear to tomorrow night's reception?"

Eléonore flushed, her eyes blazing with a sensuality that caused a stirring within Avery. She shifted on the lounge and pulled the fur closer. Her hair was a soft tangle, a lock hanging across her forehead. "*Oui.* Black with sequins." She paused. "When did you become interested in fashion?"

He played with her. "When you became my wife."

She didn't hesitate. "Is that all you expect from your wife? For her to wear the latest fashions?"

Gannon leveled his eyes at her. "No. There is more, but, for now, we have other things to discuss." He rose from his chair and walked across the room and back again.

"Bedeau. Our friend is in extreme danger. Colonel Krenz has given him an ultimatum."

"An ultimatum? I don't understand."

Gannon became thoughtful. "Men like Krenz have extraordinary instincts. His instincts tell him Bedeau knows my whereabouts. That from the beginning, Bedeau has hidden me in the hotel."

"But, Colonel Krenz has searched the hotel thoroughly. On two occasions."

"That is so, but it does not change things. Krenz thinks what he thinks and right now he is certain Bedeau is the key to my capture." Gannon cleared his throat. "And, now that Heinrich Müller is paying him a visit, he is more than frantic to find me."

"Müller?"

"Sorry. Göring became ill and has returned to Berlin. Müller will arrive on the 1:19 train tomorrow."

"And the reception?"

"Still on. Our most special guest is now Müller. Back to Bedeau, Krenz expects Bedeau to reveal my whereabouts by midnight tonight or he will have Madame Bedeau shot."

"No! Impossible that he suspects Bedeau! How did this happen?"

"Remember, his instincts are strong."

"What are you going to do? Bedeau must be moved to safety, as well as his wife."

Gannon said nothing. He paced the room, looked out the window across the Place de la Concorde and sighed.

"Well, what are you going to do?"

Gannon looked across the room. "Nothing. Absolutely nothing."

Eléonore flushed with anger, her voice shrill. "So you are going to allow his death?"

The smile from Gannon's lips was cunning. "Your assumptions amuse me, Madame."

CHAPTER FORTY-EIGHT

The taps on the door at 308 sounded like an angry wood-pecker, impatient and annoyed. When Gannon opened the door, Plomion entered with his usual flamboyant flair. He didn't bother to remove his beret or take off his worn coat. The urgency with which he paced was typical. He was a highly-charged man despite the amount of whiskey he drank. As usual, his eyes blazed as black as the depths of a dungeon. From his thin stature, he rose on his heels and looked at Gannon.

"It is my wish, Monsieur Gannon, that you keep me abreast of all that is happening." Plomion crossed his arms and waited.

"It would be my pleasure, Olivier. Anything special you'd like to know?"

Plomion grunted. "Bedeau tells me you will not be moving him to safety. Is that true?"

"That is true, Olivier."

Plomion lifted his eyebrows. The look he gave Gannon was not pleasant.

Before Gannon responded to the surly Frenchman, he looked at Eléonore. "Eléonore, it would please me if you listened carefully to what is being said." He paused. "Your input is valuable." He held her gaze a moment before returning to Plomion.

"Our Colonel Krenz has given Bedeau a deadline for midnight tonight to reveal my whereabouts. That is not too soon for what we have to do. It will give us more time."

"More time? Time for what?"

"Your bombs, Olivier. *To make your bombs.*"

CHAPTER FORTY-NINE

Gannon and Plomion found Bedeau in the massive hotel kitchens where he rummaged around the gas ovens. Gleaming pots hung from a suspended rack above the countless bottles and cans of spices that stood like miniature armies atop shelves that seemed at any moment would collapse from their weight. Madame Lefébvre, the hotel's only cook and house-keeper stood nearby, her hands whipping something in a large ceramic bowl, whose floral design was reminiscent of the lavender fields of Provence. Her wide, ruddy-colored face grimaced in devoted concentration to her task.

"Monsieur Bedeau, do you have a moment to discuss the reception?" Gannon smiled at the obviously distraught man.

"But, of course!" he growled. "I have only twenty-four hours to borrow two chefs from the Café Procope, approve the menu, the wine, the liquor. And wait staff! I must hire at least three more waiters! I am just one man!" He stopped his ranting and looked at the two men. "My apologies," he said with apparent atonement. "What is it you wish of me?"

Plomion glanced at Madame Lefébvre and raised his eyebrows. Bedeau nodded and walked to the worktable. "Madame, please pour yourself a cup of coffee and rest in the lobby for a few moments." The woman said nothing as she placed the crockery on the table and retrieved a cup. She looked up once while pouring and found Bedeau watching her. A rare smile lifted the corners of her mouth. "Monsieur Bedeau, please do not let the croissants overcook." All three men watched silently as the stout woman left the kitchen.

The two men looked at Bedeau. "We have a plan, monsieur."

"A plan? What plan?"

Plomion eased forward. "The reception."

"The reception. What of the reception?" Bedeau swung his head back and forth between the two men, waiting, his eyes alert.

Plomion hesitated a moment and spoke softly. "Heinrich Müller and many other high-ranking Germans will attend the reception. What a pity for us if we did not." He smiled.

Bedeau's eyes narrowed. "May I assume the "us" and the "we" are *les libérateurs de la France?*"

"Yes, you may," said Plomion.

From the lobby, the notes of a piano drifted to the kitchens. Bedeau lifted his chin and leaned his ear into the soft sounds of *The Skaters' Waltz.* He smiled. "A French composition. Give me everything French," he said, his eyes glistening with tears as he looked back at Plomion. "Exactly what do you have in mind?"

"Ah, such a simple plan, my friend. The Germans will eat our food, drink our wine and be served a course of bullets for dessert. Let us say *un dessert chaud.*"

Gannon interrupted. "It's not quite that simple." Again, his compulsion to control the tiniest details of any mission surfaced. It was what he had learned at Whitehall, as well as his experience as a spy. He had been taught caution, a deliberate, calculating and purposeful approach to any operation. For the life of him, he could not imagine proceeding without a thorough discussion of every aspect of the *un dessert chaud.* Again, he thought Plomion almost cavalier in his view of the operation. The man's glib perspective in all likelihood would get them all killed.

"Non?" Plomion shifted his body to face Gannon. He became defensive when there was no need to be.

All Gannon wanted was cooperation and reminded himself he was to work *with* the Résistance, not run it. Perhaps he was the pompous Englishman so despised by the French. Nonetheless, he was in France to be neither pompous nor offensive to the French people. He was here to thwart the Germans in every way possible. It just so happened his most honed skill was assassinating Germans, any German, but preferably high-ranking Germans. He admitted to himself that his unique skill had placed upon him the burden of being the most wanted spy in all of France.

He maintained a calm, steady voice. "Monsieur Plomion, let us go over the details of the plan in another place. For now," Gannon looked at Bedeau, "we will provide Monsieur Bedeau the information we feel is necessary at this time." It seemed Gannon had taken control after all.

Plomion did not seem deterred. "What information?"

"I will assume your plans are to have members of the Résistance in positions as waiters at the reception. How many men will you assign?"

"I'm thinking four."

Gannon looked at Bedeau. "Do you have uniforms?"

"If your men are not the size of elephants, I am sure I can accommodate them." Bedeau smiled at his own remark. "What else?"

"Can the room be fully staffed and ready for guests by 7:00?"

"Yes."

"Do you have a guest list from Krenz?"

"Yes, he sent one this morning."

"May I see it?"

Bedeau nodded and left the kitchen. When he returned, he held a file. "Here is all I have."

Gannon opened the folder and shoved it toward Plomion. "Fifty-one guests. Müller, Krenz, me, Eléonore. The rest are officers. I see three officers are traveling with Müller. The rest from Paris facilities. Lt. General von Boineburg-Lengsfeld, Colonel Helmet Knochen."

"They will be heavily guarded."

"True. Inside the hotel and out."

"Our best chance for success is to simply show no type of activity on the streets that would suggest an attack. Keep all signs of Résistance at a minimum, give the appearance all is well in the City of Light." Excellent strategy on Plomion's part.

Gannon nodded. "Bedeau, you must instruct the waiters on their duties. How to serve?"

He looked at Plomion. "Choose men with clean nails, well-groomed, men who have some semblance of refinement. Is that possible?"

Plomion rolled his eyes. "But, of course. But, wouldn't you say the first requirement should be their skill in shooting a weapon?"

"That goes without saying, Olivier. Your best men, of course."

"Where and what time shall we go over the plans with my men?"

"Since there is the curfew to contend with, I would say day-light tomorrow morning. Meet here – in the kitchens. Do you think you can get your men in? They will be here all day."

Plomion thought a moment and looked at Bedeau. "Give me their uniforms now. I will have them arrive dressed for the reception."

"They will be searched." Gannon lowered his voice. "Perhaps we can smuggle the weapons in and keep them here in the kitchen."

"Why not?" asked Bedeau. "I will transfer food from the Café Procope in the morning. Have your men here and I'll take two of them with me. We can load the weapons at some point between here and the 6th Arrondissement. Horse and wagon, of course. The Germans see me often at the open market and then unloading at the rear entrance. This time will be no different."

"Do they search you?"

"No." Bedeau shook his head. "It seems they approach the wagon only for food."

"Where is the wagon now?"

"Out back."

Gannon looked at Plomion. "When we leave here, let's inspect the wagon, see if it will, indeed, hide weapons."

"It will," said Bedeau casually. He walked to the coffee pot and poured into a large cup. "The wagon has carried weapons before."

Surprised, Gannon and Plomion looked at each other.

Bedeau sipped his coffee and made a bitter face. "Damn Germans. This coffee is deplorable! Potatoes and acorns!"

"Carried weapons before?" asked Gannon.

"But, of course. Have you forgotten The Great War, our time on the Western front? That wagon, not the horse, has traveled many miles loaded with war supplies. A mere few guns for our *un dessert chaud* is nothing." He shrugged and, against his better judgment, sipped the coffee again.

"Excellent!" said Gannon.

Olivier smiled. "You old man! I forget your age and your history in The Great War. Here you are again, a willing patriot."

Appearing thoughtful, Bedeau gazed at the high ceilings in the hotel kitchen, his eyes clear and resting someplace far away. Perhaps somewhere on the battlefields of France when he was young and virile, wearing red trousers and a blue and gold trimmed jacket. When he spoke, his voice was as soft as a meadow breeze.

"A patriot?" He turned his eyes to the two men who had stilled themselves and waited. "I was born a patriot."

CHAPTER FIFTY

Gannon and Plomion exited the hotel at *de concierge et les livraisons*, where a large wagon had been pushed to the side of a wooden shed. Laden with snow, it had not been moved since the onslaught of the two-day blizzard that had left Paris cold and shivering.

"We must remove the snow," said Plomion as he pulled his body onto the sides of the wagon and jumped inside. "Surely, there is a shovel inside." He pointed to the delivery door and Gannon stepped into the small alcove, the same alcove that had hidden him only days before. He remembered a shovel leaning against an old cupboard and in moments was handing it to Plomion.

Gannon watched him a few minutes. "We have more to discuss. After I visit Gestapo Headquarters, can you meet me back in 308? Say five o'clock?"

"I'll be there," panted Plomion as a volley of snow landed in the alley. As an afterthought, "Too bad you will not need the MAS 36. Our little reception will kill more Germans than we could have imagined." A peal of laughter spread throughout the alley.

Gannon said nothing. An assassination attempt at the train station had been a bad idea from the beginning.

***

When he returned to the kitchen, he found Bedeau sitting quietly, trance-like, unmoving. He lightly touched him on the shoulder. "My friend, we must talk."

Bedeau turned slowly toward Gannon, seeming not to recognize him, with shrouded eyes that perhaps saw only his imminent death as well as the death of his lovely Hélène. Then, as if a bell had rung somewhere in the Universe, he blinked. "Yes. I know."

Gannon moved closer, his words reassuring. "It saddens me that you are troubled. Plomion has told me of your plight. Of Krenz' ultimatum." He pulled a chair and sat across from Bedeau and continued. "There is no need for you to carry this burden alone."

Bedeau's old eyes searched Gannon's face. "Indeed, I am wondering what is to be done."

Gannon nodded. "Let me assure you there is a plan."

Bedeau stirred in his chair and looked at Gannon, lifting his wiry eyebrows into his forehead. "Would you be so kind as to discuss the plan with me?"

At first, Gannon thought Bedeau's question had been asked with surly sarcasm, but then realized the man's newfound humility had been a relief to him, his willingness to diminish his own misplaced view of his independence had freed him. He was ready to share the weight of his heavy heart.

"Your Hélène will be moved to safety immediately. You do not need to worry about her."

"How can you do that? There is Gestapo everywhere."

Gannon leaned back in his chair. "My friend, you underestimate our friend Plomion."

A smile from Bedeau. "There is no underestimating a man who is as obstinate as Plomion."

Gannon could not help but laugh. "I can't agree with you more. Shall we allow him to do what he does best? Thwart the Germans?"

Color seemed to return to Bedeau's skin, a brightening of his eyes. There was hope.

"Now, let's discuss this ultimatum that Krenz has so heavily placed upon you. It is my understanding that you must turn me over to Krenz by midnight tonight. Am I correct?"

Bedeau nodded.

Gannon rose from his chair and paced the long stone floor of the kitchen, his thoughts racing. He found his hatred of Krenz mushrooming into what was already a despicable opinion of the man. He knew he could not allow Krenz to have control. He also recognized Krenz' only leverage was Bedeau and Bedeau's knowledge of his whereabouts. It was apparent to him that Bedeau would remain alive as long as Krenz needed information.

And, therein, lay the answer to their dilemma. Bedeau would not turn him over to the German, therefore averting his own demise. At least not at midnight, as demanded by Krenz.

He looked at Bedeau who sat waiting in the dim shadows of the kitchen. A feeling of exhilaration overcame him. Bedeau would gladly give his life without ever telling Krenz his whereabouts. Yet, why should he? Why should he when he held all the cards?

Gannon returned to his chair and sat down.

"My dear man, do you think perhaps you could be an actor? A cunning, deceitful actor who could convince the devil to dance?"

***

Gannon walked back through the hotel lobby, the ever-present Gestapo loitering at the entrance. He ignored them and crossed the Place de la Concorde and turned west to Avenue Gabriel.

Turning north on Rue de l'Eysee, he turned left on Rue du Faubourg. Not much snow remained on the busy street, only dark slush where travel had melted what once had been pristine crystals of white. Several bicycles passed him, their riders bundled against the cold.

Despite the Nazi occupation, the streets and cafes hummed with Parisians who ignored the presence of the uniformed army as if they didn't exist, viewing the German occupation as nothing more than organized plunder. The Germans had infiltrated their lives with surprising ease. They made love to their French women, drank their wines and attended their churches. *Une collaboration de commun accord.* A collaboration of mutual agreement.

He saw 12 Rue des Saussaires in the distance, the Hotel de

l'Elysée a façade of stately stone with ornate iron grilles that softened the harshness of its walls. Behind the walls, men, whose purpose was to promote the cause of the Third Reich by torturing and killing innocent men and women, filled its rooms and defiled the beauty of the once grand hotel.

Perpetually cautious, Gannon wondered if Eléonore had unobtrusively inspected his hair and the black shoe polish that proclaimed him Édouard Delafloté. She had been meticulous in her design of him, his clothes, his shoes, his nails. Even his jewelry had been ceremoniously chosen and placed in the perfect way women seem to have. He looked down at his cufflinks, an elaborate scroll of the letters "ED." And, what of his tie clasp? Another elaborate display of wealth and nobility that so easily elevated him to a count in the French courts of so long ago.

Her dressing of him had been brilliant. So brilliant, she declared him her husband and made love to him as fervently as if it had been their wedding night. He had obliged her without restraint. Even now, he thought of making love to her again. His grandmother would be appalled.

At the entrance to the l'Elysée, he straightened his jacket and felt for his identification papers. In the quiet hush of the Paris afternoon, he became Édouard Delafloté.

Inside, he walked to the first person he saw, a woman sitting at a desk where two telephones were placed in front of her. "Mademoiselle, would you please direct me to the office of travel applications?"

She smiled, revealing crooked teeth behind narrow lips. She wore no lipstick on a face that was somewhat pretty, but harsh with eyes that did not emit warmth of any kind. "Through the lobby, first door on your right. Past the stairs."

"Thank you," he said and left her watching him. It was the clothes again, rich and tailored by Chanel, a beacon of wealth. He was sure his perceived wealth would not matter in the least to the Germans who would examine his identification papers.

As he passed the winding staircase, he heard his name. "Herr Delafloté!" A wave of cold passed through his body. Krenz.

Gannon slowed and turned. He smiled warmly. "Ah, Colonel Krenz."

"Such a surprise," Krenz' right eye swiped across Gannon's face, his hair, his eyes. Then, down the length of his coat, resting on his shoes a moment before lifting his curious inspection to Gannon once again. "Come! You must come to my office. Visit a while. I'm sure my assistant can find us some hot tea and a croissant." He turned abruptly and proceeded up the stairs, certain Gannon would not decline his invitation.

Gannon followed, each step taking him closer to the one man he had, at all costs, intended to avoid. He heard Krenz chattering aimlessly in front of him, an animated cheerfulness that immediately caused within Gannon a heightened awareness. After all, deep below him in the bowels of the hotel, torture rooms had seen men just as he come and go with bloody regularity. He knew well of the execution chambers in the dark cellars where bodies were removed and dumped into the Seine at regular intervals.

With a sweep of his hands, Krenz bowed slightly and waved Gannon into his office. "Such a pleasure, Herr Delafloté. Sit!"

Gannon removed his fedora and sat in a plain wooden chair that, to him, seemed to be missing its arm straps and shackles. He crossed his legs and let his eyes wander around the dimly lit room. Austere furniture, a small cot in the corner, the home of a fanatic who had heard the cry of Adolf Hitler.

Krenz sat at his desk with contrived enthusiasm. "My assistant will serve tea momentarily." He clapped his hands once and leaned back. "So! What brings you here, Herr Delafloté?"

Everything he had learned at Whitehall as well as his experience in the field flooded his mind. *Tread softly.*

"My travel papers. I have none. Madame Delafloté and I will be leaving on Friday to return to Senlis."

"Ah, yes, that is a requirement before you may ride the trains. Just a formality though. I'm sure you have everything in order." He paused. "Your identification papers as well as Madame Delafloté's."

Gannon nodded and said nothing.

Krenz held his gaze a moment, and then furrowed his brow. "Tell me, Herr Delafloté, do you smoke?"

An odd question, thought Gannon. "Occasionally."

Krenz seemed to deliberate. "Any special brand?"

Gannon's instincts rushed forward. He well knew the tactics of a good interrogator. Be friendly, casual, all the while administering aimless questions, questions that most certainly would lead to bigger, more important questions.

"No."

"No preferences?"

Gannon smiled. "Ah, of course." He noticed Krenz' body still, his breath quicken. "There is nothing like – "

A knock at the door and Krenz' assistant entered with a tray. "Your tea, Colonel Krenz."

"Thank you. You may pour." He smiled at Gannon. "Sugar?"

"No."

"Two sugars in mine, please." Both men watched as the young corporal prepared their tea. When he finished, Krenz, who had retained the same grin as when they met in the lobby, gestured to Gannon. "Please. Enjoy."

"Thank you," said Gannon as he reached for his cup. His hand was quite steady, a fine example of his steely resolve.

"So! Where were we? Ah, yes, cigarettes. You were saying there was nothing like . . . "

Gannon sipped his tea. "Delicious. Yes, definitely a prefer- ence. A cigar with a smooth sip of Scotch has to be my preference, Monsieur Krenz."

Krenz seemed disappointed in Gannon's answer. He nodded and stirred his tea. "I have another question for you. Your wife, Madame Delaflotè. Where did you meet her?"

Gannon pretended to enjoy his tea while the mechanisms of his brain sought an escape from what he knew was a coming onslaught of entrapment. He and Eléonore had never discussed the time and place of their first meeting. A serious flaw in their plan to fool Krenz. He felt certain Krenz was relying on his instincts to guide him to any weaknesses he may have.

"My darling Eléonore. I shall never forget our first meeting. It was at her family's estate near Senlis."

Krenz smiled. "You don't wear a wedding ring?" His gaze did not waver, but bore into Gannon as if he were at the end of his gun site.

"A silly thing," he said casually. "A family heirloom which is so valuable that it is kept in the family vault."

Krenz stared at Gannon's hands. He had recently interro- gated someone who had also seemed very casual, self-assured. It was the businessman from Andorra, the man who survived tor- ture, but failed a bullet. The man he knew was a spy. A glint of familiarity stirred within him.

Still, he was smiling. "Are you often in Paris?"

Gannon lifted his cup and held it in mid-air, looking over the rim at Krenz. "When necessary."

"How frequently is that?"

"Several time a year."

"When was the last time you visited this lovely city?"

"Ah, let's see. I believe it was prior to my trip to Greece." Gannon returned his cup to the tray and reached inside his coat and pulled his passport. "Should tell us right here." He had studied the passport carefully the day before, had memorized every detail, knew precisely when and where Édouard Delafloté had traveled. "Ah, here it is. The date of my trip to Greece was December 3, 1940. Prior to that I stayed in Paris for a few days."

Gannon returned his passport to his coat and stood. "Your hospitality is appreciated, but I must file for my travel papers. Friday will be here before I know it." He picked up his fedora.

Krenz did not rise; instead, he fingered the knob on the desk of his middle drawer. He wanted to look at Avery Gannon's picture and compare it to the man who stood before him.

"But, of course. I'm sure they will find everything in order. Tell them I said to process your request quickly." He lingered a moment. "Travel is so precarious, you know. We are currently searching for an assassin who seems intent on murdering Germans."

Krenz let his words fall casually in the room, words like *assassin* and *murder* seeming so casual in their entry into the conversation. Yet, his comment was well orchestrated and purposefully placed. He waited for Gannon to comment.

The German's tactics were quite familiar to Gannon. How could they not be? His skill at subterfuge was brilliant. Krenz, however, was fishing. He knew many things; he just could not put them all together. Not yet.

"An assassin? Here in Paris?"

Krenz never took his eyes off Gannon. "In Paris," he said, without emotion.

Gannon wanted to smile. He felt his adrenalin pump higher as his saw himself holding his MAS 36 and sighting his target. Felt himself align with his heartbeat as his finger squeezed the trigger and the bullet found its mark.

His role as an aristocrat surfaced. "Monsieur, my heartfelt apologies that my country does not afford its captors the respect they deserve."

Krenz nodded slightly while he seemed to process Gannon's words. Finally, he stood. "Good day, Herr Delafloté."

Gannon left Krenz' small office and walked down the stairs, past the woman who sat at the desk with the two telephones and found the travel office. Inside, he saw a long line of applicants, all Parisians, all wanting to get out of Paris. He, too, wanted to get out of Paris. But, not before he finished the one thing that brought him here.

CHAPTER FIFTY-ONE

Krenz' office fell into an almost morgue-like quiet, dark and void of any movement. He remained seated and watched Édouard Delafloté as he passed through the doorway leading to the stairs. He heard his own breathing, smelled the sugar that remained in the bottom of his teacup.

Édouard Delafloté bothered him. He was a perfect Frenchman. Handsome, mannered, obviously intelligent; yet, there was something missing in this suave member of nobility known as Count Édouard Delafloté. He wondered where his weaknesses lay. Then, he wondered no longer. He knew. He must find an opportunity to chat with Madame Delafloté, without the presence of Monsieur Delafloté.

Krenz leaned forward and pulled open his desk drawer, retrieved Gannon's file and opened it. Such a poor photograph, small, blurred. Could it be? He leaned over and picked up his telephone. "Corporal Bauer, get me Gestapo Headquarters in Berlin."

CHAPTER FIFTY-TWO

Gannon hurried across Avenue Gabriel. Curfew was only minutes away as well as his meeting with Plomion at 5:00. The temperature had dropped considerably since his exit from Gestapo Headquarters where his travel application had been approved and was tucked inside his coat. It had been a simple process, one that did not require the mention of Colonel Krenz' name. He and Eléonore would be able to travel on Friday without complications, if all went well.

Crossing the Place de la Concorde, he saw Bedeau standing in front of the entrance doors. The old man looked almost grand in his hotel uniform, his ever-present wool cap arranged on top of his unruly hair. If given the chance, Eléonore would pull out her scissors and cut away at the almost humorous flyaway strands while Bedeau sulked in obvious loathing.

"Monsieur Bedeau, it is time to go inside. The cold is unmerciful. Please. Come." Gannon touched his arm and opened the wide door. He scanned the lobby carefully. No one sat in the armchairs nor the velvet couches. The piano was still, the chandelier above reflected in its highly polished wood. For an instant, he wondered if Marlene Dietrich had ever sung at the Crillon. He must remember to ask Bedeau. Somehow, he could imagine the sultry femme fatale sitting atop the Crillon's piano, smoking a cigarette and singing in her deep contralto voice "*Je suis la sexy Lola." I am the sexy Lola.*

"You are ready?"

"But, of course. I have been ready."

"Any questions?"

"*Non,*" Bedeau answered casually. "I will have no trouble doing what you have asked, Monsieur Gannon."

Gannon smiled and removed his fedora. "Your confidence strengthens me, monsieur." He paused and fingered his hat. "More than that, it is your bravery that moves me so."

Bedeau smiled in return. "It is a French thing, you know. At least, the old French." His eyes glistened. "I find it quite invigorating to say "no" to the Germans, don't you?"

"Yes."

Bedeau hesitated. "I also find it quite powerful to be in control of my destiny to some extent. *Oui?*"

Gannon searched Bedeau's face and saw the history of his life in his gray hair, his bright blue eyes, the fissures of years that lined his face. He was humbled. The Frenchman had so much to lose, yet never wavered when it came to his beloved France.

He looked across the grand lobby. "Where is the reception to be held?"

"This way," said Bedeau. Gannon followed Bedeau past the majestic staircase and into a room that was grand enough for King Louis XVI. Ceiling to floor velvet draperies hung like butterfly wings across the tall leaded windows that faced the Place de la Concorde. The carpets were of the finest wools, dyed in deep purple and gold. The furniture, of course, was Louis XVI, magnificent.

Bedeau swept his arm through the air. "The Germans will find this room to their liking, I am sure."

"By all means. Is this the only entrance?"

"No, over there is where the kitchen staff will enter and exit." He pointed to the opposite wall where double doors, framed with ornate mouldings and painted floral designs, disguised the doors as large paintings. Gannon walked to them and pushed them open, revealing a hallway that wrapped around and led to the hotel kitchens.

"Where does that door go?"

"That is a lounge for the ladies."

Gannon poked his head inside and saw a large room filled with elegant couches and chairs, a few commodes and tables. "Any exits from this room?"

Bedeau looked at Gannon. "Not at the moment. Shall we make one?"

"Make one?"

"That wall there is thin." Bedeau pointed to the wall on their right, "An obvious attempt on the part of the architect to allow for expansion at some future date. On the other side is an area the size of this one."

"Interesting. If we made a passageway, could it be concealed with furniture?"

"Easily."

"Can you do it without detection?"

"Easily."

Gannon looked steadily at Bedeau. "My friend, is there anything you can't do?"

"Ah, you Englishmen. Without fail, you underestimate us French."

Gannon walked back into the main reception room and quietly registered the layout. "Where will you place the serving tables?"

"There, along that wall."

"Good. Close to the doors leading to the kitchen."

"Shall I show you anything else?"

"No, but let us walk the hallway that leads to the kitchens."

Gannon followed Bedeau through the double doors and down the dark hallway. He estimated the distance at about twenty-five meters. When they arrived in the kitchen, Madame Lefèbvre, dressed in her coat and scarf, looked at Bedeau with obvious disdain.

"It does not please me, Monsieur Bedeau, that you allowed my croissants to burn to a blackened crisp."

CHAPTER FIFTY-THREE

In Room 308, Eléonore stood before the armoire and admired her dead husband's fine jackets and trousers. The reception the following evening would require formal dress, an easy task for her to perform for Avery Gannon. For herself, she had chosen a slim black dress with a v-neckline and a low scoop in the back, cap sleeves dotted with rhinestones. Pearls. She planned to combine a string of pearls with the glittery rhine-stones. Black net stockings with suede pumps. Classically simple.

It had been a while since she had attended a formal function, instead she had spent her time waiting for Édouard. She had been a lonely woman, longing for his touch, watching the streets for his return. In was all in vain; in the end, she lost him.

Melancholy, she approached the credenza and poured Cognac. She felt she was waiting for something or someone. *The Englishman, of course.*

CHAPTER FIFTY-FOUR

He smelled her perfume before he tapped on the door of 308. He leaned against the door and chastised himself for his sensitivities to this beautiful woman. He was weak. He had not only succumbed to the flesh of a woman, but had also exposed his heart. Whatever she wanted, he would give her. Wherever she went, he would follow.

He tapped on the door and waited. He heard a soft "*Oui.*"

"Gannon."

The door opened slowly and revealed Eléonore's delicate face. "You are here," she said simply.

He smelled the Cognac before he stepped inside, watched as she walked to the credenza and poured a glass for him. When she turned to face him, he saw the yearning in her eyes. Her cheeks flushed pink, transparent.

"Your day?" she asked.

"Eventful," he said as he removed his coat and fedora. "There's much to tell you."

She lifted a glass of Cognac and held it toward him. When he took it, he felt the warmth of her fingers on the glass. *Je voudrais plonger mon visage dans tes cheveux et t'embrasser jusqu'à ce qu'il n'y ait plus d'étoiles dans le ciel. I shall bury my face in your hair, kiss you until the stars leave the sky.*

"Come. Sit with me." She walked to the lounge and sat, the ever-present black sable wrapped around her, defying the incessant chill in the room.

He sat across from her in the small chair by her bedside, sipping slowly and began to consider the words he would say to her. He smiled. "We must never run out of Cognac."

Eleonore laughed, "Nor lose the strength to open the bottle." She leaned back and closed her eyes. He saw the curve of her neck, the lobes of her ears, the place where he had kissed her the night before. He stood abruptly and left his chair and moved to the lounge. She did not seem surprised that he sat next to her. She moved over slightly and spread the tail of the fur over his legs, an act of kindness that caused a catch in Gannon's breath. He sipped again from his glass.

"The reception will not be an ordinary reception," he began. "You and I will attend, but only for a short while. At 8:00 o'clock, I'll take you back to your room and return." He cleared his throat. "That is all you need to know at this time."

Eléonore said nothing.

"Of course, while in the presence of the Germans, we must present ourselves as husband and wife."

Her response was coy. "That will not be difficult for me."

"Good. By the way, while at the Gestapo Headquarters, I ran into Krenz. He asked me where we met. I told him at your family's estate near Senlis. Is that a problem?"

"No, not at all."

"Another thing. Krenz asked why I didn't wear a wedding ring. I told him it was a family heirloom and was so valuable it was stored in a vault."

"Again, no problem," she said. "I wonder why he's so curious."

"He's working from his instincts. Something tells him there is a ruse here. What, I don't know. But, it's obvious he's having doubts or he wouldn't ask so many questions."

"What shall we do?"

"Nothing, except remain cautious." He became humorous. "And ensure the shoe polish remains intact."

He stood and refilled their glasses. From the credenza, he said, "It's possible the reception will end badly."

Eléonore sat upright. "And you are prepared for that?"

Gannon turned to face her. "Yes. The Résistance will be involved."

"Is that all you will tell me?"

He stared at her for a while, noticed her parted lips and the row of small teeth brimming her lower lip. "Yes."

She already knew the answer to the question she now asked. "Will you be in danger?"

"Yes."

***

From the door, a loud rap. Plomion, of course.

"*Oui?*"

"Plomion."

Gannon walked across the room and found an impatient Plomion. The smell of whiskey preceded his entry into the room. Oddly, he wondered if Plomion ever shaved. Even his thick eyebrows swept across his lower forehead in tangled display and obvious lack of care. Perhaps his life of deception did not allow him the luxury of occasional grooming. Of course, it didn't. He was too busy making bombs and ensuring the Germans had no peace.

Plomion nodded to Eléonore, "Madame." When he turned to Gannon, his words were urgent, as if wolves were snapping at his heels. "Let us go to the kitchens." Without waiting for an answer, he went into the hallway and headed toward the stairs.

When Gannon looked at Eléonore, she seemed complacent, accepting of the two men's need to meet in secret. The corners of her lips lifted into a smile. "It would please me, monsieur, if, from the kitchen, you would bring me a croissant."

A croissant? He was certain the only croissants in the kitchen were the ones blackened by the forgetful Monsieur Bedeau.

***

The Crillon's kitchens were cold and dark, with only a glimmer of light from the small pilot lights that glowed from the gas ovens. Plomion lifted himself and sat on the long wooden table that held a myriad of Mrs. Lefébvre's bowls. Gannon found a small chair and pulled it closer to Plomion, who predictably loosened the top of his flask and drank heartily.

Gannon waited patiently. He had become fond of the Frenchman despite his distaste of the English and their pomposity. Though somewhat arrogant, perhaps because of his small stature, Gannon decided Plomion possessed a wise intelligence. Most likely it was an intelligence honed by the invasion of his beloved France, his need to survive, to protect what he felt was sacred. Plomion had regrettably missed The Great War, too young to carry a rifle. His potential to excel as an infantry soldier was evident.

He was, however, destined to become a patriot who excelled at subterfuge, whose deft fingers made bombs that were as intricate as the workings of a fine watch. His genius not only lay in his abilities as a maker of bombs, but, more important, his extraordinary perceptive powers, powers he used for the distinct purpose of killing Germans. His refusal to accept dishonor and degradation of human values while under the occupation of the Germans easily pushed him to the front of the line when joining the Résistance.

Plomion squinted his eyes to better see Gannon. "We are set. I have four men who will be here at daylight. They'll be wearing the uniforms of kitchen staff. At some point, I'm sure Monsieur Bedeau will instruct them as to their duties at the reception."

"It might be odd if the men you have chosen are young, robust men who should be in the hands of the Germans."

"I have thought of that and chose men who look the part of refined Frenchmen. Older, thin, small." He laughed. "Like me."

Gannon smiled. "What about their handling of weapons?"

"Each one quite skillful with any weapon. It would please me to smuggle in a machine gun, but alas I would be pushing my luck."

Gannon saw a trace of apprehension in Plomion's shadowed face, a diverting of his eyes as though all was not quite perfect. "Your luck seems to be good, Olivier. You have experienced men who will not disappoint you."

"True."

In the shadowed room, Plomion pulled open his coat and withdrew a weapon. His words were a cajoling whisper. "Ah, I have been having an affair with my little *Unique 32* for most of my life. All you have to do is point it, fire as rapidly as possible, as close as possible." He brought the small pistol to his face as if it were his lover and rubbed it along his unshaven cheek before he returned it to its hiding place.

Gannon allowed Plomion his reverie for only a moment. "What of the bombs?"

"Ah, the bombs. The darling petite bombs I have made. My little girls are so beautiful." He laughed and opened his flask again, perhaps a sign of anxiety. "They will be put to good use. Once the reception is over, bombs will be detonated throughout the City as well as the train stations, a distinct advantage for us when we leave the Crillon.

"Why leave the Crillon? Why not hide here?"

"A possibility?"

Gannon nodded and left his chair. He walked around the dark kitchen and thought of the events that would take place in a mere few hours: a massacre in the reception room of the Hotel de Crillon. The bombings throughout Paris. The plight of Monsieur Bedeau. His own survival in the next twenty-four hours. His liaison with Eléonore Delafloté, a woman who had unwittingly saved his life and, at the same time, stolen his heart.

His breath came shallow as he once again acknowledged his fervent desire to confront the one-eyed colonel who had ended the life of his compatriot spy. He wondered if his impersonation of Édouard Delafloté was a mockery to his dead friend, the fellow spy who had formed a brotherhood with him, cleaned both their weapons late into the night, had talked of his beautiful wife who waited for his safe return. He felt himself weaken.

"Nothing must happen to Krenz in the foray."

"Ha! Hundreds of bullets flying around the room and you expect Krenz to remain untouched? It's foolish to think he would survive such an attack."

"You heard me, Plomion."

Plomion nodded. "Then, perhaps he should leave the room before the time of the attack."

"That is my plan. I will take Madame Delafloté to her room a few minutes before 8:00 o'clock. Perhaps I could ask Krenz to accompany us to share some private moments discussing the . . . "

"The capture of the English spy?" Plomion laughed. "I would suggest your topic of conversation with Krenz be limited to the weather or the cultural offerings of Paris."

"Perhaps."

Plomion eased himself from the tabletop and moved toward Gannon. "Regardless, at precisely 8:00 o'clock, my men and I will begin our attack."

Gannon said nothing. The decision to abandon an assassination attempt at the train station had been a good one. A reception for Germany's Chief of Gestapo would be a far better place to have a fêtes with the Germans. As Plomion had said, a delightful opportunity to serve *un dessert flambé*.

CHAPTER FIFTY-FIVE

At twenty-seven minutes prior to midnight, Monsieur Claude Bedeau stood at his post in the lobby of the Hotel de Crillon. He seemed relaxed as he hummed an obscure tune he remembered from his childhood. His uniform had been meticulously pressed and brushed. Even a crisp handkerchief, the color of *claret* wine, lay exposed in precise points from his topcoat pocket.

The lights in the lobby were dimmed, an acknowledgement of nightfall in Paris, where curfews were in force and its citizens tucked away in their homes. Only German soldiers patrolled the streets. Bundled in their wintertime wool uniforms, they smoked their cigarettes, laughed at the possibility of one day climbing the Eiffel Tower. They felt growing erections as they told stories of romantic escapades with lovely French women.

Bedeau lay down his fountain pen, closed the ink well and watched the entrance doors of the hotel. He knew his Hélène had been whisked away to safety only hours before. Where, he did not know. He would have to trust, that is all he could do.

He looked at his watch. Twelve minutes before midnight. He studied the shadowed lobby, the brocade chairs that had been in use since his first day of employment. He had returned from The

Great War emaciated, his ragged uniform of the French Army hanging on mere bones. He had been a young man when he walked from the northeast, through the Aubervilliers gate, and found the remnants of his family. Hélène had bathed him, fed him and then held him in her arms, whispering soothing words that led him into a long sleep.

Bedeau smiled when he saw the slow approach of Krenz' Horch 852, its Nazi flags limp and unfurled. The Frenchman and the Nazi, two men whose center cores were built on their individual perceptions of right and wrong, a conflict through the ages, all beginning with either a black heart or divine guidance. Claude Bedeau, a gentle man, was about to challenge the devil.

Through the tall lobby windows, Bedeau watched while Krenz' driver opened his door and the man, dressed in black knee boots, pushed himself from his car. The leather of his black overcoat glistened from the light of the nearby street lamps. Krenz straightened his field cap and patted the holstered gun beneath his coat, perhaps an ominous sign of impending doom. Bedeau lifted his chin and waited.

When the large, heavy entry doors opened, Krenz was alone. His walk to the concierge station was slow and deliberate. He didn't seem to be in a hurry as he stopped and swiveled his head slowly to his right, then to his left. He remained about three meters away when he called to Bedeau.

"Monsieur Bedeau, a most pleasant good evening to you."

Bedeau found himself smiling again and rejoiced at his sense of control. He decreed himself almost invincible, a strength spreading throughout his body that reminded him of his time in the trenches of The Great War, of the Third Battle of Aisne, where he realized his true depth as a Frenchman.

"And the same to you, Colonel Krenz."

Krenz waited in the shadows for a moment, then moved forward to stand only a short way from Bedeau. He stared a long time at the old man who stood before him, unwavering, aloof.

"It seems you and I have something of importance to discuss, Herr Bedeau."

Krenz removed his overcoat and laid it on a nearby chair. His tunic was immaculate, perfectly tailored, black, the most feared color in all of Europe. His breeches flared at the knees, the uniform a perfect ensemble of leather, wool and brass. The three and one-half inch bill on his visor gave a false impression of height. Krenz was not overly tall, the heels of his boots hoisting him up a forged inch taller.

Bedeau said nothing and watched as Krenz narrowed his eyes.

"The Englishman?"

Bedeau held his gaze for a long moment. "As you can see, he is not here."

For a moment, Krenz seemed bewildered, confused. His reply was harsh. "Do not dawdle with me, Herr Bedeau. You know very well what I expect of you."

Bedeau lifted his hands. "I repeat. He is not here."

Krenz threw his head back and screamed. "Lights! Turn on the lights!"

Bedeau seemed unaffected by the Nazi's fury. "As you wish." He slowly walked to the switches near the staircase and turned on the great chandelier hanging over the piano. When he looked back, the light had exposed Krenz' contorted face, the snarl of his lips. He was Berlin's one-eyed fanatic.

He returned to the concierge station and waited.

Through tight lips, Krenz hissed. "The Englishman, Herr Bedeau. *The Englishman.*"

"Ahhhh, the Englishman." He looked down at his podium and picked up his pen, scribbled a few words on a document and without looking up, said, "I have decided to turn over the Englishman to you at Noon on Friday." .

A hush spread throughout the lobby, leaving only air and the two men who stood before one another. Finally, a small laugh from Krenz. "Perhaps I did not hear you correctly. Would you repeat that, please?"

Bedeau looked up and said. "You heard me, Colonel Krenz. I do not plan to hand over the spy until Friday, at Noon."

The words settled on Krenz slowly, one word at a time, each one perhaps an explosion in his head. A sharp intake of his breath, then a slow, ghost-like expulsion of air. "Do you realize, Herr Bedeau, that I could simply shoot you here in the lobby of the Hotel de Crillon?"

Bedeau lifted his eyebrows. "That is your choice. You may choose the spy on Friday or my death here tonight."

Krenz' hand found his holster and pulled his weapon. He

moved closer and was only inches from Bedeau. "Your impertinence amazes me, Herr Bedeau. Do you really think you can keep the spy from me simply by telling me to *wait* until Friday?" His breath came from hot, twisted lips, his left eye wobbling as it sought a resting place.

Bedeau placed his hands on the podium of the concierge station. "Colonel Krenz, you are, indeed, in control of your weapon." He paused, the trace of a smile. "And I am in control of the spy."

Krenz jerked back. The gun in his hand aimed squarely at Bedeau, its barrel almost touching the handkerchief that protruded from his overcoat pocket. The smell of Krenz' dinner drifted around the two men. Sausages. German, most likely. After a moment, Krenz pushed the muzzle into the handkerchief with such force that Bedeau held tightly to the table for fear of falling backwards. "Not 12:01 nor 12:02, but Noon."

Bedeau, ever the arrogant Frenchman, straightened his jacket and fluffed his handkerchief. "But, of course. That is what I told you. Noon." He lifted his brow. "You will not forget our arrangement? My life for the Englishman's."

Krenz retrieved his coat, turned and walked halfway to the hotel doors. "Just out of curiosity, Herr Bedeau, for what reason must I wait until Noon Friday for our English spy?"

Bedeau sent Krenz a brief smile. "I believe he has some social commitments on his schedule."

"Social commitments?"

"Yes."

Krenz shook his head. "Your impertinence will have you hanging from the *fahnenmasten*."

***

Bedeau dimmed the lights over the grand piano and sat on the bottom step of the staircase. He smelled the burned croissants from the morning baking. He must remember to apologize to Madame Lefèbvre.

CHAPTER FIFTY-SIX

The Paris air was crisp. The glow of street lamps cast soft light on the snow that banked along the avenues. The dark winter sky soared upward to meet a band of light that Galileo had deemed the Milky Way. Exiting the doors of the Hotel de Crillon, Krenz ignored his driver and the door that had been opened for him. Instead, he turned sharply and, with steps that were stiff and measured, walked down the Place de la Concorde toward the Rue Royale. For an instant, he thought he would return to the Crillon and put a bullet into the head of Bedeau. His fingers twitched at the mere thought of it. He also dismissed a night of torture; the man would never reveal the whereabouts of Gannon.

Why Noon Friday? There had to be a significance to the safe-keeping of the Englishman until Noon Friday. But, what? Social commitments? Krenz' anger swelled as he envisioned the smug, little Frenchman – *I am in control of the spy.* When the time came, he would not forget Bedeau's words.

At Rue Royale, Krenz stopped and pulled the collar of his coat up against his neck. Bedeau was not his biggest problem. His biggest problem would arrive at 1:19 p.m. tomorrow after-noon when the train carrying Heinrich Müller arrived. So sure he would have the spy in hand, Krenz had cabled Müller: *Cap-*

ture of spy imminent. Interrogation scheduled when you arrive. There would be no interrogation by Müller. Müller's train was scheduled for departure from Paris at 6:00 a.m. on Friday, hours before the alleged hand-over of the spy.

The purpose of Müller's visit was clear: Hold Krenz accountable for the English spy and the fact he was not presently being held in a cell in the basement of Gestapo Headquarters or at least hanging from one of Paris' flagpoles. Müller would return to Berlin with a report that would go directly to Adolf Hitler and, thus, the demise of Krenz would begin.

Krenz felt weak. Bedeau was right: he had control of the spy.

Behind him, he heard the tires of his car crunch the frozen snow. He turned and waved the car toward him. He must think. Müller's train arrival was only hours away and he found himself totally unprepared for Germany's Gestapo chief.

"To headquarters," he said to his driver. Inside the car, Krenz leaned back and closed his eyes. In his mind's eyes, he saw the blurry picture of Gannon, the fedora, a cigarette between his fingers. Then, he smiled. He would wait until Noon to finally meet the Englishman.

CHAPTER FIFTY-SEVEN

Long after midnight, Room 308 lay in a subliminal calm. Dark and cold, it was a thinking man's opportunity to delve deep into all that mattered to him. Avery Gannon sat on the lounge opposite the bed and considered the important things in his life, perhaps a prelude to an onset of adversities that teased him from the shadows. He was not afraid. The *un dessert flambé* had been planned well. He had spent the past four hours turning over every detail of the operation, concluding that the simplicity of the plan was its best chance for success: grand reception for Müller, Germans, Résistance, weapons, attack.

Bedeau's performance had been brilliant. His charade had convinced Krenz that he would turn over the Englishman at noon on Friday in exchange for his own life. How ludicrous. By noon Friday, Krenz would no longer be breathing.

Gannon smiled to himself. *And, then there was Plomion.* He envisioned a ridiculous picture of Plomion at the reception, perhaps in a French army uniform, standing on one of the tables and tossing his delicate girlie bombs at the Germans. The colorful Frenchman, flamboyant in his quest to ensure the message of a free France was heard, possessed something that was rare in most men. He was afraid of nothing.

From the bed, he heard a stirring of the silk duvet. A whisper. "Monsieur Gannon, you are there?"

Her words came with a sensual breathiness. Avery uncrossed his legs and leaned forward in the dark. "I am here."

"Ahhhh. And, so you are. What time is it?"

"Three o'clock."

"How long have you been here?"

"A few hours." Gannon leaned back. At midnight, he had stood in the dark at the top of the stairs, his pistol aimed at the head of Colonel Horst Krenz. His desire to shoot him was paramount; yet, it was neither the time nor the place. As Avery Gannon, he had yet to have a conversation with the Nazi. Above all, that was want he wanted.

"I did not hear you return."

"You were sleeping soundly."

"I am awake now."

Avery smiled. "I know."

"I had a dream."

"A dream?"

"*Oui.*"

He heard her sit up, could picture her pulling the fur around her. "About what?"

"About you."

"Would you call that a dream or a nightmare?"

She laughed. "A dream about you would always be pleasant, monsieur."

Avery said nothing and waited. He knew she would tell him her dream.

In a hushed tone, she began, much like a mother telling her child a bedtime story. "I can see you now, those dark eyes so unrevealing, hiding your heart." She paused. "In the dream, we were sitting on a mountainside, perhaps *la vallée d'Ermenonville* near Senlis. You said to me, 'I have always wanted to sit on this mountainside with you'."

The room remained quiet for a few moments. "Go on," said Avery.

"That is all."

Avery stared into the dark place where he knew Eléonore sat wrapped in her fur. He could not see her face, but knew her eyes were turned toward him. Then, almost inaudibly, she said, "It would please me to sit on the mountainside with you."

He reached out and touched the bed, felt her hand reach for his. As if the dark room had suddenly filled with light, he pulled her to him, smelled love in her hair, felt her rapid heartbeat. "Eléonore."

"Please," she whispered.

Avery stood and after a few moments was naked beneath the fur, her body warm as his arms found her. She nipped at his neck and shoulders, placed one long leg over his hip. Her teeth pulled at his lower lip and he began to feel the sway of her hips. He kissed her without abandon while she pulled his hair and murmured, "*Mon, chéri.*"

Avery turned on his back and pulled her on top of him. He lifted her and gently pushed himself into her. His hands held her hips as he closed his eyes and felt her move above him. Her cries of "*Mon, chéri, mon, chéri*" carried him to another place, a place far away from war, away from the horrors of death, away from thoughts of having to leave her.

CHAPTER FIFTY-EIGHT

Morning came quickly at the Crillon. The bright sun of winter rose above the buildings on Place de la Concorde and found Claude Bedeau standing beneath the portico. Snow melted from the rooftop and ran down the icicles that hung firm to the edge of the roof. A brisk breeze unfurled the Nazi flag at the corner of Concorde and Rue Royale, a presence wholly ignored by the proud Parisians.

Bedeau watched as Madame Lefèbvre pulled her little cart down the avenue toward the Crillon. A stout, round woman, she was invaluable to Bedeau. For years, she had made the two-kilometer walk to the hotel and, at precisely 6:30 every day except Sunday, she unceremoniously pushed open the entry doors, her cart behind her, and began her daily rituals in the hotel kitchens.

Many times he had asked her to use the rear entrance, but she had only glared at him and continued through the lobby of the hotel. On Sundays, her husband placed a tub of hot water at her feet and bathed them while she read the latest anti-fascist newspapers and cursed the Germans.

"Good morning, Madame Lefèbvre."

"*Oui*, Monsieur Bedeau."

He smiled and noticed her earrings did not match.

"Have you forgiven me for burning your croissants?"

"*Non*," she said and pushed her way into the hotel.

***

Bedeau looked at his watch. 6:35. He left the entrance of the hotel and walked to the rear delivery area. The stable had sent over a horse and harnessed it to the wagon he intended to use to market. He'd seen this horse before, a lumbering nag who was as ornery as Madame Lefèbvre.

Once, the horse had been spooked and overturned his wagon. He still felt the anger of losing six-dozen eggs fresh from the countryside, quarts of milk, the most beautiful tomatoes he'd ever seen and a large beef, which was promptly dragged away by a pack of dogs.

"Do not disappoint me today, my friend," he said as he patted its rump. "We have important things to do."

From behind, he heard the crunching of steps into the snow filled alley. "Monsieur Bedeau, we are here to help you." Four men, all dressed in white pants and tunics, approached the wagon. The words *Hotel de Crillon* were embroidered above the left front pocket, opposite the pocket that read "*Dining.*"

"*Bonjour*," called Bedeau. "Were you stopped by a patrol?"

"*Oui*. And searched."

"Any questions asked?"

"*Non*. Only where we were going? And why."

"What did you tell them?"

"That we were to assist in a reception in honor of the illustrious Heinrich Müller."

Bedeau nodded. "Come inside and I'll give you your instructions." The four men followed him to the kitchens. "Be alert, my friends, Madame Lefèbvre does not like snow on her floors." Immediately, all four men returned to the outside and stomped the snow from their shoes. Bedeau smiled and thought *these men will take instructions very well.*

He found Madame Lefèbvre blending flour and lard for her croissants. "Madame, I have four men here who will be in training in our kitchens this morning. They will assist in the reception this evening."

She looked up from her bowl and frowned, the irritation on her face like a sour lemon. "Where did you get those men? I am certain they cannot boil water."

"They are from the labor pool, Madame. They are very skilled."

She gave Bedeau a sly glance. "Let me see their fingernails. Their hands," she said with gruffness.

The four men seemed stricken with fear. Bedeau smiled at them. "Come. Show Madame Lefèbvre your hands."

Hesitating somewhat, each man held out his hands. She waddled to where they stood.

"Closer!" she demanded. She lifted each hand and turned it over, back and forth, until every inch was carefully scrutinized. When she finished, she turned her scowling face to Bedeau.

"Pig farmers. Nothing, but pig farmers." She returned to her croissants with great fanfare. After all, it was her croissants that made the de Crillon the fine hotel it was.

CHAPTER FIFTY-NINE

Beneath the fur in Room 308, Avery Gannon held the warm body of Eléonore Delafloté. He had been awake for an hour listening to her breathe, had studied her black eyelashes and inspected her tiny ear lobes. He could not help himself; he leaned over and kissed her eyelids. When she opened her eyes, she smiled at him. "Monsieur, your lips are tender. Must you stop at my eyelids?"

"*Non*," he said. "And where would you like for me to kiss you?" He nibbled at her chin.

Eléonore pushed aside the fur and morning sunlight fell across the flawless skin of her naked body. "Everywhere, monsieur. Everywhere."

CHAPTER SIXTY

The mood at Gestapo Headquarters was one of heightened urgency. Everyone knew the day would not be ordinary. When they had dressed in their small rooms earlier in the morning, they fretted over their uniforms, a wayward thread, a loose button, a smudge that indicated carelessness, neglect that diminished their position in the world's most elite military.

Heinrich Müller, Chief of Gestapo of the Third Reich, who reigned as the most meticulous of all Hitler's staff, would step off the train at 1:19, only seven hours away. Herr Müller could spot a loose button from ten meters away.

Upstairs on the second floor, down the long narrow hall, Colonel Krenz slowly drank his tea, as if each sip brought him closer to his agonizing journey to the train station. If he never finished drinking his tea, perhaps Müller would never arrive. His fingers tightly held the handle of the teacup. He felt the stiffness in his body, the dullness of his brain as it sought an escape from the harrowing thoughts of his liaison with Müller. He concentrated on the beating of his heart, willing it to a slow fifty-two beats per minute.

The knock at his door jarred him. "Yes!"

The door opened an inch at a time. "Yes!" he called again.

"Colonel Krenz, a cable from Berlin." His assistant eased inside and placed the paper in front of him. Krenz noticed his shaking hand.

"Thank you, Corporal. You may leave."

The door closed and Krenz leaned back in his chair and stared at the cable. His call to Berlin had been interesting. Yes, indeed, they had a file on Édouard Delafloté. Yes, it contained a photograph. Yes, they would send the complete file immediately.

Krenz picked up the cable. BERLIN 23 JANUARY 08:00 EXPECT DELIVERY OF DELAFLOTÉ FILE VIA HEINRICH MÜLLER TODAY STOP GESTAPO HEADQUARTERS, COUNTER INTELLIGENCE E5 ZIMMERMANN

From his middle desk drawer, Krenz pulled Gannon's file. Without opening it, he slid it into his attaché case. He looked at his watch. Five more hours until the train arrived.

CHAPTER SIXTY-ONE

"*Enfer et damnation!*" Bedeau yelled and snapped the end of the reins against the horse's rump. The horse stopped in the middle of the intersection, turned her head and looked back at Bedeau. "*Oui,* you sorry nag, move or I will take you to the meat factory where your bones will become powder!" In the wagon, Maurice and Serge, his two assistants, laughed as the old man cursed again. Bedeau had lost his cap and his wild frenzied hair caused stares among the bicyclists who stood watching his tirade. Finally, the horse moved forward at her own pace into bicycle traffic, leaving no doubt that she and she alone determined when and if she moved at all.

Full of fruit and vegetables as well as fine meats and cheeses, the wagon proceeded slowly. Maurice and Serge appeared languid as they slouched in the back of the wagon. They gave a false impression to those who may have noticed the old horse and its wagon plodding down the avenue. Behind their lethargic appearances, they kept their eyes kept vigil at every turn, their senses on high alert. They noticed the patrols were heavier than usual, every street intersection manned by at least two or three gray-green uniformed soldiers.

At the Rue du Faubourg Saint-Honoré, Bedeau pulled into

the alley where rear deliveries were made to Pierre Poilâne's bakery. He and his two assistants left the wagon and entered the small shop where they were met by the fragrance of yeast and sugars. The men found themselves surrounded by baguettes, croissants, tarts and plates of *fougasse*. Among Pierre's *boulangerie-patisserie,* hidden under trays filled with loaves of bread, were some of the finest weapons in all of France.

Pierre's booming voice came from the shop's kitchen, followed by the man himself. Robust and jovial, Pierre's presence filled the shop. Covered with flour and dough, the front of his apron was rotund, hiding little of his massive frame. It was clear he enjoyed what he baked. His hair was dungeon black and combed to one side so heavily one was sure he had a list to his walk.

"*Bonjour*, Monsieur Bedeau." He nodded to the two men standing behind Bedeau. Then, moved closer and lowered his voice.

"I understand you are hosting some of Germany's most elite citizens at a reception this evening. If only Hitler could attend." He laughed heartily. "It is my privilege to provide some necessary items for this exciting event." He winked and Bedeau noticed flour in his mustache.

"*Oui,* that is so. You are familiar with the details from what Plomion tells me."

"Ah, yes. I have been informed of many things. My only regret is I have not been invited to this glorious event."

"Do not worry, Pierre. These Germans are boring. It seems that all they talk about is how powerful they are, how many battles they have won and the brilliance of their Führer."

"Ah, the brilliance of their Führer." Pierre shook his head and placed his hands on top of his massive stomach. Bedeau noticed his long, fat fingers, much like the sausages Madame Bedeau prepared in her kitchens.

Pierre rubbed his chin for a few moments and said softly, "*Non*, he is not brilliant. He is a madman."

"But, of course. As are those who follow him so loyally." Bedeau looked at Maurice and Serge. "It is time."

Pierre nodded. "*Oui.* Come with me to the kitchen. I have something in the oven."

All three men followed the big white back of the baker to the kitchen where the heat from the wood-fired ovens toasted their faces. No wonder Pierre's face was so red.

With a flourish, he pulled back the door of a small gas-fired oven that stood in the corner of the kitchen. Inside, neatly arranged as if loaves of bread, was a cache of weapons.

"Take what you will. Plomion tells me you'll be in a range of ten or fifteen meters. That so?"

"Yes. Approximately." Bedeau looked at his assistants. "Your choice, monsieurs. You know what Plomion wants."

Bedeau stood back and watched as Maurice and Serge scrutinized the weapons, picked up several, examined them and placed them aside. *"Armes parfaits. Ce seont plus que de faire le travil." Yes, they were perfect weapons.*

Pierre gathered them up and placed each one inside a long, fat loaf of bread that had been hollowed out from the bottom. He replaced the bottom of the bread, fitting it in like a puzzle piece. He then smeared a thick paste of hazelnut and sugar over the entire loaf and placed each one on a large tray. He licked his fingers and smiled, *"Bon appétit."*

"My most humble gratitude, Pierre."

The heavy man smiled. *"Pour libérer la France."*

Yes, for the liberty of France.

***

The men exited the rear door of the bakery with the fragrance of cardamom in their hair and Pierre's flour dust on their clothes. Loud shouts from behind were like a volley of gunfire.

"You there! Let me see your papers." Two soldiers approached them, hands outstretched. Bedeau turned and reached inside his coat. He said nothing as he placed the document into a waiting hand. The soldier read the document carefully, his eyes resting on the picture.

"Bedeau?"

"Yes. Claude Bedeau."

"What are you doing here in the alley?"

Bedeau wanted to laugh. It was quite obvious what he was doing. He had on the uniform of the Hotel de Crillon, a wagon full of vegetables and meats and was accompanied by two dining room assistants. "There is a reception this evening for your Gestapo chief Heinrich Müller and other high-ranking German

officials. It is the duty of the Hotel de Crillon to prepare food." He
looked at the other soldier. "We are merely making preparation."

"Your papers." He returned Bedeau's identification and glanced
at the two men leaning on the wagon. "Your papers." Each man
handed the soldier his documents and waited. The soldier looked up
and compared the photographs with the men who stood before him.
Satisfied, he returned their papers. He then moved closer to the
wagon and looked inside. "What have we here?"

Bedeau smiled. "It must be a fine reception this evening." He
spread his hand over the contents of the wagon. "For your superiors
who will arrive at the hotel quite hungry, I'm sure."

The soldier grinned and reached over and swiped his finger
across a loaf of bread covered with hazelnut confection and also
hiding a weapon. He put the cream in his mouth and smiled. "I'm
sure a loaf of this bread will not be missed at your reception, Herr
Bedeau."

Bedeau forced a smile. From the corner of his eye, he saw the
taller of his assistants, Maurice, ease himself around so he could see
the second soldier. From his left, he noticed Serge place his hand on
the wagon's edge. "I am short on the bread. Perhaps some fruit?" he
said.

"Short on bread? Ha! The whole of Paris is nothing but bread.
Go inside and get another from the baker." The German reached
over and lifted the bread.

"*Non!*" yelled Pierre as he came through the door. "You must not
eat that bread! It is the worst bread I have ever made."

Both soldiers pushed their rifles in front of them and glared at
Pierre.

"Here. You must taste my cheese-filled croissants." He gave
them a cajoling smile. "They are still warm."

Neither soldier hesitated. They reached out and took the croissants. The lead soldier looked at Bedeau menacingly. "Keep your
bread."

The men jumped when the horse neighed with enthusiasm and
stomped the ground with her front foot. Let's be on our way she
seemed to be saying. The wagon rocked slightly and Bedeau pulled
himself up into the seat. Behind him, Maurice and Serge jumped in.
The soldiers laughed when Pierre reached into his apron pocket and
retrieved two more croissants.

CHAPTER SIXTY-TWO

Avery Gannon dressed quietly while across the room Eléonore slept soundly. Their night of lovemaking had been passionate. They had clung to each other, whispered to each other and then lay spent, thoughts of an uncertain future faint and distant. Afterwards, lying still in the light of the early morning, he found himself hopeful that perhaps they would escape Paris. He cursed. In a wave of reality, he saw the incumbent truths, sobering, harsh truths. His plight as a spy was never anything more than a pathway to eventual death. He felt himself so close to a bullet that he shuddered.

From the window, he looked down onto the street where he saw Bedeau and his wagon turn into the alley. Two white-clad men jumped out of the wagon and followed it around the corner. He assumed the secret transport of weapons had been successful, allowing them to pursue their operation "dessert flambé," as Plomion had so cleverly named.

He decided to spend his morning at the train station where he would present his travel papers and purchase their tickets to Senlis for the following day. Afterwards, he and Eléonore planned to lunch at a small café near the hotel. It would be the last semblance of normalcy for the day.

Avery turned and looked toward the bed. His heart became cold as he acknowledged his most grievous act would not be his conversation with her about Édouard, but would be the leaving of her.

CHAPTER SIXTY-THREE

Krenz left his office at 1:00 o'clock and walked through the lobby of Gestapo headquarters where his staff watched in silence. He passed through the entry doors and found his driver opening the door of his car. The Paris sky seemed especially bright, the sun high in the sky. He adjusted his cap and, as always, patted his holstered gun. Behind him, he heard the footsteps of Lieutenant Vogel. Vogel would accompany him to the train station. After all, it was Vogel who had devised the security plan to protect Müller during his visit. It was the same plan he had developed for Göring .

He slipped inside the car. "Drive slowly." He was in no hurry to meet Heinrich Müller. Beside him, Vogel removed his gloves and looked out the window.

"Have you met Müller?" asked Krenz.

"No, I have not," said the young lieutenant.

"A handsome man." He paused. "The epitome of Aryan supremacy." Another pause. "No flaws."

Vogel nodded, stoic, perhaps afraid to look at Krenz. He sat to his left, close to the wayward left eye that tried desperately to focus in the same direction as the right.

Krenz smiled. "Do not be fooled by his charm. He is a snake."

He slapped his knee. "I hate snakes. They are so quiet, yet always moving. Searching." He turned to Vogel. "If only snakes made noise."

He reached inside his pocket and felt the cyanide capsule. He would not be caught unprepared.

***

At the Gare de l'Est, Krenz' car pulled into the security zone where soldiers stood smartly, their rifles held stiffly at their chests. Young soldiers, whose mothers and fathers cried themselves to sleep each night, praying for their safe return from a war they did not understand.

"The gate," said Krenz, leaving the car and walking briskly across the large expanse of yard. Vogel followed, a cold wind whipping the tail of his coat. Soldiers on each side and in the rear watched the Gestapo chief and his assistant with cold abandon. Krenz looked up and saw snipers posted at various locations.

Inside the station, the smell of diesel fuel rose in the air. Muffled sounds of rumbling engines drifted along the corridors where soldiers stood, alert and watching. Krenz looked at his watch. Only four minutes before the arrival of Müller's train. He stood erect, his arms by his side. He was a good German.

A commotion near Gate 7 caught Krenz' attention. Müller, of course. The man, stoic and aloof, stepped from the gate exit and took long moments to observe his surroundings. Krenz held his breath and watched.

He had read Müller's file long ago and memorized the details of the man who had hung thirty-seven Lithuanian goat farmers who had strayed across the German border in 1939. Forty years old, Müller had once referred to Hitler as an immigrant unemployed house painter. Obviously, he was no fan of the Führer. Nor, was he a fervent Nazi Party member. He was, however, a stickler for duty and discipline. Nowhere in the ranks of the Nazi Party would one find a more fanatical member. Yet, in truth, Müller was merely a regime functionary, someone whose alliances lay only with himself, neither the Führer nor the Party itself.

Müller looked almost regal in his long leather coat, his knee-high boots shining like polished black opals. His face, clean-shaven, resembled one of the American movie stars. Dark eyes sat beneath eyebrows the color of his hair, dark and combed over to one side. Krenz wondered if there was a Mrs. Müller. A Mrs. Gestapo? He smiled at his own joke

At the moment Müller's eyes found Krenz, Krenz took a deep breath and mumbled to Vogel. "Remember, Lt. Vogel, Herr Müller does not like to be touched. Do not offer your hand." The two men walked forward and stopped only meters from Müller. Krenz offered a stiff-armed salute. "Heil Hitler!" Müller, appearing somewhat bored, responded with a standard military salute.

"Greetings, Herr Müller. May I assume you had a pleasurable journey?" Krenz found his voice weak, almost falsetto.

Müller said nothing as he looked at Vogel.

"This is Lt. Vogel, Herr Müller. Our Chief of Security."

Müller nodded and turned back to Krenz. "The station seems to be well guarded. I noticed patrols down the tracks for approximately one kilometer. Very good positioning of men."

"Thank you, Herr Müller. Your safety is our priority."

"So it seems." He hesitated and glanced toward the snipers on the rooftops. "Your snipers are vigilant, I presume."

"But, of course. Excellent sharpshooters."

"What rifle do they use?"

Krenz turned to Vogel. "Herr Vogel, please answer."

"A Kar98k," replied Vogel. "A 5x scope. Zeiss Zielvier, I believe.

"Cartridges?"

"8mm."

Müller narrowed his eyes at Krenz. "It eludes me as to why your excellent sharpshooters were unable to ferret out the English assassin." He lifted his hand. "No matter." He turned, dismissing Krenz and began walking to a waiting car.

Krenz found he could not move. He stared after Müller until Müller turned back toward him. "Come, Colonel Krenz, ride with me." Müller sent a coaxing smile and motioned for him to follow. *Come, ride with daddy.*

Krenz' rigid body leaned toward Vogel. "You may take my car, Lt. Vogel."

Krenz began his stilted walk to Müller's car, one agonizing step at a time. How he hated to get in the car with him. He would be so accessible, so exposed.

He fingered the cyanide capsule in his pocket, turned it around in his fingers, rubbed it, felt its smooth oval surface. The size of a pea, slipped in his mouth, just a quick crack between his molars and he would be brain dead in minutes, his heart would follow moments later.

He felt a mounting anger. Why was he so angry? Then, it hit him. Müller had looked into his crooked eye the entire time he had spoken to him. Was it a mockery? Did the German's disdain of imperfection find itself feeding on the misshapen eye of Horst Krenz?

Krenz slid into the rear seat of the car. He smelled the leather of Müller's coat, the slight fragrance of pomade in his hair. When he looked at his hands, they were manicured and polished. He had never known a man who polished his nails and wondered if it meant anything significant.

He leaned back, shifted slightly to his right and, with his good eye, observed Müller's profile. A soft face, a hairline that fell high on his forehead, though he showed no signs of balding. His skin was still young. How perfect; the German had no flaws.

"The Führer is quite unhappy with your performance, Herr Krenz. Suffice it to say, I, too, am displeased. A despicable situation, to say the least. Twenty-seven of Germany's finest lost to an assassin's bullet."

Krenz saw Müller's jaw line harden, his chin protrude in frustration. When he spoke, the words left his mouth like a sadistic chant. "I will expect . . . a complete report . . . upon arrival at headquarters."

"Yes, Herr Müller." Krenz stared straight ahead and, to stay calm, counted his heartbeats. He had yet to tell Müller his arrangement with Bedeau, that the Englishman would be delivered to him at Noon tomorrow, an arrangement that allowed Bedeau to live. How could he possibly explain his negotiation with Bedeau? Germans did not negotiate; they tortured and murdered, but they did not negotiate. Yet, he knew he would have to report every detail to the Gestapo chief. No theories, no speculation. Facts. All Müller wanted was facts.

"I have a file for you from Herr Zimmermann." Müller reached down and opened his attaché case, his manicured hands pulling a file folder to his lap. With a deliberate, exaggerated flip of his fingers, he opened the folder. "Herr Krenz, I have read your file on Édouard Delafloté. I will expect to meet him."

Krenz stared at the open file and saw Édouard Delafloté looking at him from beneath a tilted fedora. The handsome face with its engaging smile seemed to be mocking him. "Meet him?" he asked. He turned away from Müller and looked out the window, his thoughts far away. The man in the photograph was very familiar, but he was not the man who presently resided at the Hotel de Crillon with his beautiful wife.

"Why did you request information on Delafloté?"

"Curiosity mostly."

"What made you curious about him?"

Krenz felt the air leaving the car. He reached up and pressed the back of his sleeve on his forehead. Perspiration ran down the back of his neck. He must have air. He stammered as he searched for words. Why was he curious about Delafloté?

"Perhaps I should say instincts instead of curiosity. My instincts tell me he is not who he says he is."

"There must be something about him that bothers you. Come. Out with it." Müller turned to Krenz and waited.

Krenz nodded slowly. "Yes. Yes, there is. A small thing actually."

"Go on."

"He's too relaxed and casual." He paused. "He should be afraid of the Gestapo, but he shows no fear."

The two men remained quiet for some moments, Müller smoking his cigarette and Krenz staring out the window.

"So you asked for his file from Berlin based on his . . . his . . ."

"He doesn't seem French to me."

"Doesn't seem French? You confuse me, Herr Krenz. Exactly what is *French*?" Müller's smirk did not go unnoticed.

"I feel he is too reserved, no spontaneity to speak of. He's quite controlled and deliberate which contrasts with the impulsive French."

Minutes passed as the car threaded its way toward the Rue des Saussaires. Krenz knew Müller was dissecting his statement, knew the man would not rest until his questions were answered to his satisfaction. It surprised Krenz when Müller changed the subject.

"There's a reception this evening, I presume?"

"Yes, Herr Müller. In your honor, of course."

"How nice. I do adore French food. Of course, their wines are the finest." He turned and looked at Krenz. "What time?"

"Seven o'clock."

"Where?"

"At the Hotel de Crillon."

Müller nodded. "Ah, the Crillon. My memory of history tells me that is where the French signed a treaty with the Americans, their little fat Benjamin Franklin. These Americans. Too afraid to get their hands dirty. They send war materials, but they will never blemish themselves by entering the war."

CHAPTER SIXTY-FOUR

The flag carrying the Nazi insignia waved high from the side of the Eiffel Tower, the incongruity of its presence like a mystery. One moment the Tower was French, the next moment German. Like a magician's swift-handed trick, all one had to do was blink and, like magic, the flag appeared. Sadly, the presence of the Nazi insignia had swept the French under an army so powerful that many believed all of Europe would soon be under the rule of the Third Reich.

Krenz' car wound its way through the city toward Gestapo Headquarters. Müller drummed his fingers on his knee and sighed. "Herr Krenz, I cannot imagine that one more fine German will be murdered by this assassin. Were it to happen, I feel the Führer would be most displeased."

The cyanide capsule in his pocket felt warm and comforting to Krenz as he rubbed his fingers around it and wished for an end to this madness.

CHAPTER SIXTY-FIVE

Gannon stood in the shadows of the Gare de l'Est and watched Germany's Gestapo chief move through the corridors, followed by his many assistants and bodyguards. In his mind's eye, he lifted a rifle, sighted the scope and fired. His eyes followed the imaginary bullet as though it were a streaming comet, a burning projectile that would end the life of one of the most dedicated members of the Third Reich.

Müller was known as Hitler's boy. Hitler, however, was not Müller's adored Führer. He couldn't stand the man, found him despicable and weak in administering the steadfast rules of discipline. He felt Hitler was a man of whims, someone who was guided by a self-imposed lunacy that pushed him into the depths of madness. How could a man like that carry Germany to the heights of her glory?

Gannon witnessed the cold exchange between the two Germans. A strange duo, indeed, as Müller did not return the stiff-armed salute from Krenz, instead barely lifted his arm in standard military fashion. Gannon observed Krenz' body language: timid, anxious, a nervous touch to his coat front. Feeling for his pistol, perhaps. Gannon saw Krenz turn to his lieutenant, then all three men looked upward. *Looking for me.*

Gannon looked around and counted the number of uniformed soldiers. Fifty-seven. Fifty-seven little Hitlers.

The barred ticket window was only a few meters away, the sign above it written in French, German and English. He would buy tickets to Senlis in a moment, but first he must have a small loaf of warm *fougasse*, filled with garlic and Parmesan.

He left the gate area and found a small café near the entrance, its small outdoor tables perfect for an inconspicuous few moments while he indulged in what he considered one of France's most priceless treasures. It was still too cold to remove his coat, so he sat with his fedora cocked a little to the right, his coat collar pulled up and his eyes ever-watching.

"*Merci,*" he said to the *serveuse* when the young woman placed the bread in front of him. She smiled at him and lingered a moment. Perhaps it was the fine clothes of Édouard Delafloté that caused her to touch his shoulder and ask him if he was having a fine day. He nodded and returned her smile. "*Oui*, a very fine day."

She left his table and he found himself watching her slim hips sway through the café door. French women had a certain way with their bodies. *Oui, they most certainly do.* A vision of Eléonore swept into his mind, sending a sudden rush of what the French called *désir brûlant.*

***

From the window of a nearby shop, a man watched as Gannon ate the remnants of his bread. He observed Gannon's surreptitious glances, his easy way of appearing casual and unaware. But, he knew that wasn't the case with Avery Gannon. He was looking at the most cunning spy in all of France.

CHAPTER SIXTY-SIX

Müller's face contorted into a clown-like picture of pure joy and had one not been aware of his sinister side, they might have laughed with him. Sitting across from him, Colonel Horst Krenz was not fooled by the man's joviality. Instead, he flinched and went to a place that gave him consolation: the pocket where a cyanide capsule lay hidden, promising him refuge in a place that would neither subject him to ridicule nor mock his crooked left eye.

"Let me understand you, Herr Krenz," said Müller, his eyes brimming with laughter. "The Frenchman, this Bedeau, told you he knew the whereabouts of the assassin, yet would not turn him over to you until a time of his own choosing?"

"That is correct."

Müller stuttered in mock amazement. "I . . . I am astonished at your weaknesses, your lack of reasonable thought! I ask you – since when does the Third Reich negotiate with *anyone*?" Müller, perplexed , stood, stared at Krenz, speechless while he paced the room. He returned to his chair and placed his head in his hands.

When the accusing eyes of Müller left him, Krenz found relief in a few reprievable moments. He was given time to *think*. Yes, at the moment, he had not captured the spy. Yes, his capture was imminent. Yes, there will be no mistakes. *Please, please. Give me a morsel of trust. That's all I ask.*

Müller lifted his head and Krenz felt himself recoil. It seemed he was even angrier, his face twisting into a question, his mouth forming the word 'why' as if he were a mime. "Why, Herr Krenz, did you not simply bring him to headquarters and place a gun to his head?

Krenz knew why. "You do not know this man. He will never talk."

Müller spread his lips into a forced grin. "They all talk. They *all* talk."

"Not this man."

Müller slammed his hand on the desk. "What is so different about this man?"

Krenz fingered the capsule and was comforted. "He is a proud Frenchman."

"Proud Frenchmen bleed!" A vehement cry left the German's lips as he leaned forward.

Krenz slowed his breathing. He felt his left eye quiver, lob side to side like a confused squirrel. "Yes, but this one . . . this one is . . .unusual."

Müller leaned back into his chair and looked into Krenz' wayward eye, studied it as if he might reach out and twist it into its proper place. When he changed to Krenz' right eye, he was thoughtful. "I would like a little chat with this Bedeau. Bring him to headquarters."

Krenz shook his head. "I think that would be a mistake, Herr Müller."

Müller lifted his brows. "And why is that?"

"Bedeau is our host tonight at the Crillon."

"Our host is an obstinate Frenchman? How appropriate, Herr Krenz." He paused and examined his fingernails. "Perhaps I can chat with him this evening."

Krenz said nothing. He had said far too much already.

Müller stood and looked down at Krenz. "It would please me if you would answer a question for me."

"Of course."

Müller looked up at the ceiling for a long while, then his gaze traveled slowly to Krenz. "Did it ever occur to you that our English assassin could continue his work between now and his capture tomorrow at Noon? You know, a little assassination here, a little assassination there?"

At that moment, Krenz felt the beginning of his demise, a slow draining away of his blood. Müller had come to do what the Führer had ordered. He would wait until after the reception, after the capture of the spy. Then, he would follow orders.

Müller stood abruptly, his back ramrod straight, and swiveled his body toward the door. He said nothing as he passed through the office doorway. Krenz stilled as he listened to the Gestapo chief's fading footsteps, each one an ominous reminder that he would, indeed, do exactly what his sense of duty required.

***

The attaché case leaned against the wall a few meters away in the corner of Krenz' office. The latch was made of brass and, like everything Krenz owned, was meticulously cared for, polished regularly and with utmost devotion to its place in his life. As a boy, he had kept his toys in boxes as if they were treasures given to him by the Kaiser. His diligent nature had led him to a position in the Third Reich that many men envied.

He stared at the case as though he heard the heinous laughter of Müller coming from within. Müller said he had read the Delafloté file, wanted to meet the man. Krenz left his chair, retrieved the case and returned to his desk. His pounding heart reminded him of the moment he had seen Müller at the train station, felt his eyes devouring him as he latched onto his crooked left eye.

His hand shook at he released the latch, reached inside and pulled the file of Édouard Delafloté onto his desk. When he opened it, the eyes of the man in the photograph stared at him with such intensity that he flinched.

For a moment, he envisioned him with a sword, a sword so sharp that a mere flick of its blade could cut a man's head off. Perspiration, like a heavy dew, fell across Krenz' brow and the back of his neck. Thick suffocation spread into his body as he studied the black eyes, the strong features that proclaimed this man a man of strength. He knew this man: the Frenchman who did not surrender to his interrogation, his torture, who stood stoically as his body was pummeled with German bullets. Édouard Delafloté was *Andorra*.

Krenz left his desk and walked to the window. He pulled it open and felt the cold air of Paris revive him; give him the breath he needed. His thoughts ran rampant. If Édouard Delafloté was dead, who was the man who so expertly impersonated him?

Sounds of Paris drifted up from the streets below, a myriad of bicycles carrying its citizens to their homes, an afternoon with a lover, a glass of wine at the Café Verlet. Krenz leaned forward, placed his hands on the windowsill and smiled. The anticipation he felt was euphoric. Monsieur and Madame Delafloté's attendance at the reception would be very interesting.

CHAPTER SIXTY-SEVEN

Eléonore Delaflolté placed a small black hat on her head. The mirror reflected a beautiful woman who smiled at herself as she pulled black netting over her forehead and swiped at the few long feathers that swept into her hair. Her lipstick covered her lips like a paste of strawberry jam. She felt chilled and looked around the room. She was alone yet felt a presence slip beside her, afraid to look back into the mirror. What if she saw another face along side hers? Hesitantly, she reached out and ran her hand through the cold air. *Are you there, Édouard?*

The sleeves of her jacket hugged her arms tightly, ending up at her wrists in tufts of soft fur. The fur collar was a gift from her mother. When she placed a string of pearls around her neck, the resemblance to her mother was evident. They had been her pearls. *To whom shall I give my pearls?* From the jewelry box, she pulled a pair of earrings, round with tiny diamonds arranged around the circle. She hoped Avery would not think her over-dressed. *Non, never overdressed for Paris*, he would say.

He had promised her a late afternoon lunch of *moules sautées au vin rouge*, a walk down the Champs Élysées where snow had softened the harshness of a foreign army in Paris. His words to her had been soothing, but she knew the fallacy of them. She knew he was not in Paris simply to make love to her. *Non*, he was in Paris to kill.

The lavish reception was only hours away. She somehow felt the reception would change everything. Monsieur and Madame Delafloté would be watched carefully, their words dissected like frogs in a science laboratory. She shuddered. Perhaps she would not make a good spy, after all.

A knock at the door. Avery. She closed the door to the armoire and crossed the room. "*Oui*," she said.

"Colonel Krenz, Madame Delafloté. I would like a word with you."

CHAPTER SIXTY-EIGHT

Avery quickened his steps and crossed the Avenue Montaigne toward the Crillon. Once he turned onto the Place de la Concorde, he saw the hotel, its lights already shimmering in the early dark of a winter evening. He thought of Eléonore and her trust of him. He had made love to her, the widow of Édouard Delafloté, with unending passion, with a desire so great he thought of running away with her, like in the fairy tales of long ago. In four short days, he had lost his heart to her, a dangerous thing for an agent of His Majesty's Secret Service. If only Édouard had not been his fellow spy, perhaps his agony would have dissipated into a realization that all is fair in love and war. But, he was not that kind of man. There was no fairness in the death of Édouard Delafloté. There was no fairness in his hunger for his widow.

Claude Bedeau stood outside the Crillon and Avery waved to him as he crossed the Place de la Concorde.

"Ah, Monsieur Bedeau, your dedication as the emissary of the Hotel de Crillon is astounding, especially in this awful cold. Your nose is red and I must ask if it is from the cold or the whiskey you drink."

"Monsieur, your curiosity is misplaced."

"And how is that?"

Bedeau leaned forward and lowered his voice. "I would suggest you be curious about the man who has been following you since you turned onto the Place de la Concorde."

Avery threw his head back and laughed. "You're a funny man, Monsieur Bedeau."

A slight turn to his left brought the man into Avery's view. Ah, yes. The same man who drank wine at the café where he and Eléonore had first dined, had sat on a bench on the Rue des Saussaies in front of Gestapo headquarters, had glanced at him at the train station. A man who was not French, but perhaps Spanish. What would a Spaniard be doing in Paris? He watched as the man meandered down the avenue. There was something familiar about him, something he couldn't quite discern.

Bedeau touched his arm. "Let us go inside. The kitchens are in pandemonium. Madame Lefèbvre has threatened to kill the chef from *Château d'Eau*. It seems he has also burned her croissants."

He shook his head. "We must be careful to honor Madame Lefébvre's croissants as though they were the hearts of newborn babies."

Inside the kitchens, the smell of charred bread overwhelmed the aroma of warm *gougères* and *salmon rillettes*. On the long table that ran the length of the kitchen, one of Chef Hermé's apprentices prepared carafes of black currant liqueur and white wine, to be served in crystal Champagne flutes to the Germans, who expected the very best from the subservient French.

Avery glanced at the four men Plomion had placed in the role of kitchen staff. They seemed acclimated to their new positions with a self-assurance that defied their association with one of the most skilled, deadly assemblages of ordinary men in all of France. Their tenacity was unequaled, their commitment as deep as the caves of *Gouffre Mirolda*. These were the men who would serve *tartine de viande des grisons* one moment and, in the next, pull their hidden weapons and fire them at the invaders of their beloved country.

From the rear door, Olivier Plomion entered the kitchens carrying a long, thick loaf of bread. The French perceived themselves as connoisseurs of their culture, a twitch of their shoulders, a shift of their heads, then a bite into their loaf of bread and they were forever French. Avery smiled at Olivier. "My friend, must you exhibit the crudeness of a mongrel dog by eating bread without the accompaniment of wine?"

Plomion nodded at Bedeau. "The absence of wine is indeed unforgivable, Monsieur Bedeau."

Bedeau shook his head. "*Non*, I cannot deny you wine." He reached for one of the bottles lined along the table and poured a few glasses, offering one to Avery and then to Plomion. He poured one for himself and raised his glass. "To the reception." Each man followed with his own glass.

Avery noticed a glint in Plomion's eyes. "You have something to tell us?"

"*Non*, I have something to show you. Follow me." He left the kitchen and walked upstairs to the first floor landing, his loaf of bread balanced atop his shoulder. He turned and lifted the bread and dug out the bottom with his knife. From inside, he pulled a MAS 38 sub-machine gun. "Thirty-two rounds of pure fire," he said in hushed tones.

Avery studied the weapon. He had memories of using one as he fought with the *Résistance* a year ago near the Maginot Line, his fellow spy along side him. "It will be a lovely reception," he said.

***

Avery left the men on the first floor landing and walked up the stairs to Room 308. He was late for his liaison with Eléonore. He thought of her perfume, her dark eyes, her beguiling smile. They would share a quick bite at some small café, a glass of wine and then a return to the Crillon to prepare for the reception. He would speak to her about Édouard. It would be difficult, but he must.

He knocked on the door and waited. A few moments passed and he knocked again. "Eléonore," he called softly. He pulled his gun. When he pushed on the door, he called again. "Eléonore." Then, he felt the chill of the room sweep past him like a phantom wind, its emptiness filling him with unimaginable fear.

CHAPTER SIXTY-NINE

At one time, the cool cellars of the Hotel de L'Elysée held the finest wines in all of France. After the arrival of the Germans, they lay empty of their wines as well as the decrepit wine steward who had so carefully guarded the cellars for over thirty years. The innovative Germans had found other uses for the dank areas that lay buried beneath the lavish rooms of the once exquisite hotel. On this day, the cellars were empty, but forever waiting for someone who most likely would never again see daylight.

Horst Krenz opened the door of his office for Eléonore Delafloté. She brushed past him and turned her thin body to face him.

"Colonel Krenz, I fail to see the necessity of my being here. An interrogation could have just as easily been conducted in my hotel room." The clipped words in her raised voice filled the small room like flying bullets, each one finding the ears of the impudent German.

"Please, Madame Delafloté, sit." Krenz extended his hand toward a chair. He looked at her coldly. "May I remind you that you are in the presence of an officer of the Third Reich and you are in no position to make any demands? I can do anything I like with you."

Eléonore stared at Krenz with deliberating eyes. Her next words were spoken with such certainty that her host eased himself back into a shadowed corner of the room.

"My dear Colonel Krenz, your words are foul. Did they blister your tongue? Did you expect them to bruise my heart, slice my soul in two?" She laughed. "Who do you think you have here? A woman who falters at the sight of a Nazi uniform?"

She stepped closer to Krenz, her breath warm as it fell on his cheek. "You may ask me all the questions you like, but the answers will be my own."

Krenz' hand shot out and found Eléonore's soft cheek, the blow so hard that the small hat Eleonore wore flew across the room along with one of her small diamond earrings. Blood trickled from her nose and ran into the red lipstick that she had applied so carefully. She turned her eyes back to Krenz.

"Did that make you feel powerful, Monsieur Krenz? Hitting a woman who weighs one hundred ten pounds? I assure you I am no closer to answering the questions of the Third Reich than I was before you hit me."

Krenz' body slackened. His left eye wobbled toward the window while his right eye bore into her with undeniable anger.

"We shall see, Madame."

He walked to his chair and sat at the desk where he knew Édouard Delafloté's' file lay in wait. There was so much to ask. Where should he begin? He leaned back.

"Sit."

Eléonore ignored him and walked across the room and picked up her hat. One of the feathers was crushed against the floor beside her broken earring, her mother's earring. She stared at it until her eyes watered, then picked it up and placed it in her pocket. Without hurry, she returned the hat to her head and patted it as if it were a cat. Without turning around, she said, "Monsieur Krenz, may I ask *you* a question?"

Krenz studied the back of the woman. He wished he could see her face, her eyes. There was something about her that was unsettling. He could never be afraid of her, yet his instincts were at play. It was as if he could never truly know what she was thinking. She was unreadable, mysterious. His felt himself lean forward in anticipation. "I am listening."

Finally, she turned and looked at him.

"I am curious about your eye, Monsieur Krenz. Can you see out of it?" She held his one-eyed gaze.

For a moment, Krenz was not sure he heard her correctly. He stared without blinking into her black eyes. He couldn't breathe. Perhaps the mentioning of his wayward eye had turned him to stone.

He licked his lips slowly and heard the thudding sound of his heart beat in his ears, a hollow sound as though he had fallen down a deep well in the caverns of some obscure mountain. No one would ever find him. They would ask: whatever happened to that one-eyed German? *Wait, wait, he screamed, I am here. I am still one-eyed, but I am here.* He gasped and regained his breath. He looked at the woman for a long moment.

"Can I see out of it?" he asked.

"Yes," she said softly. "Is your eye . . . working?"

He wanted to laugh. *Why, of course, it's working. It belongs to a circus where odd, freakish people show their most unusual body parts. You know, a third foot, a second head, a crooked eye that is forever searching for its brother.*

Suddenly, almost as if it were a divine intervention, Krenz felt an unusual completeness, two-eyed instead of one. He was whole and all because someone had asked about his eye. He smiled at her.

"Your question is asked with kindness, I assume?"

She looked at him and returned his smile.

"Everything I do is with kindness, Monsieur Krenz."

She walked to the chair opposite him and sat. She crossed her legs, swiped at her hair and settled back into the chair as if she were at the opera. Her skin glowed in the pale light, reminiscent of a queen who reveled in the adoration of her subjects. She was no ordinary woman.

Krenz picked up the file and opened it. He studied it in silence while Eléonore followed the track of his eye. When he looked up, she was ready.

"Madame Delafloté, I have here a file on your husband, Édouard Delafloté. It's quite interesting."

Eléonore remained silent for a few moments while she gathered a handkerchief from her pocket and dabbed at the blood below her nostril.

"My husband has always been interesting. I am curious why you are interested in him."

Krenz smiled with such width that the missing tooth at the rear of his upper molars projected a black hole where a myriad of objects could be stored. Eléonore could not take her eyes away from the hollow space.

"Your husband is . . . shall we say . . . void of credibility."

"Credibility?"

"Yes, it seems he is sometimes alive and sometimes dead. How can that be?"

Eleonore lifted her chin. "Your ambiguity confuses me, Monsieur Krenz."

Again, the hollow hole in his molars. "I find your husband is two men."

"Your words amuse me."

Krenz pushed the file toward Eléonore. "This photograph. Your husband?

Eléonore leaned over and saw the photograph, found the eyes of her husband. Dark and brooding, they promised her a night of fervent lovemaking, a walk down the Champs Élysées, a glass of wine under the shadow of the Eiffel Tower. Her heart fell. His lips turned up slightly at the corners, seductive, enticing her to reach out and touch the picture with her finger.

"*Non*, this man is an imposter," she said in a far-away voice.

"I assure you that is Herr Delafloté, Madame," he said, tapping his thin finger on the photograph. "I personally saw to his death and yet inexplicably he rooms with you at the Hotel de Crillon?" He raised his eyebrows and waited.

Eléonore heard the bells of Notre-Dame as though they hung only meters above her head, their vibrations lifting her up and swinging her out into the universe with such clarity that she smiled. Such perfect sounds, she thought, as the photograph blurred.

"You saw the death of my husband?" she asked, in her far-away voice.

"Saw his death? My dear woman, I rejoiced in his death! He was a pigheaded Frenchman."

The words *rejoiced in his death* were like knives stabbing into Eléonore's heart, piercing it with such pain that she felt the air leave her lungs. She placed the handkerchief to her bloody nose and looked at Krenz. *I will rejoice in your death.* She pulled the handkerchief away and stared at the red stain.

***

Krenz sat alone in the dark of his office. Perhaps time in the cold cellars of the hotel would encourage the Madame to become more cooperative. So far, he felt she had been oblivious that he could, with one command, end her life. She had been in her ivory tower too long. Either that or she was the most cunning woman he had ever met.

He left his desk and walked to the window. Only a few hours before the grand reception. Any moment, Édouard Delafloté's imposter would walk through his door. He knew he would come for her.

CHAPTER SEVENTY

Gannon walked slowly around the room, his gun held tightly in front of him, like the head of snake, ready to strike. He smelled Eléonore's perfume, saw her opened jewelry box, a scarf draped across a small chair. Hanging on the edge of the armoire door were formal evening clothes, a lavish black gown for her, a tailored suede jacket for him. A cummerbund of gray silk lay against a pair of cuff links initialed with the letters *ED*. An ordinary scene except for one important detail: Eléonore was not there.

He rushed to the window and examined the street below. The fading light of day fell across the facades of shops and cafés along the sidewalks where busy Parisians rushed toward their homes to comply with the curfew, their bicycles whizzing with obvious urgency. In the distance, the Eiffel Tower was barely visible, its iron legs and tip blending with the ashen color of the sky. At that moment, the lights blinked on along the delicate lace of the tower and the structure became alive in the near nighttime sky.

Gannon lifted the window and craned his body outward. And, there it was. Just what he was looking for. A Horch 852 glided around the corner and out of sight. He slammed the window shut and raced out of the room, down the stairs and across the hotel lobby.

"Plomion!" Gannon yelled as he headed toward the kitchens. "Plomion, where are you?"

***

From inside the kitchens, Olivier Plomion heard Gannon's frantic call and immediately pulled his pistol. He ran toward the front of the kitchen where the big doors swung open and revealed a frenzied Avery Gannon waving his pistol.

"It's Eléonore. I'm certain Krenz has her. Did anyone see him?

"*Non*, monsieur." Plomion shook his head and looked around the room.

"Let's go!"

"The curfew."

"Fuck the curfew!"

"Wait!" Plomion held up his hand. "Let's not be foolish. The reception is a mere two hours away. We cannot jeopardize our plans."

Gannon leaned forward and pushed the muzzle of his gun into Plomion's belly with such force that the Frenchman grimaced.

"Monsieur Plomion, it is quite clear to me that our plans have changed." His eyes blazed as he pulled his weapon from Plomion. "We will go to Gestapo Headquarters and arrive, hopefully, before Eléonore is taken to the cellars."

Plomion nodded, but the doubt in his eyes was obvious. "What will we do once we get there? If we get there?"

Gannon backed away and began to pace along the long walls of the kitchen. When he stopped, he looked up to the ceiling above him. Without turning around, he said, "If we have to, we'll trade the English spy for Eléonore Delafloté."

Plomion stared at Gannon's back. "You're a dead man."

His shoulders taunt, the Englishman turned around and smiled. "Really? What makes you say that, Olivier?"

Plomion studied Gannon's face carefully. "What makes me say that? Because it's true. Krenz will parade you directly to the cellars where he and Müller will delight in interrogating you. After all, you are their most-wanted assassin. You will not survive."

Gannon sauntered around the long table and stood by Plomion. "Once again, I find you a pompous, know-it-all Frenchman, who lacks imagination."

Plomion held Gannon's stare. He had been called pompous before. "Once again, I find you an arrogant Englishman." A slight smile creased his face. "And this imagination I lack? I assume you have it?"

"Enough for the both of us."

CHAPTER SEVENTY-ONE

Gannon met Plomion in the alley behind the hotel. They left the Place de la Concorde and made their way to 12 Rue des Saussaies, both men pedaling their bicycles leisurely, simply two Frenchmen on their way home from work. They passed soldiers at every turn who stared menacingly at the confluence of ordinary Parisians ending their day. When they sang *Et La Java* as they weaved through the streets, a few soldiers seemed amused at their repertoire and shook their heads at the loud off-key notes.

On Rue des Saussaies, as bicycles streamed by, Gannon braked and leaned his bicycle on a tree trunk, Plomion behind him, and stood in the shadows. "Assume a few of your *girls* are with you?"

"*Oui*, I have the little darlings."

"We have little time." Gannon looked at his watch. "It's 5:00. At 5:10, I'll plan an entry by the kitchen door. If that doesn't work, it will have to be the main entrance. I will depend on your *girls* to divert attention away from me if you see I have to go through the front entrance, so keep a close eye on me."

Gannon eyed the Frenchman. His confidence in him was unparalleled, a man who had remarkable instincts. Too bad he was a surly Frenchman.

He hesitated, a hardness creeping up his jaw line. "If I do not leave with Eléonore, you know what to do."

"*Oui.*"

At the rear of the building where kitchen deliveries were made, Gannon melted into the shadows. Once, while in Paris, a few years before the fall of France, he had stayed at the L'Elysee and, now, as he observed the large wooden door, he remembered he had made love to a woman in the grand suite where candles glimmered softly and skimmed her naked body with golden light; a compatriot of his, who later died on a mission in Poland. Sadly, he could not remember her name, only that her lovemaking was as passionate as her commitment to her cause.

He didn't have long to wait as the door opened and two young men pulled a garbage cart to the rear alley. Gannon slipped inside and made his way to the second floor where he knew Krenz sat at his desk waiting for him.

***

The hallway lay in semi-darkness, its sconces dimly lighting the ceiling above, while below a rug absorbed Gannon's steps, steps that brought him closer to the doorway of Krenz' office. He didn't want to kill Krenz. Not yet. His presence at the reception would be necessary if their plan was to be successful.

When Gannon arrived at the doorway, he pressed his body against the cold wall. He breathed deeply as he slipped his hand into his coat and felt his weapon. He could feel the thump of his heart. From inside the small office, an almost friendly voice called out.

"Do come in, Herr Delafloté, and let's have a little chat." The words were honey-filled, from a voice that hid the presence of malice, but made one pause and consider its source.

Gannon smiled to himself. The Gestapo chief had not disappointed him. He stepped through the doorway and found himself face to face with a smiling Krenz.

"By all means," he said. "Let's do have a little chat."

The room became still as the two men observed each other, a slow scrutiny that seemed to permeate their very skin. Gannon could almost smell a Nazi stench in the air, like a poisonous gas that promised instant death. He found himself wanting to pull his weapon. This was the man who had murdered Édouard Delafloté.

"Where is Madame Delafloté?" he asked.

"Nearby," Krenz answered.

"Where?"

Krenz shrugged his shoulders. "Near."

Gannon reached behind him and closed the door. He swept his eyes around the small office, a bed in the corner, a small chair near the window. The room was austere for the chief of the Paris Gestapo. It was cold, dimly lit, a perfect place for the brewing of evil.

"What is the purpose of bringing Madame Delafloté to Gestapo Headquarters?"

Krenz leaned forward on the desk and folded his hands in front of him. "There are some things troubling me."

"What does Madame Delafloté have to do with those things?"

Krenz smiled broadly and gazed at the ceiling. When he looked at Gannon, his right eye narrowed, devil-like.

"Everything."

Gannon moved slowly from the doorway and sat in the chair opposite Krenz. He studied the man's face, the crooked eye, the lopsided smile, knowing he must suppress his anger if he were to see Eléonore. "I'm listening," he said in a calm voice.

Krenz opened the file on Édouard Delafloté and turned it around. "See this man's picture?"

"Yes."

"Recognize him?"

Gannon stared at the photograph and saw his fellow spy. *Hello, Frenchie. I'm here, my friend. Your Eléonore needs help. I didn't mean to involve her in my life; it just happened.*

"No, I do not recognize him."

"I find that strange," he mused. "Madame Delafloté said the same thing. That is what troubles me."

Krenz stood from his chair and walked to the opposite side of the room. "If you are Édouard Delafloté, who is the man in the photograph?"

"Where did you get the photograph?" Gannon felt himself waver between his perspicuity as a spy and his surmised innocence as a French aristocrat. He knew Krenz was on the brink of putting all the pieces together, the cusp of a discovery.

"The file and the photograph came from Berlin. I am sure of their accuracy." Krenz stopped at the window and looked out.

Gannon pulled the file closer. A formal Gestapo file on Édouard Delafloté. But why? Did Berlin suspect his affiliation with the Allies from the very beginning of Hitler's storm across Europe? He scanned the file quickly and saw the comments under "status." *Possible agent for England as well as France. Long periods of absence from residence. Association with suspected members of the French Résistance. Keep under surveillance at all times. 1940 August 16.*

August 1940. Delafloté had made a trip to England just after the German invasion into France and returned as an agent for MI6. Obviously, he had been watched all along. *Wonder when they acquired the photograph?*

"That's odd," said Gannon, his brow in deep furrow.

Krenz turned and looked at Gannon. "What is odd?"

"The photograph. The man in the photograph looks a lot like me. The similarity is amazing."

Gannon shook his head. "I am mystified. Wonder who he is?" He kept his voice light, a passing interest in the photograph.

Krenz licked his lips, a nervous habit he had acquired when he was six years old, on his first day of school. He remembered the scrutiny of his classmates as he walked across the classroom, every eye on him as he found his seat, his skinny little legs barely reaching the floor. Even the teacher had observed him with curiosity. He had looked around the classroom in hopes another child might also have a crooked eye. To his dismay, he saw that they were all perfect.

"So, you think the man in the photograph is not Édouard Delafloté?"

"But, of course not. I am Édouard Delafloté." Gannon smiled at Krenz in an almost condescending gesture. "I am curious, Monsieur Krenz. Why would you doubt my identity?"

The face that held the crooked eye turned hard. No more pleasantries as Krenz returned to his chair and studied Gannon.

"I arrested the man in the photograph." He leaned back, lifted his chin and turned his face to the left, giving Gannon only his right eye.

His next words were smug. "Not only did I arrest him, I shot him. An obstinate chap, he was. Almost belligerent. I am certain he was Édouard Delafloté."

Gannon felt a rise of his body heat. His fingers twitched, his trigger finger burning and searching. It would be so simple to slip his hand inside his coat, pull his weapon in a matter of seconds and fire. The act would alleviate his growing rage. But, what would follow? A barrage of Germans who would strip him of his power to find and rescue Eléonore. He forced himself to stare stoically at Krenz. He must find Eléonore. He then playfully patted his chest.

"But, Édouard Delafloté is sitting across from you at this very moment." He allowed his eyes to soften.

The silence that followed permitted the thoughts of both men to wander. Krenz suspected the man who sat across from him was not Édouard Delafloté, yet who was he? Gannon saw the German deliberating, vacillating between an outright accusation and a deliberate hesitancy. It was obvious Krenz faltered, but why? Then, it hit him. Krenz did not want to fail. He craved perfection, a perfection that would astound Müller, astound Berlin with his brilliant, though one-eyed, self.

Gannon stood. "The reception is in one hour. I would like to take my wife with me so she may dress for this illustrious event?"

Krenz jerked as if awakened from a deep sleep. "The reception. Yes, I'm sure Herr Müller will not be late. He is anxious to meet you." He smiled and let his eye slowly wander across Gannon's face. "Whoever you are."

Krenz did not fool Gannon. The man had no intention of leaving the mystery unsolved. He had the way of a serpent, a serpent that whispered foul words of malevolence as though he were the devil himself.

Gannon turned toward the door only to hear Krenz' final words.

"One more thing. The English spy. Herr Bedeau tells me the spy will be in my hands at Noon tomorrow." His small hands closed the file on Édouard Delafloté as he looked up.

"Perhaps you will ensure that Bedeau delivers as promised." Krenz reached for the attaché case and slipped the file inside. He then casually straightened the belt that carried his weapon, his long, thin fingers grasping the leather and positioning the holster meticulously in place. He gave Gannon a half smile,

"Bedeau delivers the spy, I give you Madame Delafloté."

Gannon kept his eyes on Krenz'.

"Madame Delafloté will leave Gestapo Headquarters with me." Gone was the facade of a suave gentleman of the French aristocracy; a hardened man who had no intention of acquiescing to his enemy had replaced it.

Krenz laughed and shook his head. "Ah, you Frenchmen. You are so forgetful." He placed his hand atop the flap of his holster. "May I remind you that you are in a city occupied by an enemy? You may do nothing unless I say you may."

Gannon released his hand from the doorknob and walked a few steps to Krenz' desk. The power of his lean body would fool anyone who saw him. Beneath the fine wool jacket was a man who could simply reach out and crack a neck so quickly his victim would never see it coming. Now, as Édouard Delafloté, Gannon felt himself tense. It was at this moment he must suppress the rage he felt. He hesitated. When he spoke, his words were cajoling.

"What makes you think Monsieur Bedeau knows the whereabouts of the spy?"

Krenz threw his head back and laughed heartily. His shoulders shook, his eyes squeezed shut. Abruptly, he stood and walked to within a few feet of Gannon, his grin wide.

"You may take Madame Delafloté with you. That is how certain I am that Monsieur Bedeau will deliver the spy to me as promised." He walked to the door and opened it. "She's in the next room." He straightened his jacket and adjusted his holstered gun. "A charming woman. I look forward to seeing you both tonight." His eyes narrowed. "Don't be late."

***

Krenz returned to his desk and leaned back in his chair. His placed his legs across the desk and closed his eyes, letting his thoughts remain on Édouard Delafloté. He was certain he was an imposter and a brilliant one at that. Try as he might, he could not discern exactly what it was about him that seemed fraudulent. But, it was there, nonetheless. He could not have studied Delafloté any deeper than if he had opened his skull with a scalpel and exposed his brain. He spoke like a Frenchman, looked like a Frenchman and, as Frenchman do so well, escorted a beautiful woman around the City of Paris.

Krenz' eyes snapped open, his breath catching in his throat. He stood and walked to the window where the lights of Paris seemed brighter than ever. *He smelled the blood of an Englishman.*

CHAPTER SEVENTY-TWO

Gannon left Krenz' office and walked a few steps down the hall. To his right, a closed door. When he opened it, he saw Eléonore standing at the window, the fading light of day touching her face. She turned and looked at him. "Is that you, Édouard?" He moved closer. Her eyes were dull, the lids half closed. She fell into his arms. "Hold me, Édouard."

CHAPTER SEVENTY-THREE

Olivier Plomion watched as Gannon and Eléonore left Gestapo Headquarters. "Come, we must hurry." Only a few short moments of Paris daylight remained as all three hurried to the Crillon.

"I was hoping to use some of my little girls for you, but I see you were successful."

"Barely." He squeezed Eléonore's arm and felt her shiver as he pulled her along. When they crossed the avenue, Gannon slowed his walk and turned to Plomion.

"As soon as we get to the hotel, we'll dress. Meanwhile, I'll see you a few minutes before 7:00 in the kitchens. Brief your men as necessary." The Frenchman was in charge, not him. He spoke quietly. "The plan is the same, I assume. During the reception, a few minutes before 8:00, I'll take Eléonore back to the room. Then, return."

Plomion nodded. "We are ready."

***

The lights in the Hotel de Crillon were festive. Three large chandeliers hung in the ballroom in a display of opulence, something the French did well. Outside the entryway, along the sidewalks, soldiers walked in pairs along the Avenue. Except for those attending the reception, the streets would be deserted in minutes.

In the kitchens, Monsieur Bedeau and Madame Lefèbvre worked feverishly on final details of food and presentation. Thankfully, Madame Lefèbvre had forgiven Bedeau for burning her croissants and, humming happily, had miraculously turned the four men from the *labor pool* into acceptable kitchen staff. Their hands and nails were immaculate, their uniforms meticulously cleaned and pressed. She had even trimmed their mustaches and beards.

At twenty minutes until 7:00, she poured them each a glass of wine and gave them final instructions. She was an extraordinary woman even though it was well known throughout the city that she trapped the cats that roamed her neighborhood and stewed them for Sunday dinner.

Upstairs in Room 308, a silent Eléonore dressed in her black gown. Gannon sat on the small lounge across from the bed and drank Cognac and watched as she dabbed perfume behind her delicate ears. He had poured a glass for her and placed it next to her jewelry case. "Come sit with me a moment."

She clasped a string of pearls around her neck and looked at him. Her eyes were pensive; a dark brooding veil of anger had surfaced there and stayed. He noticed her hands shook; red splotches lined the contours of her neck. She was an angry woman. "In a moment," she replied.

Before their arrival at the reception, she must gain control, thought Gannon. If she didn't, she cannot perform, as she must.

"I am here," he said quietly. He could do nothing more than wait. When they had returned to the room, she screamed and cursed, had buried her face into a pillow to smother her sobs. She tore at her hair, threw her shoes across the room. When she finished, she lay in a heap in the middle of the room. At last, a reckoning. Her Édouard was dead. The German had told her so.

She finished dressing and looked at him. Her face had hardened, hiding the innocent, child-like wonder of a life without war and death. Make-up hid the mark on her face where the Gestapo chief had slapped her. "I am ready."

He smiled. "Of course, you are. You are lovely."

A slight smile and she looked away. He, too, had dressed and evolved into the handsome and debonair Count Édouard Delafloté. The Germans adored the aristocracy of France, the culture, the titles. When she looked at him, he knew she no longer saw him as her husband, but rather the imposter he was. The German had killed more than Édouard Delafloté; he had also killed the woman who was his wife. Now, as her shadowed eyes watched him, he felt a deep sadness.

"You have forgotten your cufflinks," she said.

"So, I have. Would you put them on for me, please?"

She nodded and crossed the room and sat beside him. Her delicate hands lifted the cuff and attached the monogrammed jewelry. "I like your hands." Abruptly, she looked at him. "They kill Germans, don't they?"

Gannon's dark eyes softened while he reached up and touched her cheek. "They do. But, they can also be tender."

She remained quiet while she attached the second cuff link. Her fingers were nimble. Oddly, Gannon envisioned them holding a weapon and pulling the trigger. Could such lovely hands perform such heinous acts? He reached out and pulled her to him. "What can I do except love you, Eléonore?"

At last she answered. "You can never leave me."

CHAPTER SEVENTY-FOUR

A soft tap on the door. Avery approached and placed his hand on the doorknob, but did not open it. *"Oui?"*

A moment of silence. Spanish words. *"Se sabia que venia. Hay que hablar."* Yes, he knew he was coming. Yes, they needed to talk.

"Si. Un momento, por favor," he replied and turned to look at Eléonore. "I'll be a moment." He pulled open the door and stepped out into the dimly lit hallway.

In the shadows, a figure emerged and extended his hand. "Gannon."

Gannon nodded. "I wondered if they would send someone." He swept his eyes across the dark face. "I see I was right."

The Spaniard said nothing as he handed Avery a cigarette and lit one for himself. When he inhaled a long, slow breath, he looked around the hallway. "Safe?"

"Safe enough?"

Gannon had known the Spaniard a while. Juan Castillo, a veteran SIS operative. An agent prized by Britain, Castillo was assuredly one of their most efficient and versatile spies. He had run missions from Poland to Spain to Russia. His Spanish citizenship gave him a neutrality that allowed his movement all across Europe. As far as anyone knew, he worked for Franco, the Germans, the Russians, but never the British. How wrong they were. Castillo was as British as if he had been the offspring of the King and Queen themselves. It was no surprise His Majesty's Secret Service had sent him to bring home a wayward spy, a spy who had ignored a summons by MI6 as though it were a frivolous request to play rugby on the lawn of Kensington Palace.

"You're in a lot of trouble." There was a wry smile on Juan's lips.

"What do you base that on?" A hint of irritation crossed Gannon's face.

Juan shrugged and let the smoke from his cigarette cloud above them. "The fact you have disobeyed very specific orders."

Gannon nodded and tapped the ash of his cigarette on the edge of the doorframe. "What else?"

"Delafloté? What happened?"

Gannon felt the air leave his lungs in a long sigh. "Mission gone wrong. He took too many chances. Nothing I could do. The Gestapo captured him at the train station."

"He was a good man."

All at once the air in the hallway seemed suffocating. Gannon closed his eyes. "Yes. Yes, he was."

"The woman? His wife?"

Gannon raised his voice. "What about her?"

Juan's eyes narrowed. "Are you involved with her?"

Gannon shook his head, the words leaving his mouth like dangerous projectiles. "She's jeopardized nothing."

"That's not what I asked." Juan placed his cigarette in his lips and waited.

"I know what you asked me, Castillo. Yes, I'm involved."

"You stayed because of her?"

There was hesitation on Gannon's face. "No."

"I do not believe you." Juan stamped out his cigarette. "Get your things together and meet me at the safe house at 10:00 o'clock. The Service won't wait another day."

Gannon stiffened. "Can't oblige you."

Juan said nothing as he buttoned his coat and placed his worn fedora on his head. "I've spoken with Olivier Plomion at length. He tells me of your planned raid tonight at the reception. If you survive it, you and the woman come to the safe house.

With any luck, we can get out of France alive."

Juan's words were matter-of-fact. Gannon studied his face carefully and saw the weariness in his eyes. His own words were brittle, chillingly unambiguous.

"Nothing must happen to the woman."

Juan reached in his pocket and pulled out a pack of Melachrino cigarettes.

"Here. I brought you these. Know they're your favorite." He began to walk away, but stopped after a few feet and turned. "I am aware of your plans regarding Krenz. Don't let that be the end of you." Unlike the hardened agent he was, his face softened. "Or the woman."

In a moment, Castillo's thin frame disappeared down the hallway. It was if he hadn't been there at all, merely an apparition that had simply appeared to impart a few sage words. Gannon smiled to himself. MI6 had sent the legendary Juan Castillo to save his hide.

CHAPTER SEVENTY-FIVE

At 6:50, Gannon escorted Eléonore to the elevator. He had no weapon; he knew he would be searched. He felt stirrings of the same defiance that had steered him away from his grandmother's prickly command that he become a priest. It was the same resolve he carried with him on every mission: an alertness to his task, a simple desire to stay alive. But, this time it was different; his desire to stay alive was two-fold. He must protect Eléonore. His arrangements with Bedeau and Plomion had been specific. In the event of his death, they would ensure her safety. Was that too much to ask for the Englishman who had come to France and murdered Germans for eight months? They owed him that, didn't they? And, what about his fellow spy? He must avenge Édouard Delafloté's death.

The elevator opened in front of them and they stepped inside. Gannon smiled when he saw Bedeau. The old man was dressed in his finest wool suit, a deep, charcoal gray, brushed to perfection. It appeared as if Madame Lefébvre's scissors had found his hair. No longer did it fly in rebellious tufts around his head, but lay in perfect order, as if summoned by a king to obey.

"Monsieur Bedeau, your handsomeness is sure to sweep Madame Delafloté off her feet." Avery chuckled softly.

Eléonore laughed. "Monsieur, my heart is beating so quickly, I cannot breathe."

Bedeau blushed. "Ah, the magic of a woman. Madame Lefèbvre tied me to a kitchen chair and breathed her foul breath on me for twenty minutes while she cut away. She used the same shears she uses to cut up poultry. Most likely, I smell of wet chicken feathers."

Such banal conversation in the prelude to their meeting with the Germans. In moments, everything would change.

CHAPTER SEVENTY-SIX

The splendor of the ballroom at the de Crillon fell quietly on the Paris evening, its elegance belying the plight of the Parisians, who had little to eat and who shivered in the cold of a bitter winter. In times past, guests had listened to magnificent orchestras and danced on a floor of marble that had been imported from Italy, the same marble used in the Catherine Palace in St. Petersburg. Eléonore herself had danced there as a young girl, her shimmering gown reflected in the gilded mirrors that graced the tall windows.

When Gannon and Eléonore entered the room, a sea of German uniforms greeted them, men whose tunics held the medals that proclaimed them the heroes of the Third Reich. The slaughterers of innocents all across Europe puffed out their chests with self-importance, confident in their belief that Germany would rule the world and they, as the supreme beings they were, would reap the rewards. They moved about the room to the cadence of peacocks, while their hearts beat with a blackness that defied any semblance of humanity.

Gannon's hand rested on Eléonore's elbow as he guided her to a shadowed corner. He felt the Germans watching as he handed her a glass a wine.

"Smile, Eléonore. You have nothing to fear," he said softly. He lifted a glass to his lips and glanced casually around the room. He saw Horst Krenz in animated conversation with Heinrich Müller. Both men held champagne flutes, filled but untouched. Their Führer promoted abstinence and they always obeyed their Führer.

To Müller's left, a stout, balding man with a red face listened intently. He was Carl-Heinrich von Stülpnagel. Gannon recognized him from his training at MI6, where photographs of Germany's hierarchy were pinned to large boards in their classrooms. He never forgot a face.

From his vantage point, he observed the four uniformed kitchen staff. They worked as though they had served large events their entire lives. They were unobtrusive and hardly observed. Madame Lefèbvre must have threatened them with the wrath of her kitchen knives if their performance was anything but perfection.

The men were calm and focused on their work; a subterfuge that would allow them to carry out what was to come. Not once did Gannon see any indication that they weren't who they pretended to be. The Germans were oblivious. Even Krenz, whose instincts were razor-sharp, seemed totally involved in the circle of officers around him, his one good eye darting nervously to Müller, careful to twist the wayward eye as far from his right as possible.

From the Germans, Gannon's gaze turned to Bedeau, who had just entered the room from the main doors. He, too, seemed unusually calm. He smiled as he nodded to Gannon and Eléonore. The esprit de corps of the two men went unnoticed, hidden in their own little secrets; they knew something no one else knew. Together, they would fight the Germans the best way they knew: their intellect. Bedeau played his role well; humble and accommodating. Yet, within his own thoughts, he moved about the room as if he, and he alone, had the power to overcome the evil that lay hidden beneath the uniforms of the Germans who surrounded him.

At that moment, Gannon saw Krenz and stilled. He would kill him before the next Paris sunrise.

Sandwiched between Müller and Von Stülpnagel, Krenz eyes found Gannon's. The two men stared at each other a long moment before Gannon tipped his head slightly in greeting, then turned to Eléonore and smiled.

"You are the most beautiful woman in Paris." He moved closer, a gesture of reassurance as he saw the slight shaking of Eléonore's hand.

Quietly, almost a whisper, "I am going to walk across the room and subject myself to our German friends."

The bitterness in Gannon's words caused Eléonore to smile. "Englishman," she said softly, "this is no time to be pompous." She touched him lightly on the arm. "Don't be away long."

Gannon placed his hand on top of hers. "You know very well I cannot be away from you for more than a moment." He stepped away and realized her hand had been as cold as the ice that hung from the rooftops.

CHAPTER SEVENTY-SEVEN

The long strides across the room seemed kilometers instead of a few meters. The knowledge that in less than an hour the room would erupt into the dessert *flambé* that Plomion had promised loomed heavy in Gannon's gaze as he swept his eyes across the stand of Germans he now faced.

Müller was the first to speak. "Ah, Herr Delaflotè, at last we meet." His somewhat handsome face broke into a half smile. His eyes, however, were hard and calculating. He continued in a booming voice.

"I hear great things about your philanthropic endeavors on behalf of this war. How courageous of you." He ran his gaze quickly over the fine jacket Gannon wore, finely resting on the gold monogrammed cuff links. He paused as though he had made a decision.

"Your position in the French aristocracy permits you to wield your money and power in any way you choose." A slight chuckle. "How interesting you've chosen to immerse yourself into this war by helping those who suffer the wounds of battle."

From his peripheral vision, Gannon saw Bedeau ease to the side of Eléonore. He counted the four Frenchman who served wine, two to his right, two to his left. He caught a glimpse of

Madame Lefèbvre lighting candles near the entryway. He heard the strike of the match and smelled the phosphorus as the flame flushed orange. It was though his senses were heightened, magnified into something bigger, stronger, closer.

He felt his body steel into the man who for eight long years had carried his favorite assassin's rifle and whose finger had rested on its trigger only an instant before a bullet tore out of the barrel and found its target.

He smiled warmly at Müller. "A privilege, I assure you, Monsieur Müller. I am a Frenchman and my heart belongs to my country." Casually, he pulled out the small package of cigarettes Juan Castillo had given him and placed one between his lips. He puffed gently as the flame of a match touched the end.

Across from him, Krenz moved slightly toward Gannon. "I would enjoy one of your cigarettes," he said as he extended his hand.

Gannon shook the pack and watched as Krenz's thin fingers pulled one out. "Of course."

Krenz fingered the cigarette for a moment. "An unusual cigarette." He pretended to study it closely. "I seem to remember your telling me you preferred a fine cigar, Herr Delafloté."

An awareness of danger spiked Gannon's heart rate. Krenz had asked him questions about cigarettes at Gestapo Headquarters.

"A fine cigar with a sip of fine Cognac, if I recall our conversation correctly." He paused. "And you, Monsieur Krenz? Do you recognize this cigarette as a Melachrino, an Egyptian tobacco?"

Krenz hesitated. "As a matter of fact, I do." A slight smile broke his stone face, as if he had been given the answer to an age-old mystery.

Gannon nodded but said nothing. He turned slightly to his right and caught Bedeau looking his way, saw the stoic face and wondered what the old man was thinking. He jerked when Müller called across the room to Bedeau.

"Herr Bedeau, I would like a word with you." Müller looked at Gannon. "Would you excuse me, Herr Delafloté. Herr Bedeau and I have some important things to discuss."

Gannon watched as Müller met Bedeau halfway across the large room. He noticed Bedeau walked slowly, perhaps the same walk when he returned to Paris at the end of the Great War, savoring the air, the strength of life that pushed him toward home. He marveled at Bedeau's demeanor, a self-assured Frenchman, besotted with patriotism like no other man on earth. He was from the old France and it showed. Now, as the German closed in on him, Bedeau's height seemed to rise, his presence like that of a matador who is faced with a ferocious bull.

Colonel Horst Krenz's decided he would, indeed, sip his glass of champagne. A celebration was in order. The revelation had come to him with quiet brilliance, perhaps by a divine vision. His smiling lips touched the edge of the crystal flute as he watched Delafloté in animated conversation with Von Stülpnagel. *You are the English spy. And, how do I know this?* He almost laughed outloud. *Who else could you be?*

He would arrest him at the end of the reception, in the presence of Germany's Gestapo chief, in front of some of the Third Reich's most powerful men. *Such a grand moment.*

CHAPTER SEVENTY-EIGHT

Heinrich Müller's swagger toward the Frenchman was meant to intimidate. It did nothing of the sort as Bedeau smiled warmly at the German. "Monsieur Müller, I trust you are enjoying the evening."

Müller seemed surprised at Bedeau's calm words and watched him with interest. "It has been very pleasant." He leaned forward in an animated cower, lowered his voice to a conspiratorial whisper.

"Herr Krenz tells me of your plans to turn over the English spy tomorrow at Noon."

He paused and frowned. He stammered his words in a pretense of confusion. "How troubling to me that you cannot give him to us . . . at this very moment." Müller raised his eyebrows high on his forehead in feigned perplexity, while casually, but with a grand show of intention, rested his hand on his holstered weapon.

Bedeau's eyes twinkled as though Mrs. Bedeau had exposed her enormous breasts to him and made promises of grand lovemaking. He lifted his wine glass and sipped thoughtfully. His eyes searched the room, the grand chandeliers, the ornate paintings of French artists Manet and Degas and finally the black knee-high boots of the Germans. With the utmost care, he lifted his chin and stared into the eyes of the German.

"And it is troubling to me that you occupy my country and force my countrymen to eat only bread." He smiled with contrived sincerity. "Perhaps then, we are even?"

The fingers on Müller's right hand tightened on his weapon while a red streak of anger pulsated across his brow like a crawling insect. He was momentarily speechless, thrown into a frozen statue by a shriveled up old Frenchman whose height barely reached the epaulets of his uniform. The stiffness of his jaw magnified the fury in the thin set of his lips as a cold smile creased his face.

"At this very moment, you are only moments away from a sure death. Did you know that?" His words were meant to sear the skin from Bedeau's face.

Bedeau nodded. "All Parisians have been in danger of death since your army marched down the Place de la Concorde and under the Arc de Triomphe." He shrugged.

Müller unsnapped his holster and removed his pistol, a growl of anger in his throat. He looked across the room at Madame Lefèbvre, who busily arranged dessert dishes on the tables.

"I shall put a bullet through her head and then we'll see if that troubles you."

Bedeau did not move, did not turn around and look across the room at Madame Lefèbvre. Instead, he sipped his wine. "Do whatever you wish." He paused, his blue eyes calm, his voice like the softness of a morning fog. "And I will do the same."

From behind, Gannon watched the two men in conversation, saw Müller remove his pistol, saw Bedeau casually sip his wine.

In a corner of the room, Krenz's back was turned as he stood close to Eléonore and placed a glass of wine in her hand. The four French waiters remained stoic, but caught the infinitesimal shake of Gannon's head that warned them to hold their positions.

When Müller returned his pistol to its holster, Gannon, with a forced nonchalant gait, meandered across to the center of the room and, ignoring Müller, spoke to Bedeau.

"Monsieur Bedeau, is it my imagination or did you somehow find Château Latour for our grand reception this evening?"

Bedeau responded with an almost comical wave of his arm.

"Indeed. The Ritz' Chef Escoffier allowed his wine steward to give me the key to his cellars. Quite generous of him, I assure you."

Still smiling, Gannon turned to Müller. "Let me pour you a glass of this excellent Bordeaux, Monsieur Müller."

Müller, his voice gutteral as if from the bowels of hell, narrowed his eyes and looked from Gannon to Bedeau.

"You may keep your wine." Shoulders stiff with anger, he left the center of the room and found his staff watching him with discerning eyes.

When Gannon spoke, he seemed almost reverent. "My dear friend, if it wouldn't cause a scene, I would fall to my knees in rapt admiration."

Bedeau swiped his fingers across the mustache Madame Lefèbvre had so meticulously trimmed. "The bastard," he said quietly. "Before this night is over, I shall happily hang his testicles from the Eiffel Tower."

"Your knowledge of the English spy is the only thing that has saved your skin, you know."

"Of course." Bedeau finally looked into Gannon's eyes. "How badly they want you, monsieur. Hitler himself waits for word of your demise." He shook his head. "Ah, the joy I will feel when this is over."

Gannon leaned closer and with a quiet tenderness said, "You realize that you and Madame Bedeau will be transported to the safe house later tonight and then to England."

Bedeau nodded. "Yes, I am aware." He took a breath. "It is my hope that Madame Bedeau will be doused with laudanum before she is packed into a sack for the journey. She is not an agreeable woman when it comes to crossing the Channel."

"I'm not sure about the laudanum, but certainly we can find a large bottle of vodka."

Both men laughed and sipped their wine. Gannon turned around and his eyes found the corner of the room where he had left Eléonore. It was empty. Quickly, he scanned the entire ballroom. There was no sign of her. More disturbing, there was also no sign of Krenz.

CHAPTER SEVENTY-NINE

Colonel Horst Krenz' hand rested on the elbow of Eléonore Delafloté as they left the ballroom and walked to the hotel elevator. "You are so kind, Colonel Krenz, to accompany me to my room. A coat will diminish the chill I feel. It will only take a moment."

"My pleasure, I assure you."

They said nothing more as Eléonore opened the door of Room 308 and stepped inside. Krenz followed and watched as she removed the luxurious black sable from the armoire.

"Colonel Krenz," she said, as she pushed her arms into the sleeves of the coat, "It occurs to me that you and I did not discuss some important things while I was in your office earlier today."

Eléonore's words were like fine whiskey; smooth and captivating; yet, simmering beneath was a trace of something more.

Krenz raised his eyebrows in interest. One of the Gestapo's most skilled interrogators would never miss discussing something of importance. His brow furrowed deeply as his mind seemed to skim across the time he had spent with her.

"I find that hard to believe." He moved closer. "What is it that you feel we have missed?"

Eléonore slipped her hand in a pocket of her fur and pulled out a small photograph of Édouard. She looked at it intently, saw the tenderness in his eyes, the curve of his lips as they formed a slight smile. Almost absentmindedly, she rubbed her thumb across the paper and was taken back to the time of their first meeting. When she looked up at Krenz, her eyes were half closed, like that of an animal in rapt focus before a kill.

"I don't believe you have seen this picture."

Krenz reached out and took the photograph, bringing it closer to his good eye. Eléonore saw the eyeball in his crooked eye jump sideways in a rapid back and forth movement. She also saw redness creep up his neck and across his face. He looked at her.

"This is the man arrested at the train station."

Eléonore nodded. "It is also the man you murdered." She lifted her chin and stared into Krenz' right eye.

"Madame, it is obvious to me that I was right all along." The smugness of Krenz' words touched Eléonore's skin and covered it like a plague, her hair rising along the back of her neck.

"I did, indeed, murder your husband. And that leads us to the next topic of conversation." Krenz rubbed the leather of his holster as tenderly as the breast of a woman. "The demise of the imposter who calls himself Édouard Delafloté. The English spy."

Eléonore's lips spread wide in a haughty grin.

"Why, my dear Colonel Krenz. Indeed, he is the *English* spy." She threw her head back and laughed.

"You foolish man, you." Her expression then turned bitter, her eyes thinned into slits that bordered on a demonic trance. Her words spewed like poison. "If you had had *two* good eyes, it would have been quite obvious to you from the beginning."

Krenz said nothing as his hand became still on his holster, a rage seeming to build within him. His mouth twisted into an animal snarl. "You French bitch." He unsnapped the flap on his holster and pulled out his gun.

Without the slightest hesitation, Eléonore's finger pulled the trigger of the gun nestled in the pocket of her fur. She fired a second time. A third bullet found the heart of Krenz as he slumped to his knees. His face was upturned and watching her, his expression confused, then angry. The fragile French woman was not so fragile after all.

CHAPTER EIGHTY

In the grand ballroom of the Crillon, Gannon looked at his watch. In ten minutes, Olivier Plomion and his men would begin their attack on the Germans. In a haze of bullets, men would die and their blood would stain the rich rugs once owned by the King of France. His glance around the room went unnoticed as the Germans continued their discussions of battles across Europe and the war that would make them the rulers of the world. He turned and walked hurriedly from the room. Once outside, he smiled at a soldier who stood at the entryway. "Good evening. I was wondering if Herr Krenz has been this way?"

"No one has passed this way in the past hour," he said.

From the lobby, he ran to the stairs, perspiration wetting his body, his heart thudding. In seconds, he was racing down the hall to Room 308. With both hands, he pushed opened the door and stepped inside. Panting, his mouth dry, his eyes swept the room and then found Eléonore.

"My God, Eléonore," he whispered. In seconds, he was holding her. "My love, my love."

Her lips inched slowly into a smile.

"Englishman, you must never worry about me." She stepped away and stood over the body of Krenz. A voice like the whispers of angels fell quiet in the room.

"I may never become a spy, monsieur," she said, "but, most certainly, I can fire a pistol." She turned to him, her face serene. "He deserved to die. He murdered my husband."

Avery pulled a blanket from the bed and spread it across Krenz. "Indeed, he did."

When he stood, he reached out his hand.

"We must talk. Come." They sat together on the bed where he had first nestled to her back and hid from the Germans, where she had aimed her pistol at him and determined his French accent hid a slight flavor of English, had discovered he was a spy for the Allies.

"What is it?" she asked, eyes wide.

"Édouard."

"What about Édouard?"

In his mind's eye, Avery saw himself running across a French meadow, the coattails of Édouard Delafloté flapping in the wind in front of him. Behind them, a farmer's goat, a large buck with his testicles swinging wildly, chased them, his hooves kicking up the soft dirt of the field. They had jumped the fence and collapsed laughing in the soft grass. That was the first time Édouard had told him about Eléonore, about the woman who waited patiently for his return.

"Though I didn't realize it in the beginning, it was Édouard who was a . . .a compatriot of mine. I knew him only as *Frenchie*."

"A compatriot?" The question floated in the room and finally returned to the bed and to the man and woman who had been thrown together through no choosing of their own. It was simply fate, the universe touching them with a power that neither quite understood.

"Yes. Compatriot. We worked together. For the Allies."

"Together." Eléonore's gaze flitted around the room, to the dead German, to the chandelier that hung above them. When she looked at Gannon, she smiled.

"So Édouard was a spy also." Not a question, but a statement.

Avery nodded. "A brilliant spy."

She lifted her chin and stared at him. "So you have made love to the spy's widow," she said matter-of-factly.

Gannon contemplated her words. Perhaps her understanding was frayed, filled with uncertainty, bewilderment. Then, as if the heavens had decreed a divine pardon, she reached out and touched Avery's cheek.

"It occurs to me that Édouard would have wanted you to care for me," she said softly.

Gannon felt a burning in his throat, a need to grieve the death of his friend, but at the same time, he wanted to fall to his knees and place his head in the lap of Eléonore Delafloté. He grasped her hand and pressed it to his face. "Édouard loved you very much."

"I know."

CHAPTER EIGHTY-ONE

From the back of the ballroom, four members of the French Résistance pulled weapons from beneath the long tables and lifted them toward the stunned Germans. Gunfire cracked the grand room, the sounds reverberating off the walls like rapid claps of thunder. The French fired with a fierceness that startled even the Gods. Plomion's small bombs rolled across the floor to the crowd of Germans where the explosions tore through them like the fires of hell.

Olivier Plomion pushed Claude Bedeau and Madame Lefèbvre to the floor.

"Crawl to the rear door. You know where to go."

He then found his favorite weapon and like a rabid dog, snarled and snapped his way across the room toward the Germans. His first bullet hit the fat German who had eaten an entire plate of fresh plump mussels. He watched as the man grabbed his throat, blood spurting through his fingers and covering his medal-filled tunic. He pitched forward and hit the floor with a heavy thump.

Plomion's next bullet found the tall, pompous German who decreed London would fall in a matter of days. He delighted in sending a bullet into the center of his forehead and, then, the expression of surprise on the German's face as he crumbled backwards, his wine glass still in his hand.

When bullets found the chandeliers, the room plunged into darkness, bullets blazing and zipping through the air like comets. There were fifty-one German guests when the grand reception welcomed Herr Müller at 7:00 o'clock. At 8:11, there were none standing. Smoke and the smell of cordite twisted together in a thick haze that covered the bloodied room and the prone bodies lying on King Louis XVI's glorious rug.

A few seconds of quiet before a barrage of soldiers rushed into the room, their boots hammering the floor, their guns drawn.

**

The escape of Olivier Plomion and his men took only seconds. They slipped through the rear exit of the room, through the ladies' lounge and into the secret room Bedeau had prepared for them. Their last act was to move the giant armoire in front of the passageway, hiding the doorway and themselves until the smoke and the Germans had left.

"All accounted for?" whispered Plomion.

"*Oui.*"

Plomion heard a groan and turned to Bedeau. "Monsieur, you are injured?"

Bedeau's raspy voice alarmed Plomion. "A slight wound."

"We must be quiet. No light," said Plomion as he moved toward Bedeau. "Where is your wound?"

There was no response. Plomion reached out and touched his arm. "Monsieur?" he whispered. He leaned over and touched his chest, listened for a breath. There was none.

The voice of Avery Gannon came from a darkened corner. "Plomion," he whispered. "We must not talk. The Germans are on the other side of the wall."

CHAPTER EIGHTY-TWO

Near midnight, the streets of the 8ᵗʰ Arrondisement were overrun with soldiers who stepped quickly and brandished their weapons at every turn. Sporadic gunfire and explosions splintered the quiet of the night as Olivier Plomion's *girls* blasted throughout Paris, a diversion that would allow the escape of Avery Gannon and Eléonore Delafloté from the City of Light.

They left the body of Claude Bedeau in the hidden room at the Crillon, where it would rest until his compatriots tenderly removed it and placed it in a grave near Bougival, a village where Bedeau, as a young boy, watched Claude Monet paint beautiful scenes along the Seine.

They all mourned his death, but Eléonore could not be consoled. She caressed his face and kissed his hair as though he were a baby. Her hands found his and held them, tugging on them as though she could pull him back into the living. Avery watched as she removed a diamond pin from her hair and placed it in the lapel of his wool suite. "*Un cher*," she murmured over and over.

"Come! We must hurry." Plomion led them from the rear of the hotel to a small storage barn in the alley. From there, a passageway through an abandoned building allowed them to separate themselves from the hotel by a good distance. They found Juan Castillo waiting for them along with the drugged Madame Bedeau. She lay in a heap in the corner, snoring and sputtering and cursing the Germans with frequent murmurs of "*bastards*." She had yet to learn her precious Claude lay cold in the Crillon.

From the alleyway, the boots of five soldiers stomped across the stone, closer to those who huddled in the vacant building. Plomion shrank back into the dark shadows like a crab between two rocks and whispered to Gannon.

"They will find us in moments. Take everyone behind the building," he pointed to the window. He licked his lips and lifted one of his *girls*. "I'll make my way to the front and toss this." He grinned and rubbed the small explosive as if it were his lover. "That should give you some time. I'll be right behind you."

Gannon nodded and turned to Juan Castillo. "We'll have to carry Madame Bedeau."

Plomion snarled at them both. "Leave her here. She will only slow you down."

"*Non*," cried Eléonore. "They will shoot her." She grasped the old woman's arm and pulled her vodka-filled body to a sitting position. "She must come with us."

Plomion cursed, "They're going to shoot all of us if we don't move. Now!"

Gannon pulled Madame Bedeau up over his shoulder. "Let's go."

***

Plomion, a weapon in one hand, an explosive in the other, made his way to the front of the old building, where perhaps ghosts were waiting to welcome the soon to be dead to float with them in the air above. He watched silently from a dark corner as the five soldiers cautiously entered, a flashlight beam sweeping the room, the mutter of whispered German. The instant the flashlight beam found Plomion, he fired his gun and caught the lead German in the chest, followed by a loud grunt as the bullet struck and propelled him backward. While his gun fired, he threw the explosive, dove to the floor, rolling into a ball, covering his head and waiting for the blast. From his rear, he heard the firing of a pistol. Gannon.

The two men crawled toward each other, each one firing their guns through the haze of smoke and debris. A lone German, the only survivor of the blast, fired repeatedly, keeping them pinned to the floor. Plomion spoke into Gannon's ear, the words almost cavalier, a mocking of the quandary in which they found themselves.

"Englishman, it occurs to me that you are about to be saved by a Frenchman." Even in the dark, Gannon could see Plomion's grin. At that moment, Plomion rolled to his right and pushed himself to his knees, his arm lifting into a firing position, his finger squeezing the trigger as though it were a cow's teat. Gannon saw the spurt of fire from Plomion's gun, smelled the gunpowder and then saw the Frenchman pitch forward.

In seconds, Gannon edged to where the unmoving Plomion lay, his right hand spread forward, still holding his gun. "My friend," he whispered. In front of him, he heard the boots of the German scrape along the floor, through the rubble and menacingly closer. *No bullets. I have no more bullets.* Across the room, the German paused, focusing his eyes through the floating haze, searching for the blood of his enemy.

Inching forward, Gannon ran his hand down Plomion's arm and touched his weapon. Gently, he lifted the Frenchman's hand and pointed the gun toward the approaching German and, placing his finger on top of Plomion's, fired.

***

Cinders from the explosion of Plomion's little bomb floated in the air like a homecoming, like a gathering of truths where unknowns had once been. They fell on the body of Olivier Plomion, the one who carried the flag of freedom for his beloved France, the same as Claude Bedeau. Gannon, his body shaking, laid his head on the arm of Plomion, smelled the cordite on his skin, felt the roughness of his shirt, tasted the glory of battle. He felt warm tears roll down his face and into his mouth, where he tasted the sweetness of friendship and then the grief of loss.

EPILOGUE

Under cover of darkness beneath a cloud-filled sky and pushed by a cold January wind, Juan Castillo and two members of the French *Résistance* led Avery Gannon and Eléonore Delafloté across the fields of France, through tiny villages where they found safety in the homes of stout French citizens who cursed the Germans for the devils they were. They left a sleeping Madame Bedeau with her sister in Amiens, a small village a few miles north of Paris, a near-empty bottle of vodka in her bag. From there, they hid in a truck carrying fence posts and followed the coast to Dieppe. In Dieppe, they slept for a few hours before arriving in Etaples, where the British had established a rendezvous that carried them across the Channel.

Upon arrival in London, Avery Gannon removed the shoe polish from his hair and his eyebrows. In minutes, he was the salt and pepper haired Avery Gannon. Édouard Delafloté had been washed away in the black sudsy water that ran down the sink and into the sewers of London. He removed Édouard's clothes and dressed in his own. His razor swiped away the beard that shadowed his weary face. Their resemblance to each other had been remarkable, even without the disguise. Gannon studied his image in the mirror and saw himself as the

Englishman he was, solemn and amazingly judicious as one of the SIS's most renowned agents.

He was immediately escorted to the office of the head of SIS for debriefing, which lasted an agonizing five hours and recounted his eight months in France and, of course, the death of his fellow spy. Édouard Delafloté' s file was closed, but not before he was posthumously heralded as a courageous agent for the Allies.

His widow was also debriefed, her statements regarding the death of Colonel Horst Krentz were entered into a file established within the SIS office. She was inducted into Britain's Secret Intelligence Service at the request of Avery Gannon, who proclaimed her an impeccable spy.

Heinrich Müller and three other German military officials escaped the carnage that took place at the grand reception at the Hotel Crillon. Müller left immediately for Berlin in great distress; he would have to tell Hitler the famed British assassin had not been captured.

The war continued until August 1945, five years after Avery and Eléonore became one of the most prolific spy duos in British history.

COMING FALL 2013

Sneak preview

"GRANDMA TAKES A LOVER"

The author tucks away her titillating spy novels for an entry into the world of hot romance as she introduces Adela Queen Harper, a Rita Hayworth look-alike who lives an idyllic life in Ivy Log, Georgia, a small town where gossip seems to be the favorite pastime of its citizens. Adela's life is turned upside down when a scoundrel by the name of Frank Carberry, a retired U.S. army general, piles crisis upon dilemma upon her life. After a forty-year absence, Frank returns to the Carberry mansion, which sits just across a picket fence from the beautiful widow's small lake cottage. Adela discovers she is more woman than she thought when she battles with the man who has not yet learned how to treat one.

See a preview of "**Grandma Takes a Lover**" on the author's website: www.suechamblinfrederick.com

Sue CHAMBLIN Frederick

She is known as a sweet Southern belle, a woman whose eyelashes are longer than her fingers, her lips as red as a Georgia sunset. Yet, behind the feminine facade of a Scarlett-like ingénue lies an absolute and utterly calculating mind – a mind that harbors hints of genius – a genius she uses to write books that will leave you spellbound.

A warning! She's dangerous - only six degrees from a life filled with unimaginable adventures – journeys that will plunge her readers into a world of breath-taking intrigue. Put a Walther PPK pistol in her hand and she will kill you. Her German is so precise she'd fool Hitler. Her amorous prowess? If you have a secret, she will discover it – *one way or the other.*

The author was born in north Florida in the little town of Live Oak, where the nearby Suwannee River flows the color of warm caramel, in a three-room, tin-roofed house named "poor." Her Irish mother's and English father's voices can be heard even today as they sweep across the hot tobacco fields of Suwannee County, *"Susie, child, you must stop telling all those wild stories."*

She divides her time between the piney woods of Florida and the lush mountains of North Carolina where she is compelled to write about far away places and people whose hearts require a voice. Her two daughters live their lives hiding from their mother, whose rampant imagination keeps their lives in constant turmoil with stories of apple-rotten characters and plots that cause the devil to smile.

Made in the USA
Columbia, SC
16 January 2018